Large Print Lor
Loring, Emilie Baker.
A certain crossroad

A Certain Crossroad

*Also by Emilie Loring
in Large Print:*

Behind the Cloud
Here Comes the Sun!
Lighted Windows
Uncharted Seas
With Banners
Give Me One Summer
As Long as I Live
High of Heart
There is Always Love
Stars in Your Eyes
Rainbow at Dusk
I Hear Adventure Calling

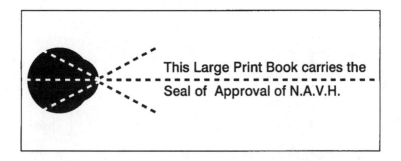

This Large Print Book carries the
Seal of Approval of N.A.V.H.

A Certain Crossroad

Emilie Loring

Thorndike Press • Waterville, Maine

Published in 2001 by arrangement with Little, Brown and Company, Inc.

Thorndike Press Large Print Romance Series.

The tree indicium is a trademark of Thorndike Press.

The text of this Large Print edition is unabridged.
Other aspects of the book may vary from the original edition.

Set in 16 pt. Plantin by Myrna S. Raven.

Printed in the United States on permanent paper.

Library of Congress Cataloging-in-Publication Data

Loring, Emilie Baker.
    A certain crossroad / by Emilie Loring.
      p. cm.
    ISBN 0-7862-3715-5 (lg. print : hc : alk. paper)
    1. Large type books.   I. Title.
  PS3523.O645 C4 2001
  813'.52—dc21   2001043397

To

V.J.L.

And sometimes the sky was like unto a great turquoise for blueness, and sometimes it was like a gray pall, and sometimes the highway wound through level radiant fields, and sometimes the rough road plunged down a steep declivity of rocks to grope blindly through dark and evil forests, and sometimes the yellow moon made mysterious twilight in the shadows. But always the Knight kept the Lady's hand close in his and always he stepped forward firmly, shining eyes straight ahead, for even in the gloom all was sharp-cut and clear to his vision.

CHAPTER I

From directly overhead the late July sun blazed down upon a bold stretch of New England coast. Pines, balsams and cedars which swept back and up from shore to skyline simmered in the heat, gave out a spicy fragrance. Under a sky pure turquoise a sea all sapphire ruffled whitely where it laved beach or rock. From the top of a fern-fringed cliff the bleached remains of an oak tree leaned out above a pebbly cove. Its white trunk and few storm-shot limbs suggested a prehistoric skeleton ready to plunge.

Suddenly the sleepy world sprang wide awake. From the green plateau of an adjacent island an aeroplane took off with a roar. More and more lightly it touched the earth till it zoomed into the sky. A dory which had been rocking idly near the island began to putt-putt out to sea. A canoe poked its nose cautiously from between glistening brown reefs. A houseboat cruiser which had been swinging idly at its mooring glided toward the outer bay.

An instant after from a peninsula of kelp-crowned boulders and crystal tide-pools strung like huge beads on a rope of sand came three sharp flashes of light. Possibly they had been but the quick reflection of the sun on the nickel of a rod, mayhap the Orb of Day had coquetted with a silver button on a gay sweater; the light might have come from a mirror dexterously handled. Whatever their cause the flashes had a curious effect. With the unwieldy haste of a fat boy in a foot-race the dory came about and waddled island-ward. The canoe shot back into obscurity. The houseboat swept in a graceful curve to its mooring. The aeroplane which had been circling climbed high above sun-burnished tree-tops to scribble in the sky.

Woods and shore relapsed into a doze. For ten minutes there was no visible stir. The air pulsed with hot sounds. Aromatic scents rose from the sun-baked kelp. A cicada shrilled his wing-drums with monotonous regularity. Gulls high in the evergreens signaled back and forth with raucous cries. The foliage of scrub alders hung as limp as painted leaves on a canvas back-drop.

Apparently there had been no human astir. Suddenly a man materialized from behind the most assertive boulder on the peninsula. He was spearing flounders. The wet back of a fish glistened like silver as he jerked it from the water and dropped it flap-

8

ping at his feet. After three more lucky jabs he picked up a basket and limped his way from rock to rock till he entered a trail on the wooded shore and disappeared in its fragrant dimness.

Five minutes more of drowsy quiet passed before the bleached oak appeared miraculously to develop arms and legs. Caterpillar-like a body wriggled backward along the horizontal trunk. Just before it reached the cliff it struggled erect and astride the tree began to flex stiff muscles. Instantly a hand with a striped sleeve above it lunged at one outflung arm. With a startled cry the victim of the assault made a futile clutch at the slippery perch and crashed down upon the pebbly beach twelve feet below.

There was the scrape of loosened gravel sliding over rock, the light crackle of dried pine-needles on an obscure trail, the shrill of a cicada, the scream of a gull. Then hot simmering silence broken only by the monotonous swish of the incoming tide as it licked whitely at the motionless feet of the prostrate figure on the shore like a sleek, predatory sea monster sniffing at its prey.

CHAPTER II

Across the bay in his garden Doctor David Sylvester had kept his eight-power binoculars on the limping figure among the boulders till it disappeared into the woodsy trail.

"What in thunder is Johnny Brewster doing on Kelp Reef at noon?" he muttered. His shaggy white eyebrows met in a frown as he looked down at his shawl-covered knees. His Mark Twainish head accentuated the thinness of his face and body. Exertion brought color to his pale skin as he propelled his wheel-chair from the patch of lawn from which he had had an uninterrupted view of the bay and opposite shore into the perrenial bordered path.

The air was fragrant with blossoms and drowsy with the hum of bees. Many paned windows set in gray weather-worn shingles under the beautiful lines of the roof of the house looked down upon the garden. Apparently, spread had been the architect's one idea for a dwelling when he had planned the Sylvester homestead. His design ran the gamut of all the ells and bays that an eighteenth century family might need. At its "raisin' " it had been called "The House" and "The House" it had remained. It was conspicuously the *pièce de résistance* of village architecture even among the summer homes of the magnificence of which the designer of the Sylvester house could have had no conception.

The garden was patched with sunlight and pitted with shadows from bordering shrubs and trees. There were columns of larkspur in every conceivable shade of blue, clouds of baby's breath, clusters of Madonna lilies, coreopsis like golden stars, Rose of Heaven petunias with a discreet sprinkling of Purple Prince. A tiny stream of clear water trickled from the stone mouth of a Chinese dragon in the hedge to splash over the mossy edge of a basin into the fern-bordered pool with its darting streaks of living gold. Robins twittered and chirped and wooed as they took their midday bath. An old-fashioned arbor, rambler-rosed, arched the garden path which led to the shore and the float to which a cabin-cruiser, fittingly inscribed *The Husky,* was made fast. In contrast to its chunkiness were the long smart lines of a speed launch which tugged skittishly at the mooring beyond.

David Sylvester navigated his chair under the arch of red roses to the expanse of green from which stretched the sandy beach. It had become one of the interests of his narrowed life to watch for the aeroplane which soared from the island each day at noon. Why hadn't Johnny Brewster been on hand to-day to help in the start, he puzzled. Had he been mistaken when he had thought that he had discerned a vague, smoky outline of letters in the trail of the flyer?

Sylvester raised the glasses and swept the rocky coast with his keen glance. The hazy line of distant hills, purple at the base, ran the chromatic scale of violet, till the color fused into sun-gilded crowns. With a stifled sigh he trained the binoculars on the opposite shore. How many hundreds of times had he traveled the highway hidden among those trees? Far up on the sky line he could see the steeply sloping roof, rounded eaves, irregularly placed dormers and red-capped chimneys which gave the house at Meadow Farm, Diane Turkin's property, an old-world quality. His attention shifted suddenly to the bleached oak which was a landmark for miles around. Were his eyes playing pranks or had something dropped from that tree? The glasses brought the boulder-strewn shore so near that it seemed that he might reach out and touch it. There was something on the beach! Was it a man?

No, the out-flung arms and legs were too small. It must be a boy. Was he stunned?

Sylvester's heart beat heavily as he blew furiously on a whistle which hung from a cord about his neck. He muttered anathemas as he realized his helplessness, realized anew that he who had been at the beck and call of every inhabitant for miles around now sat as irresponsive as a bronze Buddha while a few rods away a life was in danger. Seconds, which seemed hours to the impatient man, passed before the door of the house flew open and a silver-haired, rosy-cheeked little woman, whose figure had seen better days panted down the garden path.

"What is it, Dave?" Dorothy Sylvester demanded breathlessly as she reached the wheelchair. "I thought something terrible must have happened, your whistle fairly shrieked." Her brother lowered his binoculars only long enough to answer:

"Someone fell from the bleached oak, Dot. A boy, I think. He's lying on the shore. He hasn't moved and the tide is rising. Call Hi Cody! Quick!"

"But, Dave, how could —"

"Call Hi!" roared the doctor irascibly.

"I will, Dave. I will," soothed Dorothy Sylvester before she gave an excellent imitation of a plump tugboat attempting to emulate a submarine-chaser on its way to the barn. Sylvester had not moved the glasses from his eyes when she returned with a gaunt middle-aged man at her heels. He was coatless, his checkerboard waistcoat flapped open as he ran — his blue shirt sleeves were rolled up. Bright, snapping eyes like a terrier's, enormous ears were the outstanding features of his physiognomy. His loose-jointed figure suggested a jumping-jack. He wiggled a straw between his china white teeth and excitedly twirled a bunch of gold insignia attached to the end of his cable-like watch chain as he sent his drawling voice ahead of him.

"What's up, Dave?"

"Take the glasses, Hi. Locate the bleached oak then drop to the shore. Do you see anything?" While Cody adjusted the binoculars Dorothy Sylvester pulled the shawl closer about her brother's knees. She was of the type which seems fashioned to tuck in babies and kiss bruised spots to make them well. Her voice soothed as she queried indulgently, quite as one would question a child wakened from an ugly dream:

"Are you sure that it was a boy you saw, not a dog jumping from the bleached oak,

14

Davie?" Her brother grunted his disgust.

"My eyesight isn't impaired, Dot, if my legs are. What do you see, Hi?"

"You are right, Dave. It's a man or a boy."

"I was sure of it. Go over in *The Husky* and get him. The speed-boat's no good at a time like this. Oh, if I could help. If only I could help. Hi —"

But Cody already was half-way to the float. The two left behind watched in tense silence as the boat was pushed off. Sylvester raised the glasses to his eyes again.

"That last wave rolled to the boy's knees before it broke! Nobody will come along the shore this time of day and the tide is rising fast. Curse these wooden legs of mine! Why doesn't Hi hurry!"

His sister smoothed his mane of white hair tenderly. There were tears in her dove-like eyes as she encouraged:

"He is running the boat at top speed, dear. Don't think of your legs. Think of your hands. Be thankful that you still have the keenest brain and the most skilful pair in ten counties. Except —"

"Except Neil's. You needn't be afraid to say it. I'm as proud of our nephew as you are. If only he were here. Look, Hi's slowing down! He's getting ready to nose *The Husky* up the beach! Oh, do you realize what it means to be tied — tied when you want to help?" Sylvester pounded the arm of his chair with his binoculars and turned tragic eyes on his sister. She rescued the glasses with one hand; with the other she patted his thin shoulder as he raged on rebelliously:

"I know — I know what you are thinking, that I ought to be thankful I am no worse. I am — but my work — my work —"

"Neil is taking care of that," Dorothy Sylvester reminded gently.

"Neil! Of course he is but think what my illness has done to him! After his distinguished service overseas, his years at hospital, came his chance with one of the biggest surgeons in New York and presto, Destiny lands him in this one-horse village to carry on my practise. He has been here a year, do you realize it, a *year*."

"But think of the experience he has had."

"He would have had that anywhere. That can't make up for the time he has lost. Destiny! Hmp! It is *my* fault that he is here, but I didn't know what else to do. My people were dropping off with influenza. I was shocked into uselessness and not a physician to be secured for a country community for love or money. I got one for love. I traded on Neil's affection for me — plus his New England conscience — and here he is. I wronged the boy, though. He is thirty years old. He is cut out for a surgeon and he's spending his precious time visiting lonely homes in the hills or remote islands in my place. But, I didn't know what else to do. I *didn't* know what else to do," Sylvester reiterated brokenly.

"Davie, you mustn't get excited." His sister brushed two big tears from her dimpled cheeks with one hand while with the other she offered the glasses. With the adroitness of one who had heard the rebellious tirade many times, she sidetracked his train of thought. "What is happening now?"

The thin hands which held the binoculars tightened till the knuckles showed white.

"Hi has him! He's lifting him into the boat! Oh, if Neil were here!"

"Perhaps Fanny Browne will come first. A nurse with her experience should know what to do. Dave, have you thought that Neil might fall in love with Fanny? Sometimes such a fierce look comes into his eyes that — I wonder." This time Dorothy Sylvester succeeded in engaging her brother's undivided attention.

"Hmp! Do you think that I haven't noted that 'fierce look,' as you call it? I am sure that Fanny is not the cause. She isn't the type for Neil. She is a good nurse and a beautiful woman but she has about as much imagination as that speed-boat. As for a sense of humor — she wouldn't recognize a joke if it chucked her under the chin. A wife with neither imagination nor a sense of humor isn't a wife, she's a calamity."

"Dave! How you talk! It's — it's sacrilegious, almost. No wonder you never married. You expect everything in a woman. Fanny is the prettiest girl in the county and she is deep. Often I look at her and wonder what is going on behind her impassive face. You've said many a time that she is the best nurse you ever had to assist you."

"She is. She is a beautiful machine. Perhaps Neil will fall in love with her, propinquity is an insidious jade, but if I thought there was danger of it, I'd pack the boy back to New York if everyone in town broke out with spotted fever. Here's the boat!"

The cabin-cruiser slid gently alongside the float. Hiram Cody made it fast before he lifted a slim figure partially covered by an oilskin coat. He strode through the arbor with the wheel-chair and Dorothy Sylvester at his heels. He laid his burden on the wicker couch under the apple tree. His eyes threatened to snap out of his head as he turned to the doctor.

"Dave, it's a girl! She's one of them up-to-date females in knickers an' what the summer folks call a shingle bob. That's why you thought 'twas a boy. She's alive all right, but she ain't as much as flicked an eyelash since I picked her up. Mark my words, her head got a nasty crack."

From his wheel-chair David Sylvester leaned toward the motionless figure. Brown hair which held the high lights and deep gloss of polished mahogany waved softly back from a white face. Long lashes with up-curling golden tips lay like dark fringes on the cheeks which showed traces of blood and sand. There was a deep dimple in the softly rounded but determined chin. From the end of an arching eyebrow to the cheek bone extended a raw, bleeding cut. A fine white linen blouse clutched at the breast by a slim hand was visible beneath the rumpled green coat. One cordovan booted foot pro-truded beyond the yellow slicker. As Dorothy Sylvester started for the house she called over her shoulder:

"I'll try to get Neil or Fanny on the 'phone!"

"Come back, Dot! We can't wait for them." There was a strain of excitement in David Sylvester's voice, the old light of confidence in his eyes. "Take the girl to the office, Hi. Thank the Lord my hands are limber if my legs are balky. I —"

"What's the excitement," challenged a rich, amused voice from the house door. "Holding a post-mortem over one of Hi's catches? If you are —"

"Neil! Oh, Neil!" The words throbbed with relief, the color rushed into Sylvester's face as he turned toward the man who was coming down the garden path accompanied by a statuesque girl in the striped uniform of a nurse. "Never were you two needed more. A short time ago I saw someone fall from the bleached oak. I thought it was a boy — Hi went to the rescue in *The Husky*. When he got there he found it was a girl. Her head is cut."

The smile tightened out of Neil Peyton's fine lips. His direct, steady eyes which had been as blue as the sea darkened to professional gunmetal. In the smart perfection of his gray clothes there was no hint of the country practitioner. He was tall and lean, his skin was weather-bronzed, his features were of cameo clearness, there was a slight wave in his black hair which no amount of furious brushing could reduce to smoothness.

During his uncle's explanation he had stripped off coat and waistcoat and tossed them to the nurse. He rolled up the sleeves of his white shirt. The laughter had left his voice. It was coldly impersonal as he commanded:

"Get things ready in the office, Miss Browne. I'll bring the patient in. Do you know who she is, Hi?"

"It's the girl who's visiting at Meadow Farm. Folks say she's rich an' that Diane Turkin's going to make a match between her and Boris Stetson. Mark my words, Di's nutty about that brother of hers."

Dorothy Sylvester who had been tenderly brushing back the girl's satin-soft hair made way for her nephew. Her eyes were full of tears as she pleaded:

"She's — she's so pretty, Neil. Try not to hurt her."

Peyton half-closed his eyes in an oblique glance which made them seem brilliantly amused.

"Shame upon you, Aunt Dot! Would you have me more considerate of a beauty than of a —"

The last word froze into silence as he glanced down. The blood drained from his tanned skin. His outstretched hand clenched. After an instant's hesitation he lifted the girl. His voice was rough as he explained unnecessarily:

"I'll take her to the office."

Along the gayly bordered walk moved the

assorted procession. Neil Peyton with his unconscious burden, his aunt pattering in his wake, Hiram Cody pushing the wheelchair. A thoughtful frown beetled Doctor Sylvester's white brows as he kept his eyes on the back of his nephew. At the house door Peyton halted to protest:

"Don't come in, Aunt Dot. Miss Browne will be all the help I need."

He passed through the outer office to the operating room and laid the girl on the clinical chair which the nurse had adjusted. Deftly he tested for broken bones. He could find no evidence of injury save the cut and the slight concussion due to the force of the fall. He sent Fanny Browne to the outer office for something in his bag. In the minutes she was gone he unclenched the slim hand which still gripped the delicate blouse. His face was livid, his lips set in a hard line as he bathed and dressed the bruised cheek. When he lifted his head the dark color swept to his hair. The nurse's usually bovine eyes were alight with curiosity, her beautiful, doll-like face pink with surprise. He volunteered what he realized to be a clumsy explanation of his perturbation:

"I feared that the skull might have been fractured, but it is not. Merely a slight concussion and the cut is not as deep as it looked, no stitches needed. The color is coming back to the patient's lips. Take off those wet clothes. Get her into bed and see that she stays there for twenty-four hours at least. I will report to Doctor Sylvester and turn her over to his care. You and I are due at the Port in half an hour."

"I'll be ready, Doctor Neil."

Peyton looked down at the still figure, then at the front of his shirt. A stain proclaimed the exact spot where the gashed cheek had rested. As the patient's eyelids quivered he stepped to the door. With the knob in his hand he lingered. He saw large brown eyes open slowly, saw them contract in pain as a frown wrinkled the brow above them. He noted the puzzled glance which traveled along the white tiled walls, lingered on the X-ray and electrical equipment, on the glass cases for instruments before it returned to Fanny Browne where it rested as though hypnotized.

With a stifled exclamation the girl raised herself on one elbow. Her eyes were glazed with pain but wide with incredulity as she looked straight up into the face of the nurse and whispered unsteadily:

"*You* here! Why — *why* did you push me from that tree?"

CHAPTER III

Four o'clock shadows in the fragrant garden. Shifting purple and blue tints on the sea. Murmur of tide. Somewhere a robin twitting garrulously. White hair as silvery as the silk of milkweed. David Sylvester in his wheel-chair. In the apple tree above him a motley company of feathered tenants preparing their apartments against the night. The man's sensitive hands were folded upon an open book. His heavy brows met as his eyes swept sea and shore. At a sound from the house he looked up.

A girl was coming down the path. A mandarin's coat of pale blue satin richly adorned with golden dragons and many-hued iris enveloped her slender figure. A white patch below one temple was little whiter than her cheeks. Her brown eyes were shadowed; a slight frown contracted her brows. Not until she had dropped into the peacock chair opposite him did David Sylvester speak.

"My dear child, you should not be here. Our instructions were to keep you in bed at least twenty-four hours."

The girl smiled.

"I am quite fit, Doctor Sylvester; you see I recognize you from Miss Dorothy's description. Never in my life have I been laid up for a moment. Why should I stop now for this silly bruise? Your sister told me that barely twenty minutes elapsed between my fall and the opening of my eyes in your office. Twenty minutes! Think how boys who are knocked out in football keep on. Why shouldn't I?"

"They keep on to their sorrow — later."

"But I had a fine sleep and I feel absolutely fit. Please let me stay!"

Sylvester smiled in sympathy with the girl's wheedling voice. He should obey Neil's orders and send her back to her room, but — let Neil battle with her when he came. It would do her good to sit in the fragrant garden for a while. The concussion had been slight and her eyes showed that its effect was rapidly passing.

To the man to whom human nature had been an absorbing study for over thirty years the girl's slender hands looked capable. Her determined chin suggested self-reliance, the slightly rebellious curves of her lips a sense of humor, which to Sylvester was the gyroscope which steadied the world. There was innocent coquetry in the depths of her dark eyes but, he would be willing to wager that not one man in a hundred would presume carelessly to touch even her soft hair. No shop-worn emotions there but vividness, fresh and sparkling charm and depths of passion yet unplumbed. "She is a law unto herself," Sylvester summed up mentally.

"What is the verdict? Will I pass?"

The laughing challenge brought his keen eyes to hers.

"Our acquaintance has been too short for me to commit myself," he teased.

"*Auwe!* — which is Hawaiian for alas, in case you shouldn't know —" she came back gaily. "Your sister told me that you saw me fall. The adventure has the flavor of an old-time fairy story. A maiden in distress, a noble prince to her rescue."

Her brown eyes with a smile in their depths reminded Sylvester of deep pools reflecting stars.

"A sorry prince am I, child, chained to this chair."

"But neither your eyes nor your spirit are chained. You have been so kind to me without knowing who I am. I am Judith Halliday. Yesterday I arrived in Seaboard to visit Mrs. Turkin. I had traveled several hundred miles to get here without encountering so much as a pebble of excitement. I am consumed with mortification that I should have met with such an inglorious accident so soon after my arrival." She laid a tentative finger on the white patch.

"Don't touch it! What were you doing in the bleached oak? It was a reckless stunt for a girl."

"Not for this girl, Doctor Sylvester. I was reared under the iron rule of a boy cousin. He was a relentless taskmaster. I smolder with indignation, I flame with wrath when I think of the training he put me through."

"What lured you into that particular tree today?"

"I wonder if Destiny took a hand. You look startled. Don't mind my nonsense; perhaps I am still a bit light-headed. After Mrs. Turkin left for Bar Harbor this morning I eluded the twins and — I mean, I fared forth all by my lonesome for adventure. I saw the bleached oak, writhed out along the trunk the better to see — the view. All would have gone merry as a marriage bell had I not been inspired to stretch while still astride the tree. I lost my balance and — turn to your own line-a-day book for the continuation of the story."

Sylvester ignored the laughter in her voice. He leaned slightly forward as he probed:

"You are keeping something back about your accident, Miss Halliday. If ever you are in perplexity or trouble come to me. That little reference of yours to Destiny makes me sure that sometime I may be able to help you. As the physician of this community I have become a safety-vault for secrets. Trust me."

"Thank you, Doctor Sylvester, I will remember." The girl steadied her voice. "Is Miss Dorothy who found this lovely coat for me in a treasure-chest in the attic your only sister?"

"The only one living. My younger sister and her husband died years ago. Their son made his home with us. He lives in the house beyond the hedge. The White Cottage, we call it. He is the last of the Sylvesters and the best."

The girl's tapering fingers tapped lightly the arm of the chair as she inquired:

"Was the pretty girl in the striped gown who helped me before Miss Dorothy came your nephew's wife?"

"No, that was Fanny Browne. She has been my office nurse. She is a native girl who took hospital training. The only reason that I can figure out why she stays in this small town is to be near her mischief-breeding sister."

"Does Miss Browne know Mrs. Turkin or her — or the family at Meadow Farm?"

"Bless you, child, every resident of this community is on 'Hulloa, Di!' terms with Diane and her family. She and her brother Boris Stetson have spent their summers here since they were youngsters. All the young people, rustics and rusticators — that is what the natives call the summer people — played round together. Stetson has rushed each one of the village girls in turn. My boy — my nephew — but I mustn't start on that subject. When I do I am a garrulous old party."

"A man with a spirit like yours never is old," the girl protested with heart-warming sincerity.

"I have told you of my family, now tell me of yours. I am an advocate of reciprocity, you see."

"I have no immediate family. My parents died when I was a baby. I was brought up at schools. My vacations were spent abroad or at the home of the uncle who is my guardian and who was the guardian of the cousin of whom I told you. I had to learn to decide matters for myself. There was no older person to whom I could turn for advice, no one who loved me, I mean. I suspect that the responsibility has made me arrogant, selfish and difficult." Sylvester's eyes softened in sympathy with the strained note in the charming voice. "Last fall in a spirit of restlessness I went to St. Moritz with friends. There I met Mrs. Turkin. I liked her at once and I adored the twins. Diane invited me to visit her this summer. I hadn't been in the peace and quiet of this village twelve hours before I realized that I had made a mistake. I was tempted to dash off to Alaska, Australia, South America, anywhere for adventure."

"What are you trying to forget?"

Judith Halliday flushed warmly and answered evasively:

"Do you ever think back and wonder what would have happened had you taken the right turn instead of the left at a certain crossroad? Suppose, just suppose, that I had gone to Australia instead of coming to Seaboard? I might have been kidnapped and dragged into the bush by this time." Sylvester's laugh showed his sympathetic appreciation of the reckless diablerie in her words.

"Don't lose hope. Don't leave us just yet. Between you and me, life here may not prove as uneventful as you apprehend. Surely you are satisfied with your spectacular start. Didn't your fall register excitement enough for one day?"

The girl's eyes darkened. Her color deepened as she leaned forward and confided:

"There was something curious about that fall. I —"

"Wait!" David Sylvester warned softly as his sister trundled the tea-wagon down the garden path. In his normal tone he observed whimsically: "The arrival of a guest always proves a powerful stimulant to Dot's afternoon-tea complex."

"Laugh if you like, David," Dorothy encouraged placidly, "but I notice that you feel more cheerful after you have had your tea. I telephoned to the Farm as you requested, Miss Halliday, but Diane has not returned — don't glare at me, Davie — I couldn't keep the patient in the house — If you insist upon leaving us, my dear, when you are ready Hiram Cody will drive you over in the sedan. It is smooth running and won't jar your poor head. You may feel quite safe with Hi. He has been my brother's right-hand man since David began practise. He is sheriff and game-warden for the county, president of the Grange and a member of every fraternal organization in the state. I am not saying this to encourage your going, child. We would like to keep you here, wouldn't we, David?"

"We ought to keep her here."

"Thank you both, but as I am perfectly fit I must get back to Di's as soon as possible. Are my clothes wearable?"

"They are nicely dried and pressed. Did Davie tell you that he thought you were a boy?"

"Because of my knickers? I contracted the habit of wearing them at St. Moritz. They are the only practical clothes in which to explore. May I not wait on the doctor?"

"No, no, *no!* You must keep as quiet as possible."

Dorothy Sylvester pulled a wicker stand close to her brother's chair. She provisioned it with the lavishness of a commissary-general. Her first aid invariably took the form of food. It was her panacea for ailments of the mind, the heart and the body. As she nestled down behind the tea-cart she volunteered:

"If Fanny Browne gets back in time she will come out for tea."

"Has she a lame brother or — or husband or lover?" Judith inquired with studied casualness.

David Sylvester sensed the false note in the girl's voice. He set his cup down. She was quite unconscious of his appraising scrutiny as she awaited his sister's answer.

"Bless you, child, no. There is only one lame man in the village and he is Johnny Brewster, Fanny's brother-in-law. You will see him at Diane's. He is general utility man there. He helps Boris Stetson with the airplane, takes care of the motor-boats, works on anything which has a wheel or engine that he can tinker."

"Where have you seen Johnny?"

"I didn't know that it was Johnny when I saw him," evaded the girl. She became absorbed in her tea. David Sylvester regarded her from under his ragged white brows as he observed:

"It is curious that you should have thought of him in connection with Fanny Browne because before he went overseas folks in the village suspected that he and she were sweethearts. However, when he came back with one leg shorter than the other he could see no one but that scatterbrain Pansy, Fanny's sister. There's a perfect example of the inevitable mischief-maker for you. Having some good looks, a modicum of intelligence, a sort of feline cruelty, and a tinsel talent at the piano, she's of the type which starts her career in a movie-theatre and ends as co-respondent in a divorce court."

"You shouldn't talk so about Pansy when

you got Johnny the position at Meadow Farm so that he could marry the girl," his sister reproved mildly. "We never knew whether Fanny cared. She makes her sister's house her home. I told Neil —"

"*Neil!* Who is Neil?"

Judith Halliday hurled the question. Sudden color stained her white face. She reminded David Sylvester of a startled bird poised for instant flight. His eyes on the eyes of the girl were like firm fingers on a racing pulse as he answered for his sister.

"Neil is the nephew of whom I told you."

"But — but I thought you said 'the last of the Sylvesters.' Is — is he a physician? Does he live in the white house beyond the hedge?"

"He does. He is Doctor Neil Peyton, the only child of our house. He was called the Flying Doc. in the army. A year ago he gave up a brilliant future in New York to come here. I could get no one else to carry on my practise."

"Who — who patched my head? *Who* took off my blouse?"

"There, there dear, don't get excited," cooed Dorothy Sylvester. "The nurse took off your blouse of course and though Davie could have done it just as well, Neil patched your head, as you call it. Fortunately he arrived just as Hi brought you into the garden and he carried you into the office. He left you in our care — and you have disobeyed his orders. I don't know what Neil will do to us, do you, Davie? I expect though that he will put us on bread and water for a week. He's a tyrant." Her plump chuckle registered appreciation of her own humor.

The girl rose and set her cup on the tray. Her fingers were unsteady, her cheeks deeply flushed.

"Then I'll go before your tyrant returns, Miss Dorothy. I want to get back to Meadow Farm in ample time to dress for dinner. Diane must not think for an instant that she has an invalid on her hands. I'll say 'Good-afternoon' now, but I'll say 'Thank you' always for what you did for me this noon, Doctor Sylvester."

The man gripped the hand extended.

"You owe me nothing but if you persist in feeling in debt, come and see me often as payment," he lowered his voice. "Come soon and tell me what there was 'curious' about your fall."

"I will. Let me know when you are to be quite alone and need company and I will scuttle any engagement I may have and come."

"Take care of yourself. *Don't* go down to dinner to-night."

The girl laughed.

"I'll think it over. Good-afternoon."

She went up the garden path with Dorothy Sylvester puffing at her heels. At the door she turned and waved. Sylvester dropped his head upon the hand which once had been immune to fatigue and which now became so quickly tired.

He should have insisted that Judith Halliday stay at the house for twenty-four hours, he knew — but — he couldn't forget Neil's face as he had looked down at the motionless figure under the apple tree. In some way the girl had hurt his boy and it was better to let her go.

He frowned at the shore across the bay. The peninsula of rocks was completely inundated, all the little tide-pools had been gathered to their mother sea. His shaggy brows drew together as he summed up aloud:

"She saw Brewster on Kelp Reef — had he anything to do with her fall? What was she about to tell me when Dot appeared? For some reason she linked Johnny up with Fanny Browne — I wonder where Neil and Judith Halliday have met before?"

CHAPTER IV

Hiram Cody's terrier eyes seemed to snap up the road. The straw between his super-white teeth wig-wagged continuously as he sent the automobile smoothly and steadily on. Judith Halliday leaned back in the seat beside him with her troubled brown eyes fixed on the purple hills against the horizon. Her heart still shook her, her knees still felt like pulp as they had felt when in the Sylvester garden she had discovered that accident, or Fate, had led her directly to Neil Peyton. Determinedly she forced the embarrassment of his proximity from her mind and lined up the events of the morning for inspection.

Was the Johnny Brewster described by Miss Dorothy the man whom she had seen furtively make his way from the edge of the woods to the extreme end of Kelp Reef? She had been stretched on the fragrant needles under a group of pines, elbows on the ground, face propped in her two hands when first her attention had been attracted to him. She had crawled out on the overhanging trunk of the bleached oak the better to observe his stealthy progress. It must have been he who had flashed the light which she was convinced had been a signal to someone. Of course it couldn't have been to Boris Stetson evidently practising skywriting in his plane. What possible interest could he have in signals? It would be as absurd to connect it with Di's houseboat-cruiser. It might have been to the canoeist, it might have been to the doryman. Each immediately had changed his course. Should she tell the sheriff what she had seen? Perhaps already he suspected a mystery afoot. Was Fanny Browne an accessory? As she had opened her eyes in the doctor's office the sight of the nurse had released a flash-back of memory. With startling clarity had returned the instant's vivid impression she had received of a striped sleeve above the hand which had given her that brutal push.

Judith's brows contracted till a twinge of pain under the patch gave her pause. What could have been the woman's motive in attacking her unless she also was concerned in the signal? Had she calculated callously that the eavesdropper would fall into the water, that the tide would cover her and her knowledge of the secret forever? Gruesome thought! With a shiver Judith turned to the man beside her to find him regarding her with friendly concern.

"Not cold, are you? I was hoping you were feeling better every minute in this fine air." Hiram shifted the straw from side to side of his mouth to facilitate expression. Judith watched it with fascinated eyes. Suppose he forgot and drew it down his throat! She hastily reviewed her first-aid lore even as she answered:

"I am better, much better, thank you. Curious that I should have fallen. I have climbed trees all my life and never had I a tumble like that before."

"Guess you were raised with boys, weren't you?"

"With one only, thank heaven. Had there been more like him I should not be here to tell the tale. He was not content until I could equal him in skill. He would disown me if he knew that I had fallen from a tree. Did you see a fine platinum chain when you picked me up Mr. Cody?"

"No. Did you lose one? Maybe it caught and snapped when you fell. Don't worry. You'll find it, see if you don't. Perhaps Fanny took it off when she fixed your head."

"*Fanny!* I hadn't thought of that. Perhaps she did," agreed the girl thoughtfully. Cody shot her a quick look before he drawled:

"Ever been here before?"

"No."

"I thought I'd never seen you up at Turkin's. I get to know most everybody that comes there. Diane's a fine woman and mark my words she's an up-to-date farmer — I know, because I buy stock for her. She don't put on no airs with the villagers and she listens to my advice. She deserved a better husband than she got. Folks round here wouldn't stand for him. He was one of the kind who felt he wasn't getting all the fun that was due him unless he was stirring people up and getting them ripping mad. You know that breed. Well, I guess where he's gone he'll find 'em all poppin' round lively. Di sure makes a peppy widow. Everybody loves her but the Terrible Turks are too much like their old man to be right down pop'lar."

"Do you mean the twins?"

"That's the name them Turkin kids go by in this village. They're holy terrors and as for *Scotty,* that sawed-off, long-headed pup of theirs — he's like their father was — always stirrin' up trouble."

"Terrors? And only six years old?"

"Young lady, they may be six in years but they're twenty in deviltry. That French nurse of theirs, Toy-nette, has grown years older since she came here. Sooner or later everyone gets let in by their pranks. I'll

40

admit I haven't never had no children to train but it seems an awful pity when youngsters aren't given a chance to grow up straight."

"But Gretchen and Gregory are having every chance. They have the best of tutors, the best of homes, the best of medical care," the girl protested indignantly.

"Surely, surely, *but,* they're not having the best example and example's what counts with kids, Davie Sylvester claims. Look at their uncle Boris Stetson! Look at the friends he brings to his sister's house! Oh, they're called gentlemen, but they indulge in diversions which I'm too old-fashioned to mention in the presence of a lady. As for respect for the game laws — they think no more of smashin' them than of smashin' their clay pigeons. The twins' father was off the same bale of goods. I hope the next one Di gets'll be tender and lovin'. She ought to have married Neil."

"Neil Peyton!"

"Surely, surely, Dave Sylvester's nephew."

"Was — is he in love with her?"

"Well, I can't swear to *was* but he will be if Diane can put it across. Mark my words there's nothing so sure-fire as a young rich widow when she's made up her mind what she wants. But it looks a little now as though

Neil's best friend was kinder getting his wings singed too. Hi there, Johnny Brewster!"

With the authoritative shout Cody brought the car to a sudden stop. Judith's pulses rapped out a tattoo of excitement. The man limping toward them was the flounder-spearer who had flashed the light! Had he by any chance seen her under the tree? Had the girl who had pushed her over warned him that he had been watched? He pulled off his cap as he stopped by the side of the car but no change of expression lighted his slightly sullen face, his brooding blue eyes. His light hair was almost white, his skin which once must have been fair, was freckled and tanned by wind and sun, his lips were femininely soft, his chin lacked stamina. He leaned one out-at-elbow arm on the edge of the lowered window of the car as he looked up at Hiram Cody.

The sheriff dragged the bunch of insignia from his pocket. It would serve as a reliable sinker if perchance its collector contemplated suicide by drowning. Judith sternly checked the laugh which brimmed to her lips at the thought. Cody twirled the gold symbols tirelessly as he frowned down upon Brewster and demanded:

"Johnny, who's using your canoe, now?"

42

Judith caught the slight dilation of the pupils of the younger man's blue eyes but Brewster's voice merely was roughly good-natured as he answered:

"You sure do surprise me, Sheriff. I didn't suppose anything could happen in this burg you weren't on to. That rusticator who came a couple of weeks ago to stay with Neil Peyton hired it for the rest of the summer."

"He did! He didn't tell me."

"He sure overlooked his duty, Sheriff."

"He hasn't applied for a license. If he goes to breaking the game laws being Neil Peyton's friend won't save him in this community. It's my job to see that the laws are kept and I intend to do it."

"If you're so set on seeing the game law isn't broke you'd better watch out for something bigger that may be cracking up."

"What do you mean by that, Johnny?"

Brewster's face reddened furiously. Judith thought that the color must burst through his skin.

"Nothing. If that was all you wanted to know, about the canoe, I mean, Hi, I'll get along home. Pansy raises the roof if I'm not there in time to wash up before supper. She's one of the original Gold-Dust twins. Good-afternoon, Miss Halliday."

He had turned away before Judith had recovered from her surprise sufficiently to answer him. He knew her name! As the sedan started she looked inquiringly at Cody. The activity of the straw between his teeth indicated turmoil of mind.

"How could Johnny Brewster know who I am? Never have I seen him before — that is — never has he seen me," she added, "I hope," under her breath.

"Mark my works, there isn't a man, woman or child in the village who didn't know your name and suspect what you came for, an hour after you lit."

"What I *came* for?"

"Surely, surely. Perhaps I'd oughter say what they *think* you came for."

"Perhaps you'd oughter," the girl agreed crisply with a careful adaptation of his English. "If you know so much about me it is only fair that I know something about you. Of course you are not obliged to answer me but why are you so interested in the disposal of Johnny Brewster's canoe?"

"Well, now as long as you say I'm not obliged to answer, I won't," chuckled Cody. He tightened his grip on the wheel. "I don't see what that chap wants with the canoe with all the boats there are at the Sylvesters'," he muttered under his breath.

"What chap? The rusticator who is

staying with Neil — Neil Peyton? What is his name?"

"Oliver Fleet."

"I thought so."

"Do you know Ollie Fleet?"

"Yes. I know Ollie, I know him well. In fact he is the cousin of whom I told you."

"Well, now, ain't that curious? You and he have landed in the same town without either knowing the other was coming. Something behind that, I guess. I take it you didn't know he was here, did you?"

The girl shook her head. A slight frown puckered her brow. Had Oliver Fleet known that she was coming? In his frequent but brief letters to her he had made no reference to his summer plans. Last fall, when he had heard that she and Diane Turkin were to spend the winter in St. Moritz, he had sent them notes of introduction. She and Di had become warm friends, they had spent days together but Diane never had mentioned Neil Peyton's name. It would be just like Ollie, knowing that his best friend had settled in Seaboard, to suggest to Diane that she invite his cousin to visit her. What had Cody meant by his, "Something behind that, I guess"? He was maddeningly uncommunicative. He seemed to have withdrawn into a shell of conjecture. Could she lure

45

him out? She looked up at him with a laugh as she probed with theatrical impressiveness:

"You sizzle with mystery, Sheriff. First you hint at an underground reason for my being here, then you get unduly excited about Johnny Brewster's canoe. I wonder what your reaction would be if I told you what I had seen."

"*You!* What have you seen?"

"As long as you can't make me answer, I won't." She adapted his earlier reply with a laugh. He grinned down at her much in the manner of a big dog contemplating a mischievous kitten.

"I get you but you don't get nothing out of me. I just heard that I've got the reputation of talking too much. I don't like it. This sure is the show farm of the county," he exulted with a sort of proprietorial admiration as he turned the car between the posts of the white fence which enclosed the home grounds of Meadow Farm. Beyond a vista at the end of the ascending drive loomed the vine-patterned round turret of the house with its windows gay with boxes of flowers.

"There isn't anything Di hasn't got here. Stable, cow-barns, feed-mill, poultry houses. Them that has, gits, I tell her. Now we've heard that a couple of hundred acres of woodland up where she's got a hunting camp, that was burned over two years ago, is blue with berries. I want she should go into the canning business. She's going up to inspect the place. For once Boris Stetson agrees with me. He's been hanging round a canning factory down the bay a lot. Says it interests him. Perhaps it's Di's idea to have him run hers. Might keep him out of mischief."

"Boris Stetson overlord of a blueberry canning factory! How funny."

"Your laugh's more like a chime of soft bells than anything I ever heard but you'd better stop or you'll hurt your head. See that white building across on the island? With all the land Di has here she went and built that hangar over there because her brother insisted 'twas the only decent landing place she owned. Must take a pile of money to carry on this outfit."

"If one has it, is there anything better upon which to lavish it than a home?" Judith cleared her voice of wistfulness. "There are your Terrible Turks now! Don't they look like angels?"

"Angels! More like the cat that swallowed the canary! Mark my words, they've been up to mischief."

Cody brought the sedan to a stop in front

of the terrace. Above, in a glare of sunlight on the top of the wall, as though they had been set out to dry, perched a girl and a boy. With elbows on their knees, chins in their hands they gazed pensively down at the sedan. The gold of their short, wavy hair gave the impression of having recently — very recently, emerged from a shampoo. Their brilliant blue eyes were rimmed with red. Between them snuggled a mass of damp black fur from which blinked one wary bead-like eye. The children's clothes were spotless, creaseless.

Judith leaned from the car to wave at them. Gretchen acknowledged the greeting with an aggrieved sniff before she warned:

"Toinette says that nobody should come near us, Judy."

"What has happened, dear?"

"Nothing — to make such a fuss about. Course, grown-ups would, though. Greggy and I were playing Indians over there in the woods an' Scotty started up a black kitty with a pretty white stripe down its back and we pretended 'twas a buffalo and chased it up into the garage — and Uncle Boris was just stepping out of his nice shiny racer an' when he saw the kitty he gave a loud whoop and we thought he was playing Indians with us and —"

48

"B-but he wasn't," cut in Gregory whose articulation in moments of stress was apt to be unreliable. "He was mad. He sh-shouted, 'D-drive out that d-da— sk-sk—'" Between his limitation, his grievance and the remembrance that a certain word beginning with d had been painfully proscribed the boy became hopelessly tangled. Gretchen caught up the tale:

"And he said that he hoped some day a bear would get us and — and rip off our skins and roll them up tight and — and leave them under a tree the way they do with sheep's skins — wouldn't we look funny walking round in our bones?"

"And h-he made all that row j-just b-because our buffalo wasn't a k-kitty," Gregory concluded gloomily.

"A kitty! A black and white kitty! And they chased it right up to Boris!" choked Cody. He roared with laughter and stepped on the accelerator. As the sedan shot forward Judith regarded him in astonishment.

"What is there so funny about that, Sheriff?"

"Don't you know what a wild black kitty with a white stripe down its back is? Then take it from me, don't go chasing no buffalo that sawed-off dog starts up. I'll bet Boris was rippin'. He hadn't oughter told the Terrible Turks about the bears though. Some day they'll be missing. They will have gone too far into the woods hunting bears."

"Are there any in this neighborhood, Sheriff?"

"No, *no*. But the caretaker up at the hunting camp has seen 'em round there." He drew up at the steps. Judith smiled at him as she wheedled:

"Are you quite determined not to tell me why I came, Sheriff?"

"I'll leave you to find that out for yourself," he teased. The girl looked over her shoulder as she stepped down.

"Then I'll leave you to find out for yourself why a canoe was skulking mysteriously around Kelp Reef this morning." The speed with which Cody strangled his engine brought a squeak of protest from the machine.

"What do you mean?" he demanded. Judith laughed and started up the steps. Cody capitulated without parley. "They say you've come here to marry Boris Stetson."

"*Marry* him!"

"Surely, surely. Folks know that he crossed the ocean in the same ship with you a month ago. That's enough to set them talking. They've heard you've got money and they know he needs it." The last sentence was delivered with warning deliberation. "Now come across with your information."

The girl stepped back to the sedan. Her low voice held a tinge of breathlessness as she warned:

"Watch Johnny Brewster! At noon to-day he signalled with a mirror to a dory near the island or to someone in a canoe."

CHAPTER V

" 'By the old Moulmein Pagoda,
lookin' eastward to the sea,
There's a Burma girl a-settin',
an' I know she thinks o' me;
For the wind is in the palm trees,
an' the temple bells they s-a-a-y —' "

What the temple bells said was drowned in a splash of water and a series of voluble shivers from the direction of the shower-room as Neil Peyton entered the White Cottage. He snapped up the shade in the book-lined living-room and stared out at the crimson sun which topped the mountain like a mammoth golf ball on a giant's tee. He swung about as the voice which had been ballading with Keith-circuit abandon called:

"That you, Neil?"

"Yes."

"Don't bite. What's the trouble? Has there been another cloudburst of tropical neckties from your female G. P.'s?"

"Quit your nonsense and come out here, Ollie. I have something to say to you."

"I wait only to don the habiliments required by the National Board of Censors and I come," laughed the voice.

Peyton turned back to the window from which he could look down upon The House. It was blushing rosy red as its century old lover, the sun, flung it a last colorful good-night. Wood smoke curled from the kitchen chimney, a light gleamed in a lower window. It was the homiest home he had known, the man thought, but never had he been as glad as he was to-night that his uncle had insisted that he have his own bailiwick quite apart from the restrictions bound to be felt in the house of an invalid. Now that Oliver Fleet had come and brought his Jap it was an especially desirable arrangement.

Peyton wheeled as his friend entered the room. The fair skin of Fleet's face, of the texture which colors furiously at the slightest provocation, glowed from its recent contact with soap and cold water. His light hair was brushed smooth over his well-shaped head. His smile which was renowned for its subjugating charm was at its zenith. A green and white striped lounging robe was wrapped about him toga fashion. His bare feet were thrust into down-at-the-heel, exceedingly down-at-the-heel, slippers. His brilliant hazel eyes darkened for a moment as they rested on Peyton's face. He pulled at his slight reddish mustache as he inquired:

"What's up, old scout? Had a hard day? You look about all in."

Neil thrust his hands into the pockets of his coat as he demanded:

"Did you know that Judith was at Meadow Farm?" Fleet's fair skin crimsoned at the surprise attack. "You needn't answer. Your color betrays you. Did you send her there?"

Oliver knotted the green cord about his waist preparatory to lighting a cigarette.

"Calm down, Neil. Your lips are white and your eyes have retreated into black caverns. I did not send her there. Your acquaintance with my cousin was of the whirlwind variety, I admit, but even you must have discovered that no one could send that young woman anywhere. She met Mrs. Turkin at —"

"I know where she spent the winter. How did she happen to meet Di?"

"Through me, of course. Have you forgotten that you introduced me to Diane before Turkin shuffled along? When I heard that both she and Judy were to winter in St. Moritz I sent them letters of introduction. What more natural than that Diane should invite a rich, attractive girl to visit her, especially as she has a brother whom she would like to see settle down."

The implication slashed deep lines between Peyton's brows.

"Do you think —"

"Don't be a dog in the manger, Neil. Now, having allowed you to administer the third degree I'll take a turn at the screws. How did you know that Judy was at Meadow Farm?"

"She was here to-day."

"Here?"

"At Uncle Dave's."

"But you told me that she didn't know —"

"She didn't know my destination when I threw up the New York chance. She gave me no opportunity to go into particulars. I left your uncle's home, The Junipers, within an hour after I received Uncle Dave's appeal. Judith refused — she passionately assured me that never would she be the wife of a country practitioner. She marshalled to her defense the theories of self-realization, self-expression, all that self stuff which is raising the deuce with the people of this country. I had no time to argue. I knew what I had to do and I did it."

> " 'I could not love thee, Dear, so much
>   Loved I not honor more,' "

Fleet hummed. Peyton ignored him and went on:

"We had known one another but —"

"One month," Oliver interrupted. "When I invited my one-time hospital companion-in-broken-arms, — whose reputation as a hard-headed flier and surgeon never had been so much as dented — to visit me at The Junipers I didn't count on his first glimpse of my charming cousin setting him ablaze. But there is no combination so devastating to the male as country visiting and a moon. Did Judy see you to-day?"

"No. The sheriff found her unconscious on the shore. She had fallen from the bleached oak."

"Fallen! Boy! I thought I had her trained so that she couldn't fall out of anything. At what time did Hi find her?"

"At noon. What the dickens does the time matter? If Uncle Dave had not seen her through his glasses she would have been drowned."

"Don't cry, Neil," Fleet chuckled as his friend glared at him in speechless fury. "She didn't drown. That young woman couldn't. She's too fiery. At *noon,* you say? Was she hurt?"

"Cut on her cheek and a slight concussion. Nothing serious but I left orders that she was not to leave her room at The House for twenty-four hours. Hi took her to

Meadow Farm this afternoon."

"Don't froth at the mouth just because your autocratic commands have been ignored, Neil."

"It isn't a matter to chuckle about. One can't tell in one hour or ten what the consequences of a fall like that may be."

"There won't be any consequences in her case — so don't you worry. Judy will bounce up like a rubber ball. I wonder if Diane knows that you and she were — to put it mildly — friends."

"Don't quibble. You know that we were engaged for three days before —" Fleet interrupted with a suspicion of breathlessness:

"Before my charming cousin applied the all-for-love-and-duty-be-darned test? I am glad that you upheld the honor of our sex and refused to let the lady put her foot on your neck. I wish that you had forced her to play Katharine to your Petruchio, had thrown her over your shoulder and brought her along here. I suppose you couldn't do that, though, an engagement isn't like marriage." As Peyton swung round to the window Fleet became absorbed in lighting a cigarette. "Was there another swain hovering in the offing?"

"There may have been a hundred. Judith

can't live without gaiety. I wonder why she came to this quiet place."

"You have forgotten that any place which Diane makes her habitat ceases to be quiet. Also, you have forgotten Boris," reminded Fleet dryly. He disregarded Peyton's furious protest and went on:

"Be fair, old scout. Judith never had the chance most girls have. Like poor little Topsy, rich little Judy just growed. The child and I had no home but Uncle Glenn Halliday's and the mistress of that spent her summers in Europe and her winters at Palm Beach. The Junipers was darned little of a home. These long-distance wives and mothers are a curse. If they don't want to be on their job why do they contract for it?"

"You are a prejudiced defender."

"I am not defending Judy. She doesn't need it. She is the sweetest girl that ever lived. And let me tell you, her sense of humor will lift her high over the rocks of petty perplexities on which the nerves of so many women go smash. She won't even know they are there. But don't think that I want you to marry her. It would be the world's worst combination. You two fire-eaters are too much alike."

Peyton's eyes smiled as he mimicked:

"Don't froth at the mouth, Oliver."

Fleet grinned.

"I admit that I am touchy about Judy. I am about all she has of her own. Uncle will be her guardian until she is twenty-five unless she marries before."

"So — I have heard."

"He loved her mother who turned him down for his brother. He has taken his disappointment out on Judy. He has tried to block her at every turn. She has had to battle first with him for every move she wanted to make. She has been a good sport. The friction has not embittered her. It must be darned wearing though to have the frosting scraped off all one's fun or ambitions by opposition. Diane has Judy slated for Stetson but I doubt if she will pull it off. My cousin has one obsession and that is that someone will marry her for her money. There are so many matrimonial wrecks among her set. Did she see you to-day?"

"No. Unless Uncle David or the sheriff mentioned my name she does not know that I am in the neighborhood."

"She will soon. Have you forgotten that we are dining at Meadow Farm?"

"No, but we won't see Judith. When I raised the roof at The House because they had let her leave her room Uncle Dave said that he had told her not to go down to dinner."

"I can see her playing the invalid if she is able to crawl. You'd better dress."

"I will as soon as I have telephoned. While you are waiting for me drop in on Uncle Dave and regale him with an account of the day's adventures. What luck?" Peyton questioned in a low tone.

"Johnny's got the signal. He —" Fleet's eager voice cooled as his Japanese servant appeared at the door. "I'm coming, Soki. I will wait for you at The House, Neil."

An hour later as Peyton's low-slung, deep-cushioned roadster reached the entrance-gate at Meadow Farm the sun was giving the color-organ a run for its reputation. From its lair behind the mountain it sent shafts of rose and violet and lemon far up into the evening sky. Lights twinkled in distant cottages. From the woods stole a balsam-scented breeze, came the hair-raising screech of an owl. Off at sea a purple haze hung low on the horizon. On the houseboat, *The Blue Crane*, moored in deep water offshore, the starboard light shone like an omniscient green eye. From its deck floated the clear notes of a flute.

Neil Peyton slowed down and accompanied the instrument in a delightful baritone:

> " 'Mar-che-ta. Mar-che-ta,
> I still hear you calling me
> Back to your arms once again.' "

Magically, softly the island sent the music echoing back. As the last note drifted into the forest Fleet made a curious sound in his throat.

"That seemed like old times, Neil. Your voice always did turn my heart inside out and shake the beat out of it. I haven't heard you sing since I came."

"Too busy. Who was playing the flute?" Peyton started the car.

"The boy in that cagey crew Stetson hired for *The Blue Crane*. He's a skinny beggar, Peter McFarland. He's from the Middle West and homesick as the dickens. I suspect he's left a girl out there. He drives the skipper to profanity baying the moon with his plaintive ditties. I'll hand it to him, though, for getting real music out of his cheap instrument."

"How do you happen to know so much about him?"

"Oh, it's part of my — photography job, to keep posted on arrivals in the village. There's Diane on the terrace!"

Diane Turkin welcomed Neil Peyton with radiant satisfaction. She was a small woman crowned with a wealth of pale gold hair which gave her head the effect of a great yellow flower a bit too heavy for the slender neck which upheld it. Her features were beautiful, her skin like cream in shade and texture. Her eyes were as light a blue as the love-in-a-mist about the sundial. She was perfection except for a suggestion of I-want-what-I-want-when-I-want-it about the lips. Her frock was a sleeveless thing of exquisite white lace. The value of her string of perfectly matched pearls would have bought up most of the houses in the village below. Except for a wedding ring her fingers were unadorned. She smiled up into the intent eyes of the man looking down at her as she accused:

"Neil, you are staring at me as though never before had you seen me."

"Perhaps never has he seen the real you, Diane. Won't you say 'Howdy' to me too?" Fleet interposed before his friend could answer. He held out his hand. Diane Turkin colored as she laid hers within it. A laugh banished the spoiled-child droop of her lips.

"Ollie, you know perfectly well that when you smile like that you get anything you want."

"Do I? I will test that statement of yours sometime." With obvious effort he forced the seriousness from his voice. "How is Judy? I hear that she has been falling out of trees, has been conducting herself as no protégée of mine should dare behave."

"Only one tree, Ollie. You were right when you wrote me that I would like her. She is the most companionable girl I ever have known. How did you hear about her tumble?"

"Neil told me."

Fleet's face turned a lively and unbecoming brick tint as he caught the jealous flash in the eyes of his hostess.

"Did *Neil* take care of her head? She did not tell me —"

"She was not conscious enough to know or care who did it," Peyton explained quickly. "I left the office as she opened her eyes. Doubtless she thinks that Uncle Dave dressed the cut. Better not remind her of an unpleasant episode by referring to it. Make her keep quiet for a day or two. She —"

"Quiet! See who's here! 'You just know she wears them,' " Fleet chuckled as Judith Halliday with Boris Stetson in attendance came up through the garden. Her green frock with its over-lay of crystal beads seemed a part of the background of delphinium, spirea, London pride, hollyhocks and honeysuckle. It shaded into the verdure of the forest in the distance.

As the girl stepped to the terrace Peyton had the sensation of being slowly, inexorably frozen. She seemed iced. A lock of her burnished brown hair had been drawn down through a sparkling slide to partially cover the white patch below her temple. Barbaric rings dangled from her covered ears, diamonds glittered on her fingers, there were a half-dozen jeweled bracelets on one arm. Her costume was in theatrical contrast to that of her hostess. Was it intentional, Peyton wondered. Stetson's manner indicated possessive devotion. Boris and his sister had the same fair coloring, but where her eyes were frankly, childishly open, his were guarded. His fair hair appeared to be varnished back from a low brow. As he approached Diane laughingly reproved him.

"The next time I leave a guest in your charge, Boris, I shall expect you to take better care of her."

"Then instruct her not to run away from me. It was a rotten morning. First Judith disappeared, then Johnny Brewster failed to show up at the island. I'd like to wring his neck. I had to get McFarland from *The Blue*

Crane to help me hop-off. Next, those Terrible Turks —"

He caught the resentful flash in his sister's eyes and shifted conversational gears:

"How are you, Neil! Glad to see you, Fleet. You —"

Diane Turkin interrupted with laughing empressement.

"Judith, I want you to meet my oldest, dearest friend, Neil Peyton."

"You posted the medico with a 'No Poaching' sign, that time, Di," Peyton heard Fleet comment in a low tone to his hostess.

He kept his eyes steadily on Judith Halliday as she approached. It was her move. What would she do with the situation? She clasped her hands lightly behind her back as she smiled up it him.

"Diane is a sort of master magician, Doctor Peyton. One never knows what she has up her sleeve. That's an archaic figure of speech, isn't it, now that sleeves have gone out? I spent most of the winter with her and not once did she mention her 'oldest, dearest friend.' Now she nonchalantly produces him. I am glad to meet you. If you are as nice as your uncle I don't wonder that your patients adore you, as I hear they do. Ollie, what brought you to this part of the world?"

So — already she had made up her mind what course to pursue, Peyton thought. She had been prepared for the meeting. She must have heard at The House that he was living in Seaboard. Otherwise she could not have carried off the situation so debonairly. He was divided between a mad impulse to shake her and an irresistible desire to shout with laughter at Fleet's expression. His jaw had dropped as his cousin coolly ignored her previous acquaintance with his best friend. Neil's eyes were at their most enigmatic as he watched her. Oliver disciplined his face and patted her on the shoulder with condescending affection as he repeated her question:

"What brought me to this part of the world? I came to look after you. I have come none too soon. If you have taken to falling out of trees it's lucky I'm here to get you back into training."

"Am I the only reason you came to Seaboard?"

"There were others. Besides having appointed myself your guardian pro tem, I am engaged in the scientific if not remunerative pursuit of photography. You know the kind, 'Sees All Knows All.' As it is my laudable ambition to shoot a travel-talk in the innermost inness of Africa next winter I am practising here."

Boris Stetson regarded Fleet with frowning intentness. He busied himself with a cigarette as he inquired:

"What sort of stuff are you shooting?"

"Oh, 'shoes — and ships — and sealing wax' and perhaps, 'cabbages and kings,' " Fleet retorted lightly. "I'll get you making a landing in your plane when I'm good enough."

Stetson's fingers tightened on his cigarette until it bent. Impatiently he flung it over the terrace. There was the slightest edge to his voice as he discouraged:

"You will have mighty few chances to shoot me unless you park by the hangar over on the island. Do you realize how few suitable landing fields there are in this village? The shore in front of Johnny Brewster's cottage would be a corker if that lazy dumb-bell would show enterprise enough to clear it. I have offered to hire it done but he turned me down. I wish you'd get after him, Neil. You've been a pilot. Even if you never intend to fly again —"

"Where did you get that idea?"

"Don't snap my head off because I assumed that you had settled down to medicine. I'm trying to wake this dead town up to the importance of landing fields, that's all."

"It must cool your ardor to be obliged to

putt-putt to Shadow Island before you can hop-off. However, the plateau there is as smooth as a floor. Your plane taxies across it like a bird," commended Fleet.

"How do you know?"

"Oh, I landed there. I'll accept your suggestion. Some day when I want to shoot I'll lie in wait for you near the hangar."

"Look here, Fleet, I don't want my picture —"

Peyton's amused voice cut in.

"Don't worry, Boris. Your best friend wouldn't recognize you. I have had a private view of some of Oliver's releases and believe me, they are the funniest things outside a Keaton film. He will have to go some before —"

His opinion was interrupted by an able-bodied whirlwind as the Turkin twins, all gold and pink and blue and white with Scotty at their heels hung themselves upon him.

"Mother promised that we might sit up until you came, Doctor Neil," they chorused.

Gretchen administered a strangle-hug as Peyton caught her up in his arms. She rubbed her head caressingly against the man's dark hair as she volunteered with a suggestion of French accent in her small, shrill voice:

"Toinette says that you are to be our new father and she prays to *le bon Dieu* to put it into your heart to thrash us *beaucoup*, but you never, never would, would you, ducky?"

Over the child's golden head Peyton's eyes met the startled brown eyes of Judith Halliday.

CHAPTER VI

"Toinette says that you are to be our new father!"

The words had paged Neil Peyton at every unoccupied moment of the day. They had not been many. He looked at the sun preparing to drop behind the mountain into a crimson abyss. He had left home immediately after breakfast and was only now returning. He regretted having missed the after-luncheon smoke he and his uncle usually enjoyed together. It meant much to the elder man. It was the hour in which they talked over the condition, mental, moral and physical, of the patients whom Sylvester loved with the tenderness of an often exasperated but always understanding father.

The low-slung roadster skimmed up a slight incline. Peyton stopped the car and looked down. The view was glorious. The mountain in the distance gave the effect of a reposing camel. A patch of sunset-light was flung over its highest hump like a gay crimson saddle. Houses nestled close against its bushy sides. A clean white church, its spire tipped with flame, rose to greet a faint star.

Writhing in loops and bends like a mammoth brown serpent the highway wound from east to west. Between it and the russet-tinged shore were the cottages of summer residents. There were intensities of color everywhere. *The Husky* tied up at the float on the shore of the Sylvester garden was a white streak against an ultramarine patch of sea. Down the bay lay Shadow Island, its dark wooded expanse streaked with emerald fields like the slashed doublet of a troubadour. The white hangar shone softly like a pearl in a scabbard. The crimson afterglow tinged the boats of fishermen as they straggled out from coves along the shore. It transformed prosaic windows into squares of burnished copper. East of him Peyton could see the red roofs of Meadow Farm.

The sight of Diane's home brought back Toinette's absurd conjecture. Was it so absurd? The suddenness with which the roadster shot forward reflected the tumult of the driver's mind. What had Judith thought of Gretchen's shrill announcement? She had shown the effects of her accident. In spite of her camouflage of gaiety she had been white — until she had met his eyes. She had deliberately disobeyed orders. Had she been any other patient he would have sent her to her room and would have made sure that she went. He couldn't do that with her — now.

She had been coolly gracious to him through the interminable evening. Evidently she had determined to ignore their one-time friendship, their turbulent parting. What had she thought to accomplish with that theatrical costume? The subjugation of Boris Stetson? It was quite apparent that already he was enslaved. It was not like Judith to wear jewels. She had told him that she did not care for them but last night she had seemed frosted with diamonds.

Those had been magic days at The Junipers until into one gloriously happy afternoon had crashed the summons from his uncle. Peyton's thoughts flashed back to the hour when he and Judith had reached a parting of the ways, had had a choice of roads forced upon them. The picture in his mind of that afternoon a year ago was as clear as though he were looking at it now upon a screen. Clearer, for his vision was full of color. He could see the girl as she had faced him in white-lipped defiance in the library of her uncle's home. The stillness of the room had reminded him of the tense moment before the bursting of a shell. The snap of a smoldering log in the fireplace had

had the effect of a detonation upon his senses. It had roused him from his stunned incredulity. He had seized her by the shoulders as he demanded:

"You can't mean it, Judith! You can't!"

The blood burned his face even now as he remembered the tense repression of her voice:

"Choose between me plus your golden opportunity in New York and burying yourself in a little New England village. I refuse to encourage you in your present brainstorm. Of course you can find someone to take your place with your uncle. If you really loved me you would put me *first,* would consider what *I* want before anything else."

And he had answered stonily:

"It is not a question of my love for you, Judith. It is a question of honor. I shall start in an hour to take my uncle's practise. Will you —"

With all his force Peyton thrust the rest of that tragic hour from his mind. The times he had lived over it! He had taken the only road he could take with a clear conscience, the road which led straight to the help of his uncle and his uncle's people. There were some things which a man could not do and retain his self-respect. One of them was to ignore ruthlessly a call for help. He had been

73

needed. The noisy advocates of individualism could not shake his conviction that sacrifice and service were the only currents which could sweep back the tide of lawlessness threatening to submerge the country. If Judith had cared enough —

"But she didn't," he reminded himself aloud. "She didn't." Diane would make any sacrifice for the man she loved, his thoughts ran on. So would Fanny Browne. Phlegmatic as she seemed, she would follow a lover over red-hot ploughshares. Fanny! The name brought back the scene in his office yesterday. What a curious hallucination of Judith's that the nurse had pushed her from the bleached oak. The accusation had brought a flood of color to Fanny's usually impassive face. She had been with him — no, now that he thought of it, she had been visiting a patient at the Cove and had entered the house as he had. But the accusation was absurd, just the same.

How helpless, how at his mercy Judith had seemed as she lay with her lashes like fringes on her white cheeks. Helpless! She, the independent, the self-sufficient!

Peyton flung off the spell which memory was weaving about him. Since their parting he had felt only a chill emptiness where his heart had been, much as though that troublesome organ which once had raced and rioted with love and desire had been painlessly removed, leaving its surrounding territory still under the influence of novocaine. Just for an instant as he had looked down at the girl under the tree a tearing pain had slashed through the numbness but that wouldn't recur. He was so confoundedly occupied that he would have little time to see Judith.

What a treadmill life was. There had been times since he had come to Seaboard when it seemed as though he must burst the bonds which shackled him and rush back to his chance in New York. But he had stood by. Every day his uncle was gaining. Ease of mind about his practise had been the great remedial factor in his improvement. After all, it was so little to do for one who had done so much for him.

What was wrong with the scheme of things that to earn a living a man had to step into harness? Every college classmate whom the war had spared was working at a business or profession with sunrise-to-sunset fidelity. No standardized days for them. What was the answer? Probably to be as ambitionless as Johnny Brewster.

Brewster! There was another confounded complication. Johnny's wife was acting like a silly fool and was driving her husband to smoldering fury. Peyton's eyebrows met in an exasperated frown. He couldn't refuse Pansy medical attention, she had a tricky heart, but he would if she fluttered about him again. He and Brewster had been good friends during the summers he had spent at Seaboard but of late Johnny had scowled at him as though he could knife him with little compunction.

It was an unfortunate complication. Fleet and he needed Johnny. Cody was no good for their purpose. Did Pansy suspect that she was not wholly in her husband's confidence? Was that the reason of her silly sentimentality? Deliberately was she planning to checkmate him?

Peyton stopped the roadster with a jerk to avoid running down Judith Halliday who had stepped from the woods into the road. A soft green hat hugged her brown hair. Its color was repeated in the broad suede belt of her white frock. A V of neck was exposed to sun and wind which already had burned the delicate skin to a dusky pink. In one arm she held a happy-go-lucky mass of pine and wax-like oak leaves. Her eyes were alight with gay defiance as she approached the car.

"Don't get out," she protested as Peyton laid his hand on the door. "If you won't be bored I will ride as far as the gate of Meadow Farm. I have been waiting here for hours for a chance to speak to you," she explained with nervous exaggeration.

Without answering Peyton indicated the seat beside him. Judith tucked the greens between them and settled into the deep cushions as far from the driver as the limitations of the roadster would permit. His lips twisted curiously before he started the car and inquired with cool friendliness:

"How is the poor old head?"

"Old expresses it. It felt in the century class this morning but it has grown younger ever since. The bruise is quite healed, see." She pushed back her hat and a lock of soft hair to show the long red mark.

"Be careful that you do not irritate it. Then you have not held me up for surgical advice?"

"No. I — I thought that we ought to come to an understanding."

Peyton regarded her with amused obliqueness. His tone was slightly sardonic as he protested:

"But I thought that we had. Do you want anything more final than our last interview?"

The brown eyes flamed to anger.

"Don't be such an — an iceberg! I merely

want you to know that when I accepted Di's invitation I had not the slightest idea that this was the town in which you had settled. The mail address she gave me was Route 1, Barron. You had not told me the name of the place in which you were to practise. Even if you had, what difference would it have made? Barron does not sound much like Seaboard, does it?"

"No. The Farm uses the rural free delivery from the next town, not the Seaboard post-office. I may be dense but why should my being here make you apologetic about your acceptance of Di's invitation?"

"I have some sense of propriety."

"Have you? When did it develop? As far as I am concerned your sense of propriety may take a day off. Why curtail your pleasure for an instant? That last hour at The Junipers you accused me of having won your love — *love*, that is funny; never mind, I'll use it as a matter of form — under false pretences, of having pretended to be associated with a leading surgeon when in reality I was only a country doctor. You didn't say it, but I suspect that in your heart you accused me of being a fortune-hunter. As I remember it, you were good enough to offer to split your income fifty-fifty with me if I would stay in New York. I swore then that never would I be the one to remind you of the weeks just passed. When I make a promise to others or myself I keep it if it is humanly possible. To be frank, if perhaps discourteous, I don't care for quitters. They leave me cold. I haven't time to think about the past. My work here is absorbing and the few friends for whom I have time are eminently satisfying."

He felt the girl beside him stiffen as she retorted crisply:

"That speech is too long and too neatly phrased to be impromptu. I suspect that you have been rehearsing the last sentence since yesterday. It is a masterpiece of its kind. I suppose Diane is first among the favored few?"

The engine purred softly as the automobile coasted down a slight hill. Judith's face flamed with color. She bit her lips as though furious that the taunt had escaped them. The blood surged in Peyton's ears. Was she jealous of Diane or was it merely the average woman's dismay at discovering that the man who had loved her had transferred his affections? He felt as though they two, with hearts and souls battling, were standing on opposite sides of a yawning chasm daring one another to jump across. The knuckles of his bronzed hands were white as he gripped the wheel. His voice was strained as he answered:

"She is. Here is the Farm gate. Sorry to have to drop you in this provincial fashion but I must get back to the office. By this time there will be a cordon of patients drawn up."

Judith was out of the car before it had fully stopped. She turned and rested one hand on the door. Peyton's hat was in his hand. A busy-body of a breeze ruffled his dark hair. The strong light relentlessly showed up every line which responsibility had set, the shadows about his tired eyes, it accentuated the furrows between nose and chin. The girl's voice was low as she suggested:

"It's chancy, I know, but let's pretend that you and I had not met before I came to Seaboard. Ollie knows, of course, but why need anyone else?"

"Stetson, for instance?" Peyton's face was white, his tone one of smiling indifference as he agreed:

"I have already assured you that I keep my promises to myself, Miss Halliday. What more can I say?"

Judith ignored the question. She leaned forward as though intent on an object in the distance. With her left hand she indicated a dory which was chugging toward the island. Her voice was hardly more than a whisper as she asked:

"Whose boat is that?"

Peyton's eyes lingered an instant on the ringless fingers before he looked toward the bay.

"That belongs to your latest victim, Boris Stetson."

"Is he running it?"

"Probably not. One of the men on *The Blue Crane*, or Johnny Brewster, takes him back and forth when he wants to use the plane. Why are you interested in that particular boat?"

"I have seen it in the bay once or twice. It is noticeably different in design from the others. Mr. Stetson has a diversity of interests. He flies, he pilots the houseboat, he —"

"He is a loafer — a —" Peyton began furiously, stopped and angrily wished that he had had the sense to hold his tongue.

"You are too much of an autocrat to have patience with a person who doesn't think or work as you do, aren't you?" Judith inquired sweetly. "You are quite different from your uncle. He is so sympathetic. Yesterday I felt that I could tell him anything."

"Better not," Peyton counseled roughly as

he bent to the gears of his roadster.

The color which had flamed in the girl's face at his warning lingered in his mind as he drove home. Her angry eyes were between him and Fleet's servant who opened the door of the cottage. Soki, the Jap, was a somewhat recent acquisition of Oliver's. He looked like any one of a thousand Orientals. He was a perfect servant. He kept the wheels of the small house revolving noiselessly. His helpfulness extended to The House. Dorothy Sylvester consulted him at every domestic crisis. She was teaching him English. Apparently he revered the elder physician. Always he addressed him as Excellency.

"Has Mr. Fleet come in?" Peyton asked as he entered the living-room. His step set the pendants of the red glass candlesticks on the mantel to tinkling. He crossed to the fireplace. The hooked rug under his feet would have set a collector to smashing the tenth commandment. Behind him hung the painted head and shoulders of a tightly laced lady of the revolutionary period clothed mostly in a simper and a pink rose. An ornately gilt-framed mirror covered the space between the windows. On the wall beside the door hung a miniature Swiss chalet, beautifully carved, with weighted chains and a rhythmically swinging pendulum. Everywhere else were books and more books.

"Yes, Mr. Fleet not come in, Doctor. His Excellency command me to tell that he see all sick to-day. He make all well, yes."

"Do you mean that my uncle prescribed for the office patients?"

The Jap's face contorted into the denatured grin of the Oriental.

"Yes, Doctor. His Excellency all time plan to do so when he get better. He tell Soki, one darn long time ago. He get better each day. Soon he walk."

"Your education progresses, Soki, but I advise you to cut out that darn."

"Mr. Fleet say darn. I like hees English. He speak with great, great pepper, yes."

Peyton's laugh and the flash of his white teeth brought youth flooding back to his face.

"You mean pep, Soki. If you wish to acquire his style you should take notes. Mr. Fleet uses advance models in expression."

The tall clock on the stair-landing boomed the time of day. Instantly from somewhere at a little distance a lighter gong intoned. A bell chimed from the next room. The door of the Swiss chalet on the wall clanged open. A wooden bird hopped to the threshold and as though guiltily cognizant of the fact that he was a second late strenuously cuckooed the hour. A door slammed.

"Here is Mr. Fleet."

"Then I go draw bath, yes."

As the servant went out by one door Oliver Fleet bolted in at another. The very walls appeared to vibrate in sympathy with his excitement. He was hot and dusty. His face was crimson, his eyes glittered as he exclaimed:

"Reluctantly I'm coming round to your point of view, Neil! *All* the roar we've heard coming from the island has not been from the plane! You know the room off the hangar? It has —"

He broke off sharply as he caught the warning drop of his friend's eyelid. He followed the slight motion of Peyton's hand toward the mirror which dimly reflected a figure leaning against the door in the shadowy hall. The man's head was bent forward as though listening. Soki! Fleet's face was quite white as he finished his interrupted sentence:

"— all the requirements of a developing room. I'll ask Mrs. Turkin for the use of it."

As the reflection vanished like a spirit mist he whistled softly:

"So *he's* one of them!"

CHAPTER VII

Judith Halliday knocked at the door of the Brewster cottage. Surrounded by a white fence the pickets of which resembled nothing so much as giant toothpicks, the house stood on the upper side of a road. A by-path zigzagged drunkenly to a float on the shore. As though debauched by association the broad flat field through which it reeled its ribald way was a confusion of lobster-pots and broken-boxes in retrogressive stages of decrepitude. A brown cock with a variegated harem of slatternly hens at his spurs vaingloriously led his foraging party through the debris. The unsightly blotch of cluttered land was set in a cyclorama of unblemished beauty. The fragrant darkness of pines and spruce, the sparkle and ripple of the sea encircled it. Under a dome of Della Robbia blue conical heaps of clouds rested upon a snowy horizontal base.

The breeze which blew from the water was salty and exhilarating. Judith drew a deep breath. How glorious the air was! As she looked toward Shadow Island the memory of the dory she had seen lingering there at noon two weeks before came flooding back. She had recognized it the next day when she had seen it in the bay. Neil Peyton had identified the boat as the one used by Boris Stetson. In the full days which had intervened she had almost forgotten the flashes which had seemed significant at the time. She had been convinced then that Johnny Brewster had signaled with a mirror, it might have been to the canoe or to the dory, it might have been — she caught her breath as the possibility presented itself for the first time — it might have been to the woman who had pushed her from the tree! The striped sleeve of her assailant was identical with the striped sleeve of the nurse who had helped her at Doctor Sylvester's — Before Johnny Brewster had gone to war he and Fanny Browne had been sweethearts. The fact clicked into place in Judith's thoughts with a suddenness which took her breath.

"The plot thickens!" she murmured theatrically. Sudden determination banished the laughter from her eyes. Why shouldn't she unravel the mystery? The suggestion sent an electric tingle through her veins. The effort would at least keep her thoughts from dwelling on Neil and Diane, on the fact that she was walking on the thin crust, the extremely thin crust, over a simmering geyser. And she would be beating Ollie at his own game! Ollie who had been in the Intelligence Department during the war, who considered that only for his fatal habit of blushing he would surpass the immortal Sherlock, Ollie who now occupied himself with amateur photography while a dark and dour mystery stalked at large.

Her knock remained unanswered. Why? She had heard voices as she entered the yard. Who knew what thread of information lay behind that closed door? If she could pick it up. If only she could! Surely she was justified in an attempt to solve the mystery of her fall. With the feeling that she was plunging head-first into a brambly maze she knocked again. Her second summons met with instantaneous response. She dragged back her thoughts from the imagination-hike on which they were speeding as the door opened. Confronting her was a young woman, the angle of whose head, the set of whose rouged lips, the rural superciliousness of whose eyes challenged the visitor to question if she dared her due to admiration.

Judith observed her intently. Had there been a swift flash of fright in those eyes? Had a sudden pallor spread beneath the rouge? Undoubtedly this was Pansy

Brewster, "the inevitable mischief-maker."
She was pretty, neither beautiful nor lovely,
just pretty. The soft pink of her simple dress
was a perfect foil for her coloring. She held a
needle threaded with heavy brown silk. The
third finger of her right hand was topped by
a gold thimble.

Judith felt the woman's baby-blue eyes
appraising her from the top of her white hat
to the tip of her white shoes. She congratulated herself that she was wearing her
smartest white sports frock with its adorable
green scarf. She would be willing to wager
that Pansy Brewster was better posted on
current and forecasted fashions than she.
Her conclusions set a smile tugging at her
lips as she inquired:

"Does Johnny Brewster live here?"

The woman's eyes flamed with suspicion.

"He does. I'm Mrs. Brewster. What do
you want?"

"Your husband."

"What do you want Johnny for? Who are
you, anyway?"

Judith was quite sure that Pansy Brewster
knew who she was. Hadn't Hiram Cody said
that every man, woman and child in the village knew of her arrival and *why* she had
come? The thought of the motive accredited
tightened the smile from her lips.

"I should have introduced myself first, should I not? I am Judith Halliday, a guest at Meadow Farm. We may wish to use the motor-boat later in the day. As your husband has the key to the engine and as he wasn't to be found on the place I volunteered to look him up. I wanted the walk so we didn't telephone. Is he here?"

"He's got to work at the island this afternoon. What good will the key do? Who'll run the boat?"

"Is it your business or mine who runs the boat if the owner wants the key?" Judith inquired with friendly crispness. "Please get it for me as soon as possible. I have an errand in the village before luncheon."

Pansy Brewster deliberated for the fraction of a moment before she held the door wide.

"Come in while I speak to Johnny. He's in the woodshed."

Judith hesitated. If the confusion of the field in front of the cottage was an indication of what she would find inside she preferred to wait on the porch. But an honest-to-goodness mystery-stalker would not be side-tracked by a trifle like an untidy room, she reminded herself, and entered the house. It was scrupulously neat. The living-room furniture of a pre-mail-order period was solid and of good design. A piano stood against one wall. The ruffled muslins at the windows were immaculate. A tomb-like quiet prevailed. Pansy Brewster stuck her needle in the cushion of a work-basket and laid her thimble and a button on the table beside it.

"Wait here, Miss Halliday, while I speak to Johnny."

She darted into the hall. She was like her sister in height and figure but where Fanny Browne was stolid Pansy was like quicksilver, Judith reflected as she crossed to a window. From the rear of the house came the riffle of cautiously restrained argument, then a man's voice slightly raised:

"Fool! Why didn't you say — Where's that button? — can't wait — I — with —" The sentence trickled into a murmur.

Judith narrowed her eyes thoughtfully. There had been a familiar cadence in the suppressed anger of that voice. There had been too much spirit in it for Johnny Brewster's drawl. She had heard him speak but once but she would recognize —

She stepped back from the window as she heard the hum of an automobile. As she turned the leaves of the gold and purple Casket of Poetry on the center table she looked down at the thimble and button beside the work-basket.

The mysterious voice had inquired for that button. Judith picked it up and turned it over and over in her palm. It was a sophisticated button, a button of parts. Not the sort which would adorn a coat purchased at the village emporium nor from a mail-order house. Evidently Pansy Brewster had been about to sew it on when interrupted by the knock at her front door. On what? That polished horn product never had been part of a garment of Johnny Brewster's. Did it belong to the man who had admonished Pansy?

"Exhibit A! I have you indelibly photographed on my mind," Judith exulted mentally.

She was engrossed in a poem in the gold Casket when Pansy Brewster entered the room. Apparently the woman was wrapped in the magnificent complacency of unassailable virtue but the hand in which she extended a bunch of keys twitched nervously.

"Sorry to have kept you waiting. Johnny would have brought them himself but he has just come from the hangar and his hands are greasy."

"Thank you. Tell him that Mrs. Turkin will keep the keys at the Farm for the present. Was it your sister who took care of my head at Doctor Sylvester's?" Judith inquired as an excuse to linger. She would like to know who the man was who wasn't her husband who dared rail at Pansy Brewster with such angry familiarity, she told herself.

"I suppose so. Fanny is the office nurse and mighty toppy she is about it, too. She has a room here. She seems to feel a terrible responsibility for me — or Johnny. Just because she has had more schooling than me she thinks I know only enough to launder her uniforms."

"She is very pretty."

"Beautiful but dumb."

"Didn't you have a chance at education, too?"

"Sure. Miss Dot at The House offered to pay for any training I'd take. The Sylvesters stand ready to give anyone in this village a chance to get on but you don't catch me working like a dog while I'm young. Me for the bright lights — when I can get there."

She drew a gold vanity from her apron pocket. She solicitously regarded herself in its mirror as she deftly powdered her nose. Judith's eyes widened as she appraised the costliness of the case.

"Shouldn't every girl be trained to earn her living?"

Pansy turned with powder-pad suspended.

"What are you trained for except to marry a rich guy? Could you do anything else if you was to lose your money?"

Judith felt the hot color creep to her hair. What had she been trained to do, she demanded of herself. She had perhaps a dozen accomplishments but nothing which counted. Even so, Pansy Brewster should not know her limitations. Her voice was gaily non-committal as she parried:

"Could I? I wonder. I might be a governess. I could teach children to read and write, run a car, swim and shoot. Young as I was in 1918 I had become a fairly efficient radio operator. I —" she stopped. Now what had she said? The woman's eyes had contracted with suspicion.

"As I think it over I am sure that I could earn my bread and butter with perhaps a smatter of jam. As for work, don't you have to work to keep this house as it is? Never have I seen one more immaculate."

A gratified smile smirked the woman's painted lips but she shrugged petulantly.

"I like housework and sewing. I hate dirt. But, I ask you, what's the use my working my fingers stiff so I can't play on that piano with that nasty field out in front? Look at it! I'd like a flower garden there but I can't make Johnny clean it up. He says he hasn't time. I know that he's too darned lazy. I wish you'd urge Di Turkin to make him do it. Gee, if I could get hold of someone to help me I'd clear it myself."

Judith's imagination gave her mind an excited poke. What a chance to find out something about Brewster, his habits, his friends, why he had signaled from Kelp Reef! She struggled to appear indifferent as she proposed lightly:

"I will help you — now."

"*You!* In *that* rig!"

Pansy's tone was uncomplimentary to a degree but she could not quite douse the grudging approval which lighted her eyes as they appraised the charm of Judith Halliday's costume.

"Yes, I. I have done harder things than that. My clothes are warranted cleansable. Well? Are you a good sport or aren't you?"

"Sure, I'm a good sport. Come round to the woodshed while I get a hoe and rake and the wheelbarrow."

"If your husband is still here —"

"Johnny? Johnny's been over on the island all morning —" Pansy had the grace to crimson as she amended, "That is, he went off just as you came. He's never here but a minute at a time. This way, Miss Halliday."

Judith pondered that interrupted sentence as she waited beside the door of the woodshed. Was Brewster's wife in his confidence? Did she know that he had signaled from the Reef? If Johnny had been at the hangar all morning, who had called his wife a fool not so many minutes ago? She turned to answer Pansy Brewster's call.

Panting slightly from exertion the woman was wheeling a barrow load of tools from the shed. Judith flung aside her scarf, rolled up her sleeves and inquired:

"Where shall we begin? You had better boss the job, Mrs. Brewster."

It was noon when the workers paused to audit their time expenditure. Broad and flat and clear of rubbish the field stretched its liberated length in the sunshine. The lobster-pots were piled in a not unpicturesque heap. The ground had been thoroughly raked. The refuse was a smoldering bed of ashes. Despite shrill squawked protests and the cocky fight put up by the Grand Panjandrum of the flock the itinerant harem had been interned in the poultry yard.

With a profound sigh of fatigue and satisfaction Judith Halliday regarded the achievement. She fastened her sleeves at the wrists and caught up her scarf. Valiantly she refrained from examining her hands. They felt as full of splinters as a hedgehog is full of quills. The furious rooster had nicked one with his spur. Pansy Brewster slightly blue about the lips, a trifle short of breath, regarded Judith with grudging approval as she acknowledged:

"I hand it to you, Miss Halliday. You're some little worker. I didn't think you'd hold out. I'm obliged to you. I hope this will be an object lesson to Johnny. The field looks great, doesn't it?"

"Yes. How much larger it seems. Isn't this the place Mr. Stetson wanted cleared for a landing? He will be pleased."

"Gee!"

Pansy's clumsy attempt to turn the horrified exclamation into a cough was too late. Her consternation already had registered. Judith mentally pigeonholed it with Exhibit A.

"If you should meet Johnny don't say that to him. He — he doesn't like airplanes, perhaps because he has so much work to do on that one at the island. Won't you have a glass of milk or — something, Miss Halliday?"

"Thank you, no. I was so interested in our clean-up fest that I forgot I had promised to deliver a note at The House. I must hurry on. I shall be late for luncheon at Meadow Farm as it is. Good-bye."

Judith reproached herself for forgetting the note as she started for the village. When Diane had asked her to deliver it to Miss Dorothy, that she might explain more fully its contents, she had hesitated. Had her hostess regarded her with veiled suspicion or had she imagined it? Quickly she had consented to act as messenger. At the risk of appearing ungracious she had not called at The House since her accident. She dreaded David Sylvester's keen eyes.

The way of a deceiver was made delightfully easy — down-hill. Anger, heartache and disappointment — sickening disappointment as months passed and no word came from Neil — had fairly tobogganed her into a slough of deception.

"What should I do?"

The question had harried her this last year. Whichever way she turned it was at her heels. She had come to Seaboard determined to procure Neil Peyton's address from Oliver — wherever her cousin might be — that she might write to him. But when as she stepped to the terrace she had met his stern eyes panic seized her. She had feigned gaiety to hide it. Then had come Gretchen's:

"Toinette says that you are to be our new father."

After that could she say, "I'm sorry! I'll go with you — anywhere!"? Instead she had begged him to keep their former friendship a secret. She must have time to think. Suppose as Toinette had intimated Diane cared for Neil? Suppose Neil — If only he would thaw a little so that her heart wouldn't freeze tight when she even thought of talking with him. She couldn't continue to accept Di's hospitality without telling her of the one-time friendship between her guest and her "oldest, dearest friend."

Neil had called her a quitter. Well, wasn't she? She had been cruel, ruthless, humiliating, dishonorable. Small wonder that he looked through her and not at her when they met. Her hostess lured him to Meadow Farm on the slightest pretext. When he was there he addressed the guest of the house as seldom as he politely could. It was blatantly evident that he regretted the past as much as she.

Outside the hedge in front of the Sylvester house Judith came face to face with Fanny Browne. At the first glimpse the nurse seemed enough like Pansy to be a twin but the Brewster woman never would have submitted to being clothed in the unattractive agate-color uniform, the girl reflected. The stripes of the gown brought the memory of her accident surging back. She had searched on the beach for her chain. Hiram Cody had suggested that Fanny might have taken it. She would ask her if she had seen it.

Judith laid her hand on the nurse's sleeve as she was slipping by.

"Good-morning, Miss Browne. Did you notice a fine platinum chain about my neck the day I was brought into the office?"

The color in the woman's face ebbed as quickly as it had mounted at Judith's touch on her arm. There was a trace of Pansy Brewster's arrogance in her answer.

"Had I seen it I should have returned it to you, Miss Halliday. There was no chain about your neck when Doctor Peyton left you in my care."

With a defiant little nod she hurried on. Evidently in righteous indignation, Judith thought, as her eyes followed the uniformed figure. One might think from her attitude that it was she who had been pushed from a tree, not the girl who had accosted her. Would the mystery as to the cause of that brutal lunge unravel as she followed the thread of evidence she had picked up at the Brewsters'? Had inuendo lurked in Fanny's denial, "When Doctor Peyton left you in my care"? Did she mean to imply that Neil had taken the chain?

Why should she have colored so furiously?

The vigorous rat-tat-tat Judith administered at the door of the Sylvester homestead diverted her thoughts to stiller waters. Her summons remained unanswered. Through the screen she could see down the length of the hall which led to the colorful garden glowing in the sunshine. She would find someone there, she decided.

As she rounded the corner of the house she saw David Sylvester in his wheel-chair in the shadow of the apple tree. Bees hummed. Robins twittered. A light sea breeze took toll of fragrance from the flowers it set a-quiver. As the gravel of the pink and blue-bordered path crunched under the girl's feet the man looked up. The book he had been reading slid to the grass. Slips of paper upon which he had been making notes scattered. His keen eyes softened with pleasure as he called:

"Welcome, my dear! I feared that you had forgotten us."

Judith retrieved the book and placed it on the table at his elbow. She appropriated the peacock chair which stood near and laid her hand in his. There was a strength and vitality in his grasp which sent an electric current through her veins. She had felt that quality in Neil Peyton's touch, she remembered. Abruptly she freed her hand to pull off her hat.

"Forgotten you! After the care you and Miss Dorothy took of me! I am not quite such an ingrate. You know Diane. Dainty, appealing, but a dynamo of untiring energy. I haven't opened a book since I arrived in Seaboard. There has been something doing every moment of every day, sailing, motoring, cards, teas, tennis, et cetera and more et cetera, until this morning. And now — here I am."

She spread her hands in a gesture of laughing surrender. Sylvester caught one of them and turned it over. He frowned at the scratched, roughened palm as he demanded:

"*Now* what have you been doing?"

The girl solicitously examined the pink-tipped fingers he released. She adroitly slipped the other hand into her pocket.

"They are ragged, aren't they? Never can I do anything with the tips of my fingers. I plunge. Ooch," she ejaculated softly as she extracted a bulky splinter with her teeth. "I helped Pansy Brewster clear the field in front of her cottage."

"You *what?*"

"That exclamation was a cross between incredulity and fright. Are you afraid of

Johnny, Doctor David?" Judith teased. "His wife seems to be but in spite of her fear she and I decided to give him an object lesson in order. I hope that it registers, that not in vain have I laid my hands on the sacrificial altar. I have a note for Miss Dorothy. Are you alone?"

"The maids are in the house. Dot is campaigning in her flivver. You wouldn't expect it of such a roly-poly little woman, would you? There has been a whispering campaign started against one of the congressional candidates and she is trying to rouse the women in this district to a sense of their civic responsibility. Trying to make them realize that politics is what the voters make it, that the ballot is their chance to make this country really a government of, by and for the people. Where do you vote?"

"Never am I in one place long enough to vote."

"But you pay taxes?"

"My guardian pays them for me, I suppose."

"Do you leave everything in his hands?"

"Why not? I — I attempted to take control once with disastrous results. Why take responsibility?"

"My dear, have you not yet learned that you get out of life just what you put into it?"

"But one gets a lot of pleasure by doing what one wants to do. I am not a New Englander. *My* conscience never will wreck *my* happiness." Judith bit her lips furiously to control an unexpected quiver. "Do you think me a barbarian because I do not vote?"

"Not a barbarian but a sort of mushroom variety of American."

"*Mushroom!* My mother's people were among the early settlers of Virginia! My father's were Huguenots who fled from France to New York before it was New York. *Mushroom!*"

There was a twinkle in the blue eyes which regarded her but Sylvester's tone was grave as he persisted:

"Even so, I won't change the classification. You flit from one side of the world to the other, restless, rootless, lawless, while a stream of foreigners pours into the country for which your ancestors died, some of them to prove assets, many of them to spread disease and iniquitous propaganda."

"Take back that 'lawless,' Doctor Sylvester. I may be all the rest but I am not that. You have stripped my citizenship of its fat complacency. I can hear its bones rattle. At once I shall begin to clothe the poor skeleton in proper railment."

"Don't look so stricken, child. If Dot were

here she would scold me for preaching. Forgive me. I have acquired the habit of lecturing my helpless patients. I am sure that once an obligation is rightly presented to you you would stand by with all your strength."

Judith closed her eyes for an instant as though to shut out an intolerable vision. Her voice caught as she denied passionately:

"Oh, but I didn't! When the test came I failed."

"You! Fail!"

"Your flattery is subtle, Doctor David. I don't deserve it. I detest self-justification but I want you to know why I failed. This is only the second time I have met you. Why should I care what you think — I wonder?"

"For the same unaccountable reason that I care for your happiness — deeply."

"Do you? Then perhaps you will understand. Never in my life have I really belonged — been first. You who have so many to adore you cannot realize how passionately I have wanted someone of my very own. Oliver loves me but he has dozens of other interests. There is no one else."

"But surely, child, there have been swarms of sighing swains battering at your heart?"

Laughter flickered behind the tears in her eyes.

"I wouldn't say quite that. There have been a few but no one for whom I cared until I met a man who seemed all I had dreamed a man might be. For a few radiantly happy days I thought that I was first with him. When I found that I was not — I didn't stand by, that's all."

Sylvester laid his hand tenderly on hers.

"My dear, if the break was your fault, don't be afraid to say that you are sorry. Do you remember that line of Petruchio's? 'Little fires grow great with little wind.' A spark of anger, a tiny flame, presto a conflagration and something priceless reduced to ashes. If ever again you come to that 'certain crossroad' — sometimes we faulty humans are given another chance — remember that I shall consider it a privilege if I may be allowed to help." Quite irrelevantly, he added:

"I wish that you would lure Neil into the merry-go-round of gaiety at Meadow Farm. The boy works too hard."

Judith's heart jumped. Why should a thought of his nephew follow her confidence? Did David Sylvester suspect that she and Neil Peyton had met before she came to Seaboard? Of course not. His blue eyes smiled at her with friendly serenity. Neil had promised that he would tell no one.

"But he is within it. He does not join the day-time excursions but usually he appears in time to have one smoke and stroll in the garden with Diane."

Judith flushed with self-contempt. It was a breach of hospitality to speak of her hostess in that tone. Sylvester's dissecting eyes met and held hers.

"Why don't you like Neil?"

Judith felt the relentless color crawl to her hair.

"Not like him! Why — why —"

"My dear, I apologize. That was an inexcusable hold-up." David Sylvester's usually colorless face matched the girl's in tint. "You are not going," he protested as she rose. "Now I know that I have offended. As a measure of forgiveness stay and have dinner with us. We are old-fashioned. We dine in the middle of the day. Dot will be back soon. I promise that I won't preach again."

"But I like your preaching, as you call it. It starts my thought-centers to tingling. I am horribly tempted to stay but I must go. I told Diane that I would return for luncheon. I walked over from Meadow Farm and it will take me quite an hour to walk back. I can stay only long enough to pick up those papers I startled you into dropping."

On her knees she collected the scattered notes. As she reached for a slip which was hiding coyly behind the doctor's chair she heard a step on the gravel walk. Before she could rise a voice exclaimed:

"Uncle Dave, there's the dickens to pay. Some officious idiot has helped Pansy clear that field in front of Brewsters'. I hear that Johnny is white with fury. For once I am in sympathy with him. "If he catches the —"

Judith scrambled to her feet. She stared from Neil Peyton to Sylvester and back again before she tumbled into bewildered confession.

"I am the officious *idiot* who helped clear that field! What possible harm —"

She stopped at a growl from the arbor. Johnny Brewster stood there. Vines cast sinister shadows on his livid face. His hand tightened over the gun he held as he drawled menacingly:

"So-o, you're in with the gang, too, are you? I thought so when you set Hi Cody on my track! Well, you and your pals had better watch out. I may be small but, understand, I can lick my weight in wildcats."

CHAPTER VIII

"Johnny!"

"Brewster!" warned Sylvester and Peyton in unison.

Feet slightly apart, hands thrust hard into the pockets of her white frock, her chin at a defiant angle Judith faced the three men who were regarding her intently. For one hysterical instant she feared that she would shout with laughter. The thought of spineless Johnny licking his weight in wildcats — it was too funny! She set her teeth hard in her lips as with gun gripped threateningly Brewster limped forward. His blue eyes blazed with fury. Peyton's were narrowed. There was a tenseness about his jaw, a white line about his lips that hinted that he was about to spring. With his eyes intent on Brewster, with his hands braced on the arms of his chair David Sylvester unconsciously had drawn himself half-way to his feet. He snapped the tension.

"Drop that gun, Johnny!" As his protégé gripped the weapon harder he demanded: "Have you lost your hearing as well as your senses? I said — *drop that gun!*"

The blaze in Brewster's eyes flared out to

blue-gray ashes as he obeyed. With a sullen attempt at nonchalance he slid his hands into his trousers pockets. As Peyton took up the weapon and examined it with meticulous care Sylvester commanded:

"Neil, bring that to me!" His nephew colored and continued his investigation.

"Bring it to me. If there is to be gun-play at this party, I speak for the gun. That's right," he approved as Peyton worked the lever and emptied the magazine of the Winchester before he rested it against his uncle's chair. "Sit here beside me, Miss Halliday, till we get to the bottom of this mix-up. I won't detain you but a moment."

As Judith dropped into the peacock chair she was indignantly conscious that she was under the microscopic observation of each one of the three men; she was still more furiously conscious that the stiffening seemed to have departed from her backbone leaving in its place a trembling void, if a void could tremble. She rammed her hands harder into her pockets to steady them. What fat had she flung in the fire when she had suggested clearing that messy field? As she bit her lips to steady them she felt Neil Peyton's hand on her shoulder. Did he fear that she might escape or — or had she given the impression that she was going to pieces? How disgusted

Ollie would be at her lack of nerve! The thought — perhaps it was the light touch — steadied her. The pounding of her heart quieted as David Sylvester counseled judicially:

"Calm down, Johnny. No matter what has happened you know as well as I that you can't express your resentment in gun-shot and get away with it. Not in this country. When you crashed in on us Neil was telling me that you were in a rage because the field in front of your cottage had been cleared. What of it? You can clutter it up again, can't you?"

In spite of the lightness of the voice Judith was conscious of an undercurrent of steadying warning in the words. Brewster kicked caves in the gravel path with one clumsy shoe. His eyes evaded Sylvester's as he drawled a sullen retraction.

"Excuse me, Miss Halliday, I was mad because — because" — his apologetic tone rumbled to a growl — "Pansy told me that Neil Peyton helped her clear that field. Now I've stood for his snooping round my girl —"

"The little liar! The barefaced little liar!" Judith Halliday contradicted fiercely. She shook off Peyton's restraining hand and sprang to her feet. Her brown eyes blazed golden as she explained furiously:

"*I* helped her! You *know* that I did! You heard me tell Doctor Sylvester before I knew that you were here. Didn't you accuse me of being one of a gang? Your wife said that she wanted a flower garden in that field and that you were too — too darned lazy to clear it! Perhaps that is another of her lies. I suggested that we give you an object lesson." She stopped for breath and thrust out her hands:

"Look at those if you don't believe me! Look at those splinters! Look at that mark where your horrid mongrel red rooster gouged me with his spur!"

Sylvester interrupted peremptorily:

"Neil, take Miss Halliday to the office and dress that wound! Be quick! She hid that hand from me. Call Hi to drive her to Meadow Farm."

"It is nothing but a scratch. I won't have my hand dressed," protested the girl stubbornly. "I won't —"

"Oh, yes, you will!" contradicted a voice behind her. Before she knew what had happened Neil Peyton had gripped her shoulders and was propelling her toward the house.

"There is no time to waste in argument or dignity if I am to get you to Meadow Farm in time for luncheon and no questions asked," he observed as they entered the office. She made a furious effort to free herself. His hands tightened like steel. Her eyes blazed back at him but the expression in his sent her lids down as though they were weighted. Her heart pounded suffocatingly, her breath came raggedly as she commanded:

"Let me go! How dare —"

Peyton's curious little laugh drowned the next word.

"Dare! Why shouldn't I dare? You —" He bent his head. The girl braced her bruised hand against his arm to hold him off.

"You — you promised!"

Either the panic in the words or the sight of the jagged gouge steadied him. With a white line about his lips he released her.

"Roll up your sleeve," he commanded curtly as he busied himself with preparations.

Judith obeyed his instructions in aloof silence. The pounding of her heart minimized the excruciating smart of her hand as he worked over it. His touch was as cool and sure as though she were a plaster model, she thought furiously. When he had the cocoon varnished down to his satisfaction he deftly adjusted her sleeve and waved a dismissing hand toward the door.

"We'll go now. I will take you to Meadow Farm."

Judith opened her lips to protest, closed them as she met his eyes. In silence she took her place in the roadster. As Peyton started the car he suggested with indifferent friendliness:

"It is a thankless business to interfere between husband and wife."

"Perhaps it would be well for you to remember that."

"You don't believe that silly accusation of Brewster's, do you? You can't. It is too absurd. What took you to their cottage?"

"Diane wanted the keys to the motorboat. Peter McFarland and I have been teaching the twins to run it. We couldn't find Johnny. As I needed exercise I volunteered to walk to the Brewster house."

"Did Stetson know that you were going?"

"Boris! Of course not! Why should he?"

"He appears to be a persistent shadow. May I suggest that he is not a safe shadow?"

Judith blazed.

"You may suggest nothing about Boris Stetson which is not to his credit. What do you know about him? How do you know what he does? You keep yourself always in the background of the life here. I like him better — better than any man I ever met. I like his southern courtesy. There is none of that New England granite in his manner or make-up." She nodded toward the gray streaks in the hillside they were passing. "I am going to the island with him this afternoon. I shall walk, sail, fly with him whenever he invites me."

"Oh, no, you won't. Not until he has mixed a little New England granite with that southern courtesy you so ardently admire. From now on I emerge from the background."

Judith opened her lips impetuously, thought better of the caustic reply which burned on them and at the imminent danger of choking, swallowed it. Peyton drove steadily on. His eyes were shadowed by his soft hat; she could see only the indomitable set of his jaw and chin. She had the feeling that she was battering with bare hands against a stone wall. What had he meant by emerging from the background? It would be better not to insist upon an answer to that question. Hurriedly she forced her attention to the outer bay where the bland sea fluffed dainty meringues along the reefs as though by contrast to call attention to the colorful glory of its glinting peacock tints. A schooner under full mother-of-pearl sail was making for the hazy horizon. In the inner bay *The Blue Crane* rocked at its mooring as lazily as an elderly gossip in an hotel-veranda chair. From its deck came the notes of a flute. To emphasize her indifference to the disturbing presence of the man beside her Judith hummed softly to its accompaniment.

> " 'Mar-che-ta. Mar-che-ta,
> I still hear you calling me.' "

The music drifted into the tree-tops and was lost. With obvious effort Peyton warmed his voice to interest:

"McFarland can play but I wish that he would vary his selections. One gets fed-up after a while with his persistent wail to Mar-che-ta."

"Just wait a day or two. I have ordered a real flute and some new music for Peter. He has been so patient with the twins while teaching them to handle the launch. They adore him. He is a bit of a swaggerer but at heart he is a desperately lonely little boy. When he plays that flute he leads my heart round by the nose. It sobs or laughs or languishes at the command of his music."

"A twentieth century Pied Piper. Happy Peter to have so priceless a treasure within his control."

Judith regarded the man beside her with incredulous eyes. Could he *mean* it? There had been no tinge of sarcasm or bitterness in his voice.

"Oh!" she breathed faintly before she demanded with a reckless disregard of consequences:

"Do you realize that, for the first time since I came to Seaboard, you have spoken to me as though I were a human being?"

A smile startlingly tender, slightly quizzical, lighted Peyton's grave face. Judith felt the blood come stealing up to her temples under the laughing challenge of his eyes. Hope crept into her heart and snuggled down in a dark corner as though fearful of discovery. Her chance had come to say that she was sorry.

"More of McFarland's magic — perhaps. Didn't I warn you that I had emerged from the background?"

A shiny gray racer shot around the bend in the road ahead. Judith could feel the man beside her congeal.

"I had forgotten that you like Boris better than any man you ever met," Peyton volunteered evenly.

He stopped his car smoothly as Stetson hailed them. Judith stole a look at him. Evidently already he regretted the late thaw. Well, she could be as indifferent as he.

"Hulloa, Neil! Judith, Diane concluded

that you had lost your way in the wilds between home and village and sent me to look
you up. I began to suspect that you were
ducking the date you have with me this afternoon. Climb in here. It will save the
Doc's precious time unless he will come
back to lunch with us."

"You have no idea what a load you have
lifted from my mind, Boris. I have been stag-
gering beneath the burden of an upbraiding
conscience. Who am I that I should presume to drag the medico from duty," Judith
deprecated as she took her seat beside
Stetson.

She looked at Peyton. He was lighting his
pipe. He regarded her with oblique intentness above the flaring match as she acknowledged sweetly:

"Thank you for bringing me this far,
Doctor Peyton. Boris, Diane's thought to
send you for me must have been inspired. I
was so afraid that you would get discouraged waiting and start for the island without
me."

From the corner of her eye she saw Peyton
wave to her companion to manoeuvre the
turn of his car first. Was he smiling or had
she imagined it?

The question engaged her thoughts the
rest of the way to Meadow Farm in alterna-

tion with strained attention to the purr of an engine behind. Was Neil trailing them? As Stetson turned in between the white gate posts Peyton's roadster shot along the highway. Judith fumed inwardly. What a self-conscious idiot she must have appeared. He was on his way to visit a patient. He had not made the trip especially for her. As the gray racer stopped before the door Judith heard Gretchen's excited voice, accompanied by the angry bark of the Scottish terrier, arising from the children's play-garden.

"They *are* our eggs! They *are* our eggs, I tell you," the child shrilled.

With a hurried word to Boris Stetson Judith jumped to the ground and ran in the direction of the voice. She stopped abruptly at the white gate. As she observed the situation she laughed in relief.

Gretchen was gesticulating with an enormous spoon as she flamed with protest. Her blue eyes were dark with wrath, her golden hair ringed moistly about her flushed face, her pink rompers were smeared with egg and dirt. Gregory, her male replica except in vociferousness and initiative, nodded his head and brandished a wicked carving-knife in solemn affirmation of every explosive word from his twin. Scotty crouched between the children. With his head on one side, his black eyes as brilliant as jet beads, his red tongue dripping, the dog watched every move of irate Hi Cody who was glaring down at the twins. With hat on the back of his head, a straw between his teeth wig-wagging, his bunch of gold insignia getting under way like an incipient cyclone, the sheriff turned to Judith. His china teeth clicked out his complaint.

"I'm glad you've come, Miss Halliday. Mark my words, them Terrible Turks will land in Sing-Sing before they get through. They ain't got no respect for property rights. They've been and robbed the chicken house of eggs to mix their mud pies with, eggs from that prize poultry M's. Turkin paid a bustin'-big price for. I selected every bird and when I come up to see if they was laying as per reputation, this is what I find. Just as though I hadn't got enough to watch with lobster-snitchers infestin' the bay without watching them kids! Mark my words, their mother'll give them twins a trouncing when she finds out and I hope 'twill make them holler good. Pies! Look at that darn foolishness!"

The dewlap under the sheriff's chin flapped with every angry word. Judith smothered an appreciative giggle as her eyes followed his pointing finger. On a white seat in a glare of sunshine, arranged with beautiful precision, was a row of mud patties each one decoratively surmounted by a round, smooth substance. As she stepped toward the bakery Gretchen flung herself upon her like a whirlwind.

"You understand, don't you, Judy? So will Mother. Mother always understands. What's the use of old Mark-my-words making such a fuss about a few eggs?"

Gregory glowered at Cody as he echoed:

"Fuss a-about a f-few eg-g-gs!"

Judith steadied her traitorous lips before she placated:

"I'm sorry that you have been annoyed, Sheriff. The twins did not mean any harm. How could they know that they had taken prize eggs? Rescue those that are left in the basket and I will explain to Mrs. Turkin. No, Gretchen! No, Greg!" she protested firmly as the children showed symptoms of attacking in solid formation as the angry man picked up what remained of the loot from the poultry-house. "Come here! What *wonderful* pies! Do show them to me."

With a hand gripping the shoulder of each delinquent she approached the bakery. With his teeth clicking an accompaniment to his grunted soliloquy Hiram Cody strode from the garden. As he slammed the gate behind him Judith relaxed her hold on the children. With sympathetic interest she looked down at the row of mud concoctions.

"They look dee-licious. What kind of pies are they?"

"Raisin pies," announced Gretchen proudly. With the touch of a culinary expert she laid her finger on the shining discs on top. "They must be almost baked. See what bustin' big raisins we found for the top crust."

"Bust-t-tin' b-big raisins for the t-top crust," repeated Greg.

Judith was unconscious of the echo as she followed the child's pointing finger. Good heavens, those shiny things were buttons! Horn buttons like the button she had seen on Pansy Brewster's table! Exhibit A was own brother to those raisins now decorating the pastry in the process of baking. She seized the small cook by the shoulder.

"Gretchen, where did you get those buttons?"

The twin shook her golden hair forward over her flushed face. She tested a pie with one dirty, chubby finger as she answered in voice and intonation so like Hiram Cody's that the girl with difficulty controlled a little gust of laughter:

"Now don't go and get darn foolish about the buttons like old Mark-my-words did about the eggs, Judy. We only —"

A slam of the gate interrupted Gretchen's explanation. As Judith and the children turned Boris Stetson confronted them. His face and eyes flaunted storm signals. Instinctively the twins clutched the girl's arms as he thrust out a brown knit jacket and demanded furiously:

"Look here, you Terrible Turks! Can't I leave a thing in the garage for one hour without having it ruined? Did you cut off those buttons?"

CHAPTER IX

With knees clasped affectionately in her arms Judith Halliday perched on the crag of Shadow Island and gazed off over the unbroken green of the outer bay. Except for a languid lace-edged swirl along the beach beneath her the sea stretched in emerald blandness to the misty horizon. It was all sparkling charm. Its faint susurrus gave no hint of slumbering passion, of lurking treachery, of the rages into which it could lash itself, of the sullen swells it could roll up at the nod of its master the wind.

The girl rose and looked at the cloudless sky where a few white-winged gulls competed for altitude records. She glanced at her wrist-watch. What had detained Brewster, she wondered. She and Stetson had crossed the inner bay expecting to find Johnny waiting for them. He was to have had the hangar open and the airplane ready. Boris had had to gas it himself. Beyond the wide open doors of the white building she could see his dim figure as he stood on a wing bending over the tank.

As she crossed the smooth green field she

looked down at her high cordovan boots, at her green sleeveless coat and knickers of a wool so soft that it had the feel of velvet; at the leather coat on her arm. She had dressed to fly with Boris Stetson. For some unaccountable reason on the way over she had changed her mind. The more her companion had argued the more determined she had become not to go. Just why, she wondered. Had it been because of the thoughts and suspicions which had thronged in the wake of the discovery that the horn button she had seen on the Brewster table was identical with those that the Turkin twins had cut from their uncle's jacket? She didn't *know* that there was one missing from the garment Gretchen and Greg had stripped.

Certainly she had not retracted because she was afraid. Hadn't she been in the air many a time? Hadn't she known the breath-snatching exhilaration of flying into a sunset, the mad heart thumping when scudding ahead of a storm, the wild exultation of bucking into the wind? No, not because she was afraid had she manoeuvred the expedition into a lesson in hopping off. Just as certainly it was not because — With heightened color she tried to shut the ears of her mind against Peyton's voice saying:

"Not until he has mixed a little New England granite with that southern courtesy you so admire."

She hastened her steps as though to outspeed that authoritative voice. If Johnny Brewster did not come soon she would go back to Meadow Farm. The ground under her feet was like green velvet. Behind the hangar stretched what seemed to her unaccustomed eyes a virgin and impenetrable forest. Before it the field rolled smooth as a billiard table to the point of the crag.

She looked toward the village. In the shimmering August sunlight its white buildings glowed like alabaster; no touch of billboard blight marred its charm. In the bay the sleek wet heads of the seals wriggling clumsily on the ledges gleamed like gold. The Brewster field stretched in unbroken greenness from cottage to shore. The remembrance of the morning's work brought a glint of laughter to the girl's serious eyes. What would Boris say if he knew of her part in it? Luckily he had not noticed her wounded hand. Apparently he had too much on his mind to think of anyone but himself. Johnny had not recluttered the field as Doctor Sylvester had suggested he might. There had been veiled significance in the elder man's tone. What did it mean? What was the mystery which seemed to center about the Brewsters?

The girl's eyes lingered on the recently cleared field. From where she stood she could even better appreciate its desirability as a landing place. It was ideal. It was less than five minutes' walk from the village. It was opposite the Sylvester float. An impatient hail from the depths of the hangar recalled her thoughts to the present.

"See anything of Johnny Brewster?"

"No!"

Judith faced the village as she seated herself Turk fashion on the smooth ground.

"Confound him! I must try out the bus this afternoon."

"Can't you hop off alone?"

"I can but it's too much work."

"You promised to show me how to help," the girl reminded eagerly as Stetson emerged from the door wiping his hands on a rag. A slight smudge between his eyebrows gave a satanic twist to his expression. "After you start I'll go back in the launch. Lucky we had the key or we'd still be waiting for Johnny. If I can't find him I can bring Peter McFarland. He could help you put the plane into the hangar."

Stetson's eyes kindled as he regarded Judith's vivid face. He flung himself to the ground beside her. He laid one hand over hers on the grass; she hid the other in the pocket of her jacket. His blonde head rested against her arm, his voice held a possessive *timbre* as he protested:

"I don't want to go. It is rather nice here, Judy."

The girl shook off his touch under pretence of pulling the gay kerchief from her head.

"I put this on because I thought I might fly. It is too hot," she objected by way of explanation. Her raised arms stiffened as she exclaimed:

"There it is again!"

Stetson sat erect, intent eyes on the village.

"What?"

"A flash. This time at the Brewster cottage. There is another! Wait!" she commanded and caught his sleeve as he moved. She watched breathlessly as two more shafts of light followed. She snatched her hand away as the man pressed his lips to her fingers. His eyes were hidden as he inquired indulgently:

"What did you mean by, 'There it is again!' Judy?"

The girl caught back the explanation which quivered on the tip of her tongue. She had been about to tell him of the man who had signaled from Kelp Reef. Suddenly she had changed her mind. She evaded his question:

"If you are to take the plane up this afternoon shouldn't you start?"

"Confound it, I should. I'll give you an inside tip. I am trying this bus out for the builders. Someone has hypnotized them into buying a skywriting-made-easy patent and they have engaged me to test it."

"Is it any good?"

"It helps."

"Please show me how to start the plane. Who knows but what in an emergency I may have to hop off myself some day."

"It won't do you much good to hop off until you can fly. You'll never learn to pilot if you lose your sand about going up. You are as uncertain as a weathervane." His voice trailed behind him as he entered the hangar. "Keep out of the way! I'll trundle her out."

Judith watched the propeller emerge from the shed. It looked like nothing so much as the goggle-eyed head of a mammoth prehistoric darning-needle. The plane came slowly as though warily watching the world it was entering. Its white wings glistened dazzlingly in the sunlight. It stopped. Stetson appeared from behind it buttoning his leather jacket. His helmet was on the back of his head, goggles dangled from one hand. He looked at the sky, then at the smooth stretch of field.

"It's a peach of a day! Are you sure you won't come? What changed your mind? You dressed for it."

"Oh, perhaps I lost my courage — perhaps — oh, perhaps a dozen reasons — Why this mirror? Do you have to look at yourself as you adjust your goggles?" the girl teased as she laid her hand on a triple reflector. Even to her untechnical mind it suggested power.

"That? That is arranged so that I may watch the result of this new appliance. Ready to help?"

Judith nodded. She rolled the sleeves of her white crêpe shirt above her elbows. She couldn't be hampered by cuffs in a critical situation like the present. A soft breeze fluttered her tie, fell a victim to the magic of her eyes, caressed her lashes and gently lifted a lock of her soft hair. She felt Stetson's eyes upon her.

"Holy smoke, Judith, but you're lovely! Come here! Climb into the pilot's seat. There you are. Do you see that switch? After I have given the stick of the propeller two complete turns to draw a full charge into the cold cylinders I'll stand back and yell, 'Contact'!"

Eager interest warmed the girl's brown eyes to gold. She laid her hand on the switch.

"This? And then?"

"Throw it this way. Try it."

"This way?"

"You've got it. Then I grab the blade and whirl the propeller. The motor will start with a roar. Throttle it this way to warming speed. Then you tumble out and I'll climb in."

"Are there no blocks to pull out?"

"There should be but I won't risk having you do it. Ready?"

Judith nodded assent. It was curious how her heart persisted in getting in the way of her voice. Stetson stepped in front of the plane.

"Off?"

"Of-f!"

He gave the stick two complete turns, stood back and shouted:

"Contact!"

The girl threw the switch, the man whirled the propeller. Without waiting for the following roar he dashed to the side of the plane buckling his helmet as he ran.

"You've done the trick. Come out!" he shouted.

Judith promptly swung a smartly booted

leg over the side. Being alone in an airplane with a swirling propeller was a situation not to be toyed with. The wind from the fanning blades fluttered her sleeves, whipped her tie, blew her short hair into a Golliwogg coiffure. She evaded Stetson's extended arms and jumped to the ground. He climbed into the seat, caught and held the control. He increased the speed of the motor. As the plane crawled forward he shouted above the roar:

"It isn't too late to change your mind. Won't you come? No? Then wait for me here."

He thrust forward the control stick. Down went the nose of the plane, up went its tail. It rolled forward, touching the field more and more lightly till from the end of the crag it zoomed into the air. Raucously protesting, a flock of gulls took to their wings.

Judith watched the man-made bird settle to a speed to maintain its altitude. She dropped to the ground. Her knees still were a bit wobbly from the tense moment of responsibility in the pilot's seat. When Boris had shouted "Contact!" she had wondered if her heart had parked in her throat for keeps. She looked up at the airplane floating in circles high above the crag. Why, she asked herself again, had she decided at the last moment not to go with Stetson?

The air cleared of the fumes of gas. The roar of the motor above thinned to a purr. As though the lightest, downiest puff had been thrown across it, quiet settled down upon the island. Reassured by the stillness, birds poked tentative eyes from the shrubs before they emerged boldly to pursue the day's business. The girl barely breathed as she watched them. A pair of robins lighted on the grass and with an occasional surreptitious glance at her proceeded to dig for their meat rations. Little orange and green vireos darted among the shrubs in pursuit of the unwary fly. A ruby-throated hummingbird pried into the golden heart of a late wild rose. In a clump of white birches a brown phœbe broadcasted an entrancingly sweet solo. At the edge of the woods two chickadees flitted busily from one mossy rock to another.

Judith's thoughts were far afield as she watched them. She disliked being on the island alone with Boris but she couldn't depart taking the only boat. Where was Brewster? The signal! Had that detained him? Of what significance had been those flashes? They had meant something to Boris Stetson. They had steadied his vacillation about flying. Had the light from Kelp Reef been for him also? There had been three flashes that time, four this. She was sure that Johnny Brewster had sent that first message; this time the signal, if signal it were, had been from his cottage. This noon he had accused her of being one of a gang. Gang! Apparently he had shady affiliations himself, otherwise, why the signal? Stetson had expected him at the hangar. Why had he not come?

"Hallo-o-o!"

The prolonged hail from the village side of the island sent the feathered company and the girl's conjectures winging to cover. Judith watched the hurried flight of the birds before she turned to greet Oliver Fleet who was striding toward her with a tripod on his shoulder and a camera under his arm. He was slightly winded as he dropped to the ground. With solicitous care he deposited his burden on the grass. As he mopped his hot forehead Judith tormented gaily:

"Enter Mr. 'Sees all, Knows all,' dressed for the part in leather puttees and riding breeches just like a dyed-in-the-wool motion-picture director."

"Boy, but I got up steam to get here! A lurking demon bewitched the speed-boat's vitals as per usual and she balked. I saw the plane hop off."

"Why such a Klondyke rush?"

"Neil —"

"Neil!"

"Don't get jumpy. Keep your feet on the ground. Neil left a message for me with the beautiful but dumb Fanny — that woman has about as much fire as a coddled Chinese chow — that Boris was to hop off from the island this afternoon. He knew that I wanted to snap him in action."

"Still I don't understand the hurry. You can get him when he lands, can't you?"

"Opportunity has passed you by, Judy. You should be chairman of a government investigation committee. Your icy voice and eyes — as per present demonstration — would chill the blood of the witnesses to liquid air. I rushed to get here in time to prevent you from flying with the gallant but irresponsible Boris."

"Then you were told that I intended to fly. I wish that Doctor Neil Peyton would confine his attention to his own affairs."

"Don't purse your lips, my child, it is frightfully unbecoming, otherwise you look rather well to-day — for you," Fleet teased. He stretched his length on the grass, shaded his eyes with the brim of his soft hat and volunteered morosely:

"Don't worry about Neil's taking an

undue interest in your affairs. *Apparently* he is absorbed in another woman. Judy," his voice roughened, "have you ever heard that old admonition, 'Tell the truth and shame the devil'?"

"What do you *mean*, Ollie?"

"Nothing — to make you catch your breath like that. Forget it!"

"But —"

"Forget it!" As the drone of the airplane became clearer he pushed back his hat and stared up at the distant white wings. Apropos of nothing he observed:

"If you think that Stetson's some pilot you should see Neil handle the control-stick. It is four years since he has touched one but I'd bet on him against the world."

"Where did you see him fly, Ollie?"

"We were sent to this side from an overseas hospital together. He went at once to a flying field and I being on furlough went with him. Many a time I saw him start off in the white ship with its red cross on his way through the sky to the help of a smashed aviator. Those days make that thing above us seem like a toy. Now what the dickens —" he sat up and stared at the plane which was but a mere dot in the blue.

Judith's eyes followed his. Breathlessly the cousins watched as the dot darted down, described an enormous F, became but a trail again before it swept into an O.

"F O U R, Four," Fleet repeated. "Why should he write four?"

"He is practising, Ollie. I suppose one word is as good as another; perhaps he wanted to try out those particular letters. He is testing the plane for — I forgot, that is an inside tip. I mustn't tell." As she made the explanation she was thinking:

"Four flashes! He writes four in the sky. That test story is a blind. I wonder —" Aloud she boasted gaily, "I feel of immense importance. I helped him hop off."

"You?"

"Even I! And I could do it again. If ever a post-mortem is performed on me — perish the thought — instructions for starting an airplane will be found engraved on my heart as writing was found on the heart of king or queen something or other." She went through the motions of scrawling "Contact" on the grass. Fleet's gaze focused on the hand on her knee.

"What the dickens has happened to you now, Judy? For a girl who never had anything the matter with her you're going some. You've had something doing in the way of casualties ever since you reached Seaboard. What is that thing on your hand?"

Judith resentfully regarded the white cocoon.

"Neil Peyton put on that dressing. He and his uncle turned white when they discovered that a silly rooster had dug me with his spur."

Fleet's color faded.

"I don't wonder! One of their patients has just lost a hand because he neglected a wound like that. At the risk of appearing super-inquisitive may I ask what you were doing in the environment of a rooster's spur? You haven't added cock-fighting to your many accomplishments, have you?"

"*Auwe,* nothing so thrilling. Pansy Brewster and I embarked on a clean-up fest. A brown cock resented our curtailment of his liberty and struck. But his fury wasn't a patch on Johnny Brewster's when he espied the immaculate condition of his field. He started out with a gun."

"You cleared that field! Why did you mix into the Brewsters' affairs?"

Judith thoughtfully nibbled a blade of grass.

"I didn't stop to think at the time that it really was none of my business that Johnny was too darned lazy, I'm quoting, to clear that field. Here comes Boris. Quick, get the camera set up!"

The airplane touched the green carpet of the crag as tentatively as a gauzy winged darning-needle might light upon a swaying leaf, touched again and again and taxied to the man and girl watching it. As it stopped Stetson pushed up his goggles. With a muttered imprecation he pulled them down again. He glared at Fleet who was painstakingly grinding his camera.

"I told you that I didn't want my picture taken, Ollie," he reminded angrily.

"That landing of yours was such a knock-out I couldn't resist. If my film is a success it may establish my reputation as an artist. Be broad-minded, Boris. Give a hand-up to a struggling photographer."

Without answering Stetson flung goggles, helmet and leather coat into the cockpit. Fleet fussed about the camera before he carefully removed the film-holder and laid it on the grass. Judith looked inquiringly at the aviator.

"Can't we help put the plane back in the hangar?"

"No, that is Brewster's job. I have done enough of his work to-day." Stetson placed a cigarette between his lips and began to search his pockets. The annoyance had left his voice. It was bland as he inquired:

"Got a match, Fleet? I'm always out of

something." As he stepped forward one heel ground into the film case. He sprang back with a confused apology. Fleet's face was somewhat white but his voice was reassuringly cheery as he answered nonchalantly:

"Don't worry, it was my fault for leaving it there. There is no real harm done. You stepped on an empty case." His brilliant eyes met and held Stetson's as he tapped the camera and announced:

"I have the negative here."

CHAPTER X

With a nice sense of dramatic values the slanting sun shot a rose spot-light on the group on the terrace. It concentrated on Judith Halliday curled up on the broad wicker couch. It brought out the high lights of her hair, it daringly rouged the gold tips of her lowered lashes, it tinted the lovely arms which her sleeveless lace frock left bare. As she remained impervious to its courting it deserted her to touch first one golden head and then the other of the groomed and chastened twins who snuggled on either side of her.

Each with an elbow on her knee, each with a chubby hand supporting a dimpled chin, the children suggested the cherubs of Raphael as, intent upon the story she was reading aloud, they gazed breathlessly up at the girl. After a flash at Scotty, the terrier, sprawled at Gretchen's feet, Old Sol withdrew his unappreciated attention and sank behind the hill.

Even as she read from their favorite chronicle of the adventures of Sir Arthur's Knights Judith wondered if the children understood the meaning of the story or if it were the rhythm of the text which held them in absorbed attention. Evening shadows lightly touched the stone wall of the terrace. A hushed note crept into the girl's musical voice as she read:

" 'And sometimes the sky was like unto a great turquoise for blueness and sometimes it was like a gray pall and sometimes the highway wound through level, radiant fields, and sometimes the rough road plunged down a steep declivity of rocks to grope blindly through dark and evil forests, and sometimes the yellow-gold moon made mysterious twilight in the shadows. But always the Knight kept the Lady's hand close in his, the hand of the lovely lady who was clad in white samite which glistened with silver threads. And always he stepped forward firmly, shining eyes straight ahead, for even in the gloom all was sharp-cut and clear to his vision. For you must know that this great Knight was the crowning glory of his house and name. He was the most noble of spirit, the most beautiful, the bravest of heart, the greatest knight in all the country round.' "

The girl closed the book. Gretchen snuggled closer and observed dreamily:

"That sounds like Doctor Neil, doesn't it?

Oh, Judy, do you suppose he'll be dead before I grow up so I can't marry him all clad in white samite?"

"With g-glistening s-silver tr-treads?" supplemented Greg eagerly.

Gretchen raised appealing eyes to the girl's face. Her brother's attitude and expression were an exact reproduction of his twin's. A hot flame licked through Judith's veins. Had the child already forgotten Toinette's prophecy? Evidently both mother and daughter coveted Neil Peyton. Her cheeks flushed with humiliation. What a contemptible creature she was! She had flung away his love and now she resented Di's evident affection for him. She forced a smile as she answered Gretchen:

"It won't be many years before you grow up, dear. Make Doctor Neil take care of himself for you. Don't let him work too hard. Go find Toinette. It is time for supper."

Gretchen dug her elbow deeper into the sustaining knee.

"Not quite yet, Judy. Read a teeny, weeny bit more?"

"No. We'll finish the story to-morrow."

"But you won't be here to-morrow. You're going blueberrying."

The child's lips quivered. There had been

a battle as to whether the twins should be included in the camping party, Judith remembered. Diane had wanted to take them but Boris Stetson had insisted that if they went he should remain at home. He had won. The girl laid a caressing hand on Gretchen's head.

"So we are. I forgot. I'll finish the story the minute we return. What shall I bring you from the woods?" she suggested to sidetrack the children's thoughts from their grievance. Gretchen responded promptly. She was a glutton for gifts.

"A live Teddy-bear. Old Mark-my-words says you're likely to find them where there are berries."

"Not in this state, I'm afraid, Honey." Then as she felt Gretchen stiffen for an argument-battle, she temporized, "But I promise that if I see one I'll bring it if I can. Have you told Uncle Boris that you are sorry you cut the buttons from his knit jacket?"

The children wriggled to their feet. Sturdy legs apart, arms akimbo, the erstwhile cherubic twins regarded her belligerently. Gretchen as usual took the floor.

"But we aren't sorry, Judy. We told him what you and Mother told us to say but we aren't really sorry. Those buttons made

143

bustin' big raisins. We didn't do any harm. Toinette sewed them on again."

"She said that we l-lost one button, there was one m-missing, b-but we didn't, d-did we, Gretch?"

"Not a button. I strung 'em on grass as you sawed 'em off with the carving knife. I don't want to go in, it's so nice out here." The child looked about for an excuse to linger. "There's the moon! Where is the Man in the Moon, Judy?"

"He will come grinning along in a week or so. Don't you remember what a lovely golden path he makes on the water?"

"I remember — because a l-little boy and g-girl in our fairy b-book followed that p-path and found a t-t-treasure." Greg's eyes were big with awe and as blue as wood violets. His voice thrilled at the thought of such bold adventure.

Gretchen sniffed.

"Some day, Judy, when you all go off on a party, Greg and I are going in the launch to find that treasure. See if we don't," she threatened. "Come on, Greggy, I'm hungry."

The children dashed into the cool dimness of the house with Scotty leaping and barking at their heels. Judith curled deeper into the inviting corner of the couch and looked meditatively off to sea. Overhead scuds were blowing across the sky like a flock of woolly white sheep pelting after their leader. Toinette had reported a button missing. Her suspicion had been correct. The button which Pansy Brewster had laid on her table beside her thimble had come from Boris Stetson's knit jacket. She was sure now that it had been he who she had heard calling Pansy Brewster a fool. The intangible familiarity in the angry voice had fitted into her memory like the missing letter in a cross-word puzzle when she had seen that row of raisin pies.

Her face burned as she remembered the proprietorial note in Stetson's voice on their way home from the island. Oliver had shot off in the speed-boat and had left them to follow. After he had made the launch fast Boris had caught her by the shoulders and had made a demand which had infuriated her. The twins had saved her. The adorable twins who had popped up from a near-by boat where under the stern eye of Toinette they were doubtless making merry with its vitals as they played skipper. As their uncle had met their round blue eyes he had muttered a more forceful than elegant epithet and had released her. Judith's heart pounded at the remembrance.

Was the Brewster woman carrying on a

clandestine affair with Boris while she prodded her husband into jealousy of her physician? In spite of Neil Peyton's caustic suggestion that it was the part of wisdom not to interfere between husband and wife she was not sorry that she had helped clear that field. She had found out two things. First that there was a bond between Boris Stetson and Pansy. Second, that there was a gang at work. Did Doctor Sylvester suspect that last fact? Did his nephew?

How the twins adored Neil Peyton. Her heart still smarted and stung from that childish suggestion of Gretchen's. Why should it ache so? Why should she care whom he loved?

"Oh, but I do! I do! I do!"

With the passionate admission she flung herself face down into the pillows which billowed about her. She lay motionless as she lived over the past, all that she dared face of it. She had loved Neil from the moment she had seen him. She had loved his strength, his steel-like resistance to her the first two weeks of his visit. Later he had told her that he had decided that women should play no part in his life until he had made his professional reputation — then, then he had met her. With lids tightly closed in an effort to shut out the present, Judith could see again the flame in his eyes as he had capitulated, could feel again the fierce pressure of his arms, could hear the caressing huskiness of his voice. For the first time in her life she had realized the power of her fortune. Never need the lack of money handicap the man she loved. He could climb higher and higher in his profession without thought of finances, she had assured him eagerly. As she huddled on the couch she saw again the flash of his white teeth, his characteristic glance through half-closed eyes as he laughed down at her without answering.

And then — she breathlessly evicted the next few days from her mind, the memory hurt intolerably — and then had come the summons from his uncle, Neil's quixotic determination to fling aside his chance for fame and respond to the elder man's appeal. At first she had rebelled for his sake, then she had selfishly made his decision a test of his love. He had been such a wonderful lover. She couldn't bear the thought of sharing him with a horde of country patients. She wanted him for her very own for a while — just a little while.

She had been determined to win in the first contest of wills. He had chosen and she had tried to forget him but how could she with that insistent question always at her heels, "What should I do?" And then Destiny — or had it been Ollie — had flung her almost into his arms again. Oh, if only she were in his arms. He had promised that never would he remind her of those days at The Junipers. He would keep his vow. With his passionate devotion to the best in life, with his contempt for the cheap, the untruthful, never would he believe that a girl might love him yet be hurt so cruelly that ruthlessly she would wreck his happiness and her own.

Could she make him understand? Her heart had beaten riotously this morning as she had met the warmth of his eyes. Then they had iced again. If she told him that she was sorry, that she loved him, would he forgive and forget? It was apparent that already he had forgotten. She had not needed Oliver's intimation this afternoon at the island to confirm her suspicion that Neil cared for Diane. What ought she to do? The memory of her cousin's apparently irrelevant question at the island answered her.

"Tell the truth!"

The girl sensed the clank of shackles as they dropped from her spirit. She would free Neil from his promise and then — the next move would be his. Voices at the door! Her cousin and Di. She pressed deeper into the cushions. She could not meet Oliver's third-degree eyes now.

"I must see Judith at once."

Was that really his voice with the shaken note in it? What had happened since they parted at the island? The girl held her breath as Diane questioned anxiously:

"What is it? Neil?"

"Neil! It is always 'Neil' with you, Diane. Are you and he —"

Judith pressed her hands hard over her ears. She would not hear Di's answer. It seemed as though aeons passed before she tentatively uncovered. She heard Oliver Fleet say gravely:

"As you say, your money would mean nothing to Neil. He has a fortune of his own, besides the oodles of it which he will inherit. He is to be congratulated that you — I can't say it. I must find Judy. She may be —"

His voice trailed away into the living-room. Judith's face was white as she lifted her head. She would free Neil from his promise but never now could she let him know that she cared. Diane must have told Ollie that she and Neil loved one another. So — he had a fortune of his own and she had patronizingly offered him half of her income. His rigidly controlled voice echoed in her memory:

"You were good enough to offer to split your income fifty-fifty with me —"

Lucky that he and she had parted. He might have found out too late that it was his childhood friend for whom he really cared. He could marry Diane when — she couldn't finish the sentence even in her own mind.

In the sanctuary of her room she regarded herself in the mirror. Her lips were white, her eyelids stained. She splashed her face with cold water till it burned like fire. Lightly she dusted it with powder to restore it to normal. With a gorgeous Spanish shawl flung over her bare arm she ran down the stairs humming lightly.

A sense of impending disaster halted the song on her lips as she saw Oliver Fleet waiting for her. A grave-eyed man, a somewhat terrifying stranger, he seemed. In his hand were the pages of a letter. Judith felt the color which she had produced with effort fade as she whispered apprehensively:

"What has happened, Ollie?"

"I'll tell you — outside."

Her cousin put his arm across her shoulders. In silence, side by side, they crossed the marble floor patterned in white and black and yellow squares. The girl had a sudden sense of being a pawn pushed about a gigantic chess-board. Whose move was it

150

now, she wondered. As they stepped out upon the terrace the sonorous tones of a ship's bell striking the hour floated up from the shore. Fleet tapped the letter in his hand.

"Uncle Glenn has gone, Judy."

"Gone! *Dead?*"

"No. I wish he were. He has gone to South America."

Judith laughed in her relief.

"Is that all! Don't be a hypocrite, Ollie. You are not pretending that we should regret his departure, are you? How inconsiderate of him not to wait a year until he could turn my property over to me. Mighty selfish, I call it."

"That is what I have to tell you, dear. There is no property to turn over."

"*What!*"

Judith's eyes widened with incredulity. Her face was drained of color. She turned her back to the wall of the terrace and gripped the rough stone on either side of her as she demanded:

"Do you mean that he has stolen my money?"

"It is the old story. He lost what he had in speculation then chucked yours after it in an attempt to get his back."

"But there was such a lot of mine!"

"There was, but, darn him, he took it all except the Grammercy Park house. He couldn't dispose of that without your signature."

Quite suddenly through Judith's mind echoed David Sylvester's grave questions:

"Do you leave everything in his hands? — Have you not yet discovered that you get out of life just what you put into it?" And she had boasted that she refused to take responsibility. She had put nothing into the care of her property — according to Doctor Sylvester she would get nothing out of it. She threw back her shoulders and observed cynically:

"It looks as though I would have a chance to demonstrate an answer to the question Pansy Brewster flung at me this morning — was it only this morning — it seems centuries ago, 'What are you trained for except to marry a rich guy?' "

"You won't do any demonstrating, Judy. I shall divide what I have with you. I should have kept an eye on Uncle Glenn's manipulation of your property. Haven't we shared everything since we were youngsters? It is only a matter of luck that my inheritance came to me when I was twenty-one. Otherwise he would have chucked mine, too. If only you had married a year ago."

"Married! What difference would that have made?"

"You would have come into your property at once."

"Of course. I am dazed or never would I have asked that silly question. Think of my forgetting for an instant a fact which influenced — I deduce that the 'chucking' has been done during the last twelve months?" There was a reckless note in the voice in which she added:

"Twelve months ago! At a certain crossroad! Truly the way of the transgressor is hard."

Fleet caught her by the shoulders.

"What do you mean by that, Judy? Don't shut me out of your confidence, dear."

The girl shook off his touch then repentantly patted his hand.

"Nothing. Merely a theatrical gesture. You are a darling, Ollie, but I shall not take your money. I don't know what I shall do yet — I am stunned."

A sudden thought stained her white face with color. Neil must not know! He might think that she was freeing him from his promise because — oh, what couldn't he think! She gripped Fleet's arm.

"Have you told — Doctor Peyton?"

"Of course not. Would I tell him before I told you?"

"Keep the news of the crash a secret at present — *please*. It will spread soon enough. The papers are bound to get it. Fortunately I have a good balance in my checking account and there will be the rent from the Grammercy Park house to tide me over till I have a chance to plan. Things are not so bad." With an attempt at lightness she added:

"From now on picture me poring over the magazine pages featuring, 'Frocks for the business woman.' "

"Judy, don't embark on a crazy attempt to make money. Just now I am tied up in this infernal photography. I can't drop it to help you but my attorney is hot on the trail of Uncle Glenn and his deals. Promise to make no move until we hear from him. At the most it will be but a week or so to wait." He caught the spark of defiance in her eyes and added sharply:

"If you don't promise I will tell Neil about your financial slump and I'll tell him at once."

The brown eyes and hazel eyes clashed. The girl's were the first to waver.

"It is a bargain, Ollie. I can't believe it! That I, Judith Halliday, have nothing — nothing." She brushed her hand impatiently across her wet lashes. Fleet caught it tenderly in his. There was an attempt at laughter in his shaky voice as he comforted:

"Don't say that you have nothing, Judy, when you have me."

His words and intonation caught at the girl's throat. He was right. Never could she be poor while she had his love and devotion. The fog of emotion occasioned by the news of her uncle's treachery began to lift. She was fit and young. It wouldn't be the worst thing that could happen if she had to earn her living. The experience might be extremely interesting. The thought brought back her color, warmed her, stimulated her. She smiled radiantly at Fleet as she answered him:

"I have everything in you, Ollie. I —" as she hesitated Fleet struck in impatiently:

"I am all you need for the present, Judy. Keep Boris Stetson at arms' length. I didn't like the tone he took with you this afternoon. You are not falling for him, are you?"

The girl's eyes followed an intricate design she was outlining with the toe of her white slipper. She permitted a little conscious smile to tug at her lips for Oliver's mystification. He expected her to spread her thoughts out for him like an open book. Why should she? He did not take her into his confidence. He and Neil Peyton suspected that Boris Stetson was not on the level. She *knew* that he was not. If he were he would not be clandestinely visiting Pansy Brewster the while he was making love to his sister's guest. He had been insufferably impertinent this afternoon at the island and in the boat. Of course what he wanted was Judith Halliday's money. And Judith Halliday had none! Why not encourage him until she had solved the mystery of the flashed signals? She could not hurt him. He did not want her. He wanted her money. When he heard the truth he would cool with ludicrous despatch. Wonderful plan! It would serve a double purpose. It would free Neil from any consideration of the girl whom he considered a quitter. If she were going to cut her heart out, to sacrifice herself that he might be happy, she had better make a thorough job of it. Judith swallowed hard before she looked up at her cousin and admitted self-consciously:

"Perhaps I have fallen — as you so picturesquely if inelegantly express it — for Boris already."

"Then look out for consequences, " Fleet warned furiously. "I stood by like a fish that first night on the terrace while you pretended that never before had you met Neil. 'Diane is a sort of master magician, Doctor

Peyton,' " he mimicked. "If you don't tell the truth and tell it soon —"

"Oliver, you are registering wrath like a stern parent in a seven-reel melodrama. What has happened?" inquired Peyton's amused voice behind them.

Judith's heart bucked like a broncho and trampled her breath. Had he heard? Oh, she was not as brave as she had thought. She was not ready to sacrifice herself — yet. What did Ollie know that he kept reminding her to tell the truth? She met Neil's eyes. There was no trace of a smile in them. Was there a hint of warning in their depths?

CHAPTER XI

An hour before at The House David Sylvester had laid aside his book as his nephew entered. The living-room in which he sat had the effect of a museum of priceless Chinese antiquities. Way, way back there had been a seagoing Sylvester with a canny sense of prospective values. From under his shaggy brows the elder man regarded Peyton as he crossed to the fireplace, rested his arms on the mantel and stared unseeingly at the bronze Buddha who since the Sui dynasty had been staring back at troubled and untroubled mortals with bland impartiality. The fire in the grate had burned to red coals. It sent forth a gentle heat which was not unpleasant in the chill of the late afternoon. The mellowing, flooding light of the afterglow poured through the windows. It fused into delicate purple the blue and white of the massive Chinese porcelain vases which flanked the hearth, even the rare thirteenth century panels on the wall caught a tinge of pink, the thick rug on the floor was splashed with crimson motes.

Sylvester's hand clenched on the arm of

his wheel-chair as he regarded his nephew's profile. He noted the hard set of the jaw, the lines about the mouth. Quite unconsciously he cleared his throat before he asked:

"Did Johnny Brewster succeed in locating you, Neil?"

"Yes."

"He 'phoned the office at about three o'clock. Dot gave him a list of the calls you were to make. What was the trouble?"

"Pansy again. She overdid this morning clearing that field. She collapsed soon after lunch. Johnny was due at the island but stayed with her until she rallied. He left her to try to communicate with Boris Stetson. When he returned she was not in her room. He found her on the porch unconscious. Her fall had upset the tripod and splintered the mirror. Evidently she'd been helio-graphing again. The silly superstition about a broken mirror frightened him as much as her condition, I suspect, — anyway he sent for me. I'm sick of the whole infernal tread-mill of aches and pains!"

Peyton turned his back upon his uncle to frowningly inspect a procession of Chinese ladies of the T'ang period, protected under glass as befitted a painting attributed to the great Emperor Hui T'sing.

"Stand by, Neil! Stand by!"

Sylvester's voice was tender with sympathetic understanding. How well he knew the thoughts raging in his nephew's mind. Many and many a time had he been through a like reaction.

"I know what you are feeling. There are days when it seems as though the bottom had dropped out of the universe. It hasn't, boy, it hasn't. It is time you stopped work. You have had no let-up for over a year."

"Stop? Do you think that I would desert your — my people they are now? Forgive my fool ranting, Uncle Dave. It was reaction, that's all. I have this evening free and by to-morrow I shall have my sense of values back again."

"Just the same, you need a let-up. And you are to have it." Two red spots glowed in the elder man's thin cheeks, his eyes were blue fires, his fingers trembled ever so little as he tapped the arm of his chair. "Meade 'phoned that he will reach here to-night."

"Why did you send for him? You are taking what you call my career too much to heart. I admit that at first it was a wrench to give up the New York chance —"

"That wasn't all you gave up, was it, my boy?"

The quiet implication sent the dark blood to Peyton's hair. His voice was taut as he assured:

160

"That is all that we need consider, Uncle Dave. I have become tremendously interested in my patients here both for your sake and their own. Every moment I have spent with you has been of untold value."

Sylvester's eyes glistened but he kept his voice steady.

"It comforts me to hear you say that. In this age of rank individualism I questioned my right to ask you to pass up Opportunity and come here. But you have measured up to the best of the Sylvester tradition. Service and sacrifice for others are the invisible gold chains which hold our national life to power and achievement. If we snap them the country will drift into anarchy."

"Chains!" Peyton's fingers slid to his waistcoat pocket. "They snap easily. How did you get in touch with Meade?"

"He was a classmate of mine. I heard that he was looking for a country practise and wrote to him. He has made good in the city but he wants a change. More time for horticulture."

"Horticulture! Here! He won't care whether there is a flower in the world at about the time he returns from his first day's rounds. Horticulture!"

"He wants to try it out. I talked with him on long distance and explained the situation. I can prescribe for the office patients — when they are convinced that they can't see you. You have assured me that I will be on my feet again soon. You mean it, Neil, don't you?"

"I do."

"I knew that you would not try to deceive me. Make the rounds with the new man tomorrow then pack your bag and trek to New York. Meade will stay once he gets here. Take a long vacation before you settle down to work. Go to London for the August Congress of Surgeons."

Peyton turned his back to the betraying light which poured in at the window. With strong supple fingers he arranged and rearranged the two bronze attendants of the Buddha on the mantel.

"I should have to sail within a week. Too late to make reservations. You are right about the vacation but I won't take it in New York. I will stay here and play round with Diane et als. Tomorrow, before daylight, she starts for Turkin's old hunting camp to inspect the blueberry pastures. Cody is going with her. For the first time in their lives he and Stetson are in accord. They are both obsessed by the idea of commercializing the crop. Boris has been spending considerable time at the canning factory down the bay."

"So I hear. I wonder —"

"So do Oliver and I. Why is Boris Stetson, the cosmopolite, interested in seeing a lot of berries sealed up in cans? Why does Cody rush off to the wilderness when he should be on his job here?"

"Hi never should have been selected for the office of sheriff. He is too narrow-minded. Once he gets his nose to the ground of a clue he's like a hound on an anise trail, you can't switch him off. Just now he's possessed by the suspicion —"

"The roadster, he outside waiting, Mr. Doctor, yes."

The Jap's smooth announcement neatly sliced off the remainder of Sylvester's statement.

Peyton's eyes flashed to his uncle's.

"All right, Soki. Where is Mr. Fleet?"

"He gone on, yes."

"Get my coat from the White Cottage, will you?"

Peyton waited till he heard the door close.

"Had he been listening? For the last two weeks Oliver and I have tumbled over him every time we've moved. Spy?"

"I can't believe it of Soki but it is difficult to know whom to trust these days. Events are moving swiftly. It won't be long before we know. Think over my suggestion in regard to the congress, will you, boy?"

"Let's get Meade here first. I will take him on his rounds to-morrow then motor north and join the campers. If I leave here at midnight I would reach the lake soon after noon and get a few hours' fishing."

"Is Miss Halliday going?"

Peyton resumed his inspection of the Buddha.

"I believe so."

"Curious how that girl appeals to me."

"You have seen her but twice. You caught fire quickly. I imagined that you had her locked up in your detention-camp for testing-out character."

"It didn't take long to make that test. I was unbelievably attracted to Judith Halliday the moment I saw her on the couch under the apple tree. This morning she told me with a catch in that marvelous voice of hers that never had she had anyone of her very own."

"She told you *that?*"

Sylvester's eyes sparkled with laughter.

"I came mighty near begging her to accept me plus infirmities. *Auwe* — I learned that from Miss Halliday — 'Little fires grow great with little wind,' as you will know to your cost some day when you meet the right girl, Neil. A spark, a tiny flame, presto a conflagration. That is love — as well as anger," he added thoughtfully.

"Then as I am far too busy to stage a conflagration I will avoid girls. I promised to dine at Meadow Farm but I will leave there in time to meet Meade at the station. Don't sit up for us, Uncle Dave. Good-night!"

As Neil Peyton stepped into his roadster the burden of illness and suffering and petty ailments which he had been carrying for a year seemed to drop from his shoulders. Meade was coming! He was free! Free to assist Oliver Fleet. Free to make good his warning to Judith that henceforth he would figure in the foreground of the life about Meadow Farm. Why shouldn't he run over to London? Match to tinder. He stamped out the blaze of possibility. His lips were sealed by a promise.

As he passed Brewster's cleared field he laughed. Meade could take his place there. Pansy could practice her wiles on him for a change. Johnny would soon see through her silly pose. The speed of the roadster registered Peyton's sense of escape. He felt young, tremendously young, tremendously alive as he ran up the steps of the house at Meadow Farm. He passed through the hall as though Mercury wings were attached to head and heels. He stopped abruptly at the door of the terrace as he heard Oliver Fleet's indignant question:

"You are not falling for Boris, are you, Judy?" He felt as though he were sending roots down into the floor as he awaited the girl's answer.

"I suspect that I have fallen — as you so picturesquely if inelegantly express it — for Boris already."

Peyton barely heard Fleet's furious warning. He made a flippant comment as he stepped out upon the terrace and smiled into Judith's startled eyes. His blood which had been coursing riotously through his veins chilled to determination. This time she had gone too far. His eyes slipped on their professional mask as he looked down at Diane Turkin who had tucked her hand under his arm.

"There is a rumor afloat that your uncle has found a substitute for you. Joyful news! Is it true?"

"Yes. Uncle Dave wants me to go —"

"Come camping with us! Please, Neil. We leave at four in the morning."

"I must take the new man on his rounds tomorrow. How long will you stay?"

"Three days. Then we return, allow time for Judy to play her first match in the tournament, before we set sail on the houseboat for the weekend."

"Diane, do you never stop to breathe? You piece festivities together with the ingenuity of a picture-puzzle," commented Boris Stetson as he stepped to the terrace. "You make my head whirl. I predict glorious weather for the inspection of the blueberry fields. A wild country into which you are venturing, Judith, so be prepared."

"Tearing yourself away from the plane? How come?" queried Fleet.

"A sense of fraternal duty. I can't let Di and Miss Halliday go camping with you and the fascinating Cody without my brotherly chaperonage, can I? It just isn't done."

"Don't be cheap, Boris," his sister protested crisply. "The plan is yours. You have been insistent that we should go to-morrow. No other day would do. If you were not coming with us I should suspect that you wanted us out of the way. Come and say good-night, children."

She held out her hand to the twins who had appeared in the doorway. Their uncle frowned at them. They scowled at him darkly and made a dash for Peyton. As they scaled his legs he dropped to one knee in an effort to maintain his equilibrium. He encircled the boy and girl with his arms as Scotty playfully licked the finish from his shoes.

With a languishing glance up into his eyes and a startling imitation of Boris Stetson's voice and intonation Gretchen pleaded:

"Won't you kiss me once, Judy?"

Shocked into action Peyton pulled the chubby arms from about his neck and regained his feet. He looked at Judith whose face had crimsoned, at Oliver Fleet who had been seized with a choking spell. Boris Stetson's brow was dark with fury as he grabbed for the twins. With the agility of long practise they eluded him and ran to their mother. Of the group on the terrace she was the only member who showed a thorough appreciation of the humor of the situation. As a servant murmured in the doorway she stooped and kissed the children tenderly.

"Dinner is served, so run along to Toinette, kiddies." As they flew away as lightly as might white and gold butterflies she slipped her hand within Peyton's arm and mirthfully queried:

"Isn't Gretchen a marvelous mimic? I predict a dazzling future for her in the two-a-day. She will maintain her old mother in solid-gold comfort equaled only by that in which luxuriate the Coogan parents."

CHAPTER XII

Coals blinked fast graying red eyes among the embers of the noon fire. A slight aroma from frying trout lingered in the spicy air. A row of log cabins with brand-new tin water-pails glittering like family plate on their porches rimmed the lake at a conservative distance from its pebbly shore. Behind them loomed mammoth evergreens, before them the motionless glinting water stretched like a gigantic mirror in a forest frame.

Pipe in mouth, twirling his bunch of insignia with drowsy after-meal lassitude Hiram Cody slumped against the trunk of a stately pine. Behind it in the shadow the camp burro flapped enormous ears in a futile effort to discourage voracious insects. Flat on his back, soft cap shading his eyes, Boris Stetson stared up into the mass of green needles.

Of what was he thinking, Judith wondered, as she noted the cynical twist of his lips. She glanced at Diane Turkin in the steamer chair which had been brought from one of the cabins. The leopard skin collar and cuffs of the plain blue top coat thrown over its back contributed a touch of barbaric state. The lightest shade of blue in her plaided tunic frock might have been matched to her eyes. She seemed absorbed in a book. Had she no suspicion of her brother's intimacy with the mischief-breeding Pansy, Judith wondered. In spite of the last two days spent almost continuously with Stetson she was no nearer the solution of the mystery of his dealings with Pansy Brewster than before. Ought she to take Ollie into her confidence?

From beneath her lashes she thoughtfully regarded her cousin who was irritating a chipmunk to squirrel profanity with a fusillade of cones. Though the motor trip to the wilderness, the paddle across the lake to the camp had been replete with interest, he had maintained an uncharacteristic silence. Was he worrying over her financial crash?

Financial crash! What of it? Judith's eyes sparkled with vitality and courage. This camping experience had poured new spirit through her veins. Never had she known life as she had lived it the last forty-eight hours. Two nights she had slept on balsam boughs with the fragrance of pines and the smell of a wood-fire stealing into the window to drug her to dreamless sleep. In the early morning she had plunged into the icy water of the lake. The cold had set her teeth chattering, her eyes shining, the blood leaping and glowing through her veins.

If only Diane would be content to settle down here for a while. Not a chance of it. Before she had swallowed the pleasure she had bitten off she would have her teeth set in the next tidbit. No sooner had life shaped into a delightful form with the glorious coloring of sea and shore and sky for a setting than Di gave it a turn. Instantly like the rainbow-hued beads and glass of a kaleidoscope the bright-colored hours shifted into another pattern. What had happened that she herself no longer cared for the unceasing round of pleasure? Now she craved time to think, to recollect herself — she had seen that phrase somewhere lately and liked it. Recollect oneself. It meant so much.

A pebble flung with nice precision struck Judith's shoulder. It might as well have been a grenade dropped into the midst of her thoughts. They scattered into a thousand fragments. She looked up. Stetson smiled at her as he reproached:

"You have been in a dream for the last five minutes. I dare you to come exploring with me."

Judith became absorbed in brushing the

sand from her soft green knickers as she asked:

"Will you and Ollie come with us, Diane?"

Her hostess shook her head. She tapped white fingers over her lips to stifle a yawn before she declined emphatically:

"No, I thank you. Besides being sunburned to a cinder, and nibbled to shreds by these bloodthirsty mosquitoes I have had all the exercise I intend to take for the next month. Boris and the sheriff have dragged me over every inch of my possessions. Figuratively and literally I am fed-up on blueberries. Go with Boris, Judy. I want Oliver here with me. He rests me. All my perplexities vanish into thin air when I am with him."

Fleet withdrew his attention from the chattering chipmunk. He tugged at his short mustache; his color was high as he observed:

"It is such an unusual want of yours, Diane, that wild horses could not drag me from this spot. Is it safe for my cousin to wander about in the wilderness, Hi?"

"Surely, surely, let her go, Mr. Fleet. She can't get into any trouble and she can always holler. Don't get out of hearing, Boris, and tote your gun along."

Stetson glowered.

172

"Don't instruct me as though I were a ten-year-old, Hi."

The sheriff chuckled.

"Mark my words, we ain't none of us wholly grown-up when we are up against the wilderness, and this region comes pretty nigh being that. The most wood-wise are apt to do fool things in an emergency. Don't you go with him unless he takes a gun, Miss Judith."

The girl regarded Stetson with meditative eyes. The remembrance of his detestable familiarity on the island trip still had the power to make her hotly angry. Why hadn't her cousin come to her rescue? He had been furious when she had untruthfully intimated a growing fondness for Boris. Now he seemed rather anxious to have her go exploring with him. She would call his bluff, for bluff she was sure it was — and go. With a laughing touch of coquetry staged for Oliver's edification, she encouraged:

"I am not afraid to adventure with you, gun or no gun, Boris. Let's go."

She regretted her tone as she met the flash in Stetson's eyes. Indignantly she sensed Fleet's satisfaction in the arrangement. He had moved nearer Diane's chair and had closed the open book in her lap. If he cared so little what she did why had he

173

hurled at her that threatening:

"Then look out for consequences!"

She was still pondering the question and its countless ramifications as she and Boris reached an old wall. A pile of logs which once must have been bars lay in a crumbly heap beautified by a covering of emerald moss. Stetson mounted them and held out his hand. To the girl's intense relief he relinquished hers as soon as he had helped her over the obstruction into a clearing blue with enormous berries. The charred stumps which dotted it were a gruesome explanation of the devastation of forest which had made possible the present crop. Judith speculatively regarded the faint trail which had its beginning where she stood.

"What made this path?"

"Probably the camp donkey going back and forth from the lake to drink. The caretaker's house is just beyond here."

"From its unsteadiness I should judge that friend burro was in the habit of returning from imbibing rather pleasantly jingled. Look at those berries in the middle of the pasture! They are the biggest ever! Let's take some to Diane. Those will clinch the canning enterprise. Line your cap with this fresh hankie and we'll fill it. Come on!"

Stetson laid his gun on the mossy logs and

obeyed orders. Lured by the increasing size of the berries the man and girl followed the faint trail. With her mouth full of the luscious fruit Judith demanded thickly:

"Could bears have made this path?"

"Bears here! Don't be silly. I told you that it was the donkey."

"But the sheriff said —" Judith paused to test a specimen as large as an adolescent marble.

"Don't take stock in Cody's vaporings. If once he contracted the idea that there were bears in this neighborhood he would have them here if he had to import them. You might as well try to insert a graft in a billiard ball as to thrust an opposition plank into the sheriff's mind. We'll go as far as those trees and come back."

Stetson indicated two gigantic pines a hundred yards ahead on either side of a small space barren of bushes. They towered with the diminishing symmetry of Chinese pagodas.

"Curious that the fire should have spared those trees and devoured all the rest," Judith observed as she picked her way along. "Aren't these berries whoppers?"

"Do you wonder that I dragged Di up here? There is a fortune in this acreage. I know because I have been watching the work at a cannery down the bay."

"You! I can't picture you. Do you help paste on labels?" teased the girl.

"I — What was that?"

"The donkey braying, silly." On tiptoe Judith reached for an elusive berry. She lost her balance. She plunged head-first into the bushes. Her companion gave an excellent imitation of a competitive high-jump as he yelled:

"Holy smoke! What was that?"

The girl sat where she had fallen. She choked from the combined effect of berries and laughter.

"Bo-Boris, you should see yourself! Your eyes are round with fright. Your — your mouth is blue with berries. Good heavens! What is it?" She scrambled to her feet and clutched Stetson's arm. Her lips were as blue as his as she whispered:

"Something soft and warm brushed against my foot!"

Cautiously they parted the bushes and peered down.

"It's a bear cub! There's another! Take this one, Judith!" Stetson thrust into her arms a bunch of brown fur from which sparkled two black beads. He reached down for another. The girl hugged the treasure close.

"You adorable thing! You are as fat as

butter. Don't be frightened, Judy won't hurt you. Boris, I can feel the little thing's heart pound. We'll take these home to the twins" — she wrinkled her lovely nose — "after we've given them a bath in the —"

A rumble like distant thunder cut off the sentence in its prime. Stetson's eyes flew to hers as he demanded:

"What was that? That wasn't the donkey."

He looked over his shoulder at the crumbly bars from which direction a repetition of the sound came. His alarmed blue eyes matched to a tint by his berry-blued lips sent the girl into a paroxysm of laughter. Her smile stiffened ludicrously in response to Stetson's blood-curdling shout:

"Beat it to the trees, Judith! We can't go back! It's a bear!"

The girl waited for no second command. With the heavy cub clutched in her arms she panted along the twisting trail as though pursued by demons. Just once she looked back. Lumbering between the berry bushes was a dark shape.

"Where — where's your g-gun, Boris?" she gasped as she halted beneath a pine.

Stetson reddened furiously and ignored the question.

"Hurry! Climb this tree! Can you make it? Put your foot up! I'll give you a boost! There you go! For heaven's sake, hold on, can't you?" he puffed as she slipped back to the ground. "Try it again! Put down the cub! I'll toss it up to you! Holy smoke! Can't you stay put!"

Judith sternly choked back the laughter which was convulsing her at the ridiculous proceeding, concentrated on the ascent and made it. She reached down for the cub, clutched it in one arm and climbed higher. It was not easy to make the grade with the wriggling burden, but she held tight to her prize. Tentatively she had promised Gretchen a live Teddy-bear. This was a chance to make good. Perched on a sturdy limb she stopped for breath. She peered through the screen of green needles and watched Stetson crash upward to safety in the companion pine. From unpleasantly near came a furious rumble. The cub in the girl's arms answered it with a plaintive call.

Judith's heart pounded with the rapidity of a riveter in the hands of an expert. Cautiously she caught a sticky limb and bent forward. From between the berry bushes on the edge of the clearing protruded the head of a black bear. It turned from side to side, sniffed and gave vent to an angry growl. The girl hastily flattened herself against the tree trunk.

"All right, Judith?" shouted Stetson. "That was a mighty close shave. Who would have thought of seeing a bear here?" There was a hint of apology in the tone.

"But I told you that the sheriff —" she remembered her own impatience with an I-told-you-so addict and abandoned the sentence. "Where there is smoke there must be fire. Where there are cubs there must be —" the note of raillery in her voice was replaced by frantic appeal:

"Boris! The bear is trying to climb this tree! Get down, get *down*, you ugly thing!" The girl kicked wildly against the trunk of the pine. "Ollie-e-e! Sher-if-iff! Help! Help! Shout, Boris! Shout!"

Judith felt her color recede as she looked down at the red dripping mouth, at the snapping eyes, the clutching claws below. Into her mind flashed Gretchen's realistic description of the neat way in which bears stripped a sheep and left the skin in a nice little roll.

" 'Wouldn't we look funny walking round in our bones?' " Judith quoted in a fervid whisper.

The cub in Stetson's arms wailed. The angry bear which had been glaring up at the girl dropped to all fours and lumbered toward the other tree, making horrible sounds as it went. It set its claws in the trunk. Judith could hear the rustle of Stetson's hasty ascent as he shouted:

"She's coming up! Squeeze your cub, Judith! Make it yell! That'll call the creature off. As soon as she claws your tree I'll make this one wail. He-lp! Hi! Fleet!"

The tactics suggested proved of temporary effectiveness. Back and forth from tree to tree lumbered the bear, consuming its own fury as it went, if sounds were to be believed. Each whine from a cub evoked an answering snarl from the irate parent. Finally, it squatted on its haunches midway between the two trees and gave vent to an ear-splitting roar.

"I bet that feeble cry will bring Pop," shouted Stetson. The terror in his voice sent Judith into a little whirl of laughter. When the bear was not attacking her tree she could appreciate the humor of the situation. With the wicked realization that she was hitting a man when he was down, she tantalized:

"Do you suppose that the sheriff imported *this* bear? If he did, he is only a near-director. We need one more to give the situation real dramatic value. One for each tree. I've been craving adventure — Boris! *Boris!* She's really coming up this time! Ol-lie! Sher-iff! He-lp! Shades of the movie pioneers! Here comes another!"

She giggled hysterically.

"I see two men over by the bars! Shout, Boris! I c-can't. It's s-so f-funny."

She went off into another peal of laughter. She lost her balance. The danger sobered her. She got her voice in hand and called:

"Sher-iff! Ollie-e-e! Quick!" She heard the sound of claws below and frantically thumped her heel against the tree.

"Get down — you horrid thing! Get down!"

"Hi!" yelled Stetson. "Quick! Over here! Pines! B-E-A-R-S!"

The distance between the trees and the old wall while beset with peril was not great. Judith clearly heard the sheriff's shouted question:

"What's the mat-ter?"

"We've got some bear C-U-B-S! Ma and Pop have treed us," yelled Stetson. Distance diminished the exasperation in Hiram Cody's voice not a tinge as he roared:

"Where be the cubs?"

"We've got 'em safe!"

"You crazy critters! Drop 'em! Drop 'em!" The sheriff's voice rose in a frenzied shout and cracked into silence.

"All right!"

Judith and Stetson responded in unison

and simultaneously released their prizes. The girl regretfully watched the cub's descent. She would have liked to take the live Teddy-bear home to Gretchen. She leaned over cautiously to observe the family reunion.

Quiet settled upon the field, broken by an occasional growl from the infuriated parents. Once they advanced on Judith's pine in mass formation but a whine from their babies deflected their yearning for vengeance. After a few moments the bears lumbered off toward distant woods with the cubs padding dutifully at their heels.

As the quartette disappeared from sight Judith cautiously backed down the tree. As she prepared to drop from the lowest limb, arms caught her and held her close. Furious that Boris should have dared even in such an emergency, with an angry remonstrance she threw her head back against a tweed shoulder. She looked up. Her protest died on her lips. Neil Peyton's eyes dark with anxiety in his white face looked straight and deep into hers. In an instant he had released her. Judith dropped to the ground to conceal the fact that she was shaking with excitement. As she buried her face in her hands Peyton encouraged:

"The danger is quite over, Ju— Miss

Halliday. Hi and I were creeping up on the bears when they decided to abandon their prisoners. I couldn't fire from the wall as I had only my shotgun. One might as well try to slaughter a whale with dried peas as to make an impression on a bear's hide at that distance with bird shot."

Judith realized that he was talking to give her time to get her grip. She was furious with herself that she still shook as though with palsy. In spite of her appreciation of the humor of the situation she had been frightened. And when she had thought Neil miles and miles away to suddenly feel his arms about her — she snuggled her face deeper into her hands to hide the color which spread from throat to hair. Hiram Cody laid his hand on her shoulder.

"Don't you take on so, Miss Judy. The bears wouldn't have e't you. They might have handled you rough but they wouldn't have e't you. Those cubs must have been a late crop. I've never before seen such cute little fellers at this time of year."

The girl raised her head as Stetson approached nonchalantly brushing the pine needles from his clothes and settling his tie. The sheriff relieved his own anxiety in a caustic attempt at raillery:

"Seems to me, Boris, you're huntin'-

broke enough to know better than to leave your gun behind when you're going cradle-snatchin' in the woods. We found it over there by the wall."

Stetson remained sullenly silent. Judith hurried to his rescue.

"I insisted upon kidnapping the cubs, Sheriff. I promised that I would bring Gretchen a live Teddy-bear if I could find one."

"Mark my words, you better look out how you make such darn fool promises. Come on, we've gotter get back to camp. The folks will be anxious."

They entered the trail in Indian file. The sheriff in the lead, Stetson second, Judith at his heels with Peyton following. The girl was tinglingly conscious of the man behind her. From a mullein stalk among the bushes a bee rose, staggered giddily for an instant, found its bearings and flew straight for the woods. Cody paused in his loose-jointed stride and pointed a bony finger.

"Did you see that? That was a honey-bee. Mark my words, if you followed it you'd come upon a holler tree plumb full and dripping with honey."

For a reason which she had neither the courage nor the inclination to analyze Judith suddenly became gorgeously, riotously happy. Her spirits bubbled over at the sheriff's suggestion. Her eyes were brilliant with audacity as she glanced over her shoulder at her rear guard and suggested gaily:

"Let's follow the bee and get some honey!"

Peyton's face hardened as he met her challenging eyes. Stetson laughed. Cody growled:

"Haven't you had enough adventure for one day? If you haven't, mark my words me and Neil have. You should have seen his face when he heard your first holler. The color didn't come back till long after Boris shouted. He and me know when we've had enough. We're not hankering to drag you out of a bee scrape. An' unless Boris can show more sense than he did when he let you grab that cub I guess he wouldn't be much help. Much as I admire you, Miss Judy, I'd hate to struggle through life with only your stock of common sense. Don't you let her go on a bee-hunt, Neil."

Peyton's laugh was brief.

"She will get away only over my dead body. Go on, Sheriff."

CHAPTER XIII

With the disappearance of the sun behind the tree-tops and the creeping up of forest chill Judith's high spirits which had persisted through the afternoon unaccountably declined. As a sop to the conventions of the approaching supper hour she had slipped a skirt over her green knickers. Seated on the steps of her cabin she watched Diane Turkin and Neil Peyton push off from the float in a flat-bottom rowboat. They were laden with fishing impedimenta from landing nets and rods to the book of flies which Di carried with the solicitous care she might have bestowed upon a priceless first edition of The Compleat Angler.

Luminous pink clouds trailed reflected glory across the surface of the lake. The tips of stately pines looked down upon their doubles mirrored in the clear water along shore. The mad laughter of a loon shook the air and frayed out among the tree-tops. There was no breeze. A trout broke the surface of the lake. The water rippled into widening circles. A streak of silver flashed upward, fell and disappeared in a splash of iridescent spray. The acrid smell of wood-smoke permeated the air as it spiraled aloft from the cook-house chimney like an Indian signal. Only the cautious dip of oars broke the silence which the oncoming twilight flung ahead as a dancer might fling a mist of cloudy tulle.

With elbow on her knee, chin on her rosy palm, Judith forced her attention from the departing boat to her cousin who stood upon the float looking after it. He was tugging at his short mustache as though pondering a problem of immense magnitude. Once this afternoon she had seen him surreptitiously regarding Diane and Peyton with just that absorbed attention. They had been sitting with heads close together, he rigging his rod, she selecting flies. The utter content in the face of her hostess, Neil's boyish enthusiasm — he seemed to have shaken off years — the laughing comradeship between the two had hurt Judith intolerably. She seemed to be looking through bars at something beautiful just beyond her reach. For an instant when Neil's arms had closed about her this afternoon she had felt herself forgiven, had told herself that before the forest night closed in she would tell him that she was sorry, but he had hardened to indifference before their return to camp.

Ollie had been right. Neil Peyton was absorbed in Diane.

Unreasoning anger against him roughly extinguished the lingering glow of radiant happiness of the afternoon. He had warned her against Boris. She would flaunt her indifference to his counsel as he had emphasized his indifference to her. With the appositiveness of a stage entrance Stetson emerged from his cabin door at the extreme end of the row of buildings. Judith waved to him and called gaily:

"Isn't this an ideal night for our jacking-party, Boris?" Not until that moment had she had the slightest intention of embarking upon the expedition.

Stetson referred to her request as after supper the campers sat within the smoke protection of the fire on the shore. The burro sagged on the outer edge with his head almost in the blaze as he wagged his long ears and switched his tail to ward off mosquitoes.

"We will wait until dark before we start, Judith."

"Start where?" demanded Fleet sharply. "Didn't the bear-hunt provide thrill enough for you adventurers?"

Judith watched the light in Peyton's pipe flare and fade. Would he care if she went with Boris? He seemed superbly indifferent to his answer:

"We are insatiable thrill-collectors, aren't we, Judy? I am about to initiate your cousin into the fine art of jacking."

"It is against the law."

"Holy smoke, Sheriff, we are not taking a gun. There is no law against using a flash to light the shore."

"You will love it, Judy," approved Diane Turkin lazily. Her hair had turned to copper in the firelight, her blue eyes were luminous with content. "Don't stay late, Boris. Remember that we make an early start in the morning."

"Why don't you finish out the week here?"

There was an intangible something in Stetson's tone which acted like a spark to Judith's memory. It set afire the powder trail which led to her remembrance of his intimacy with Pansy Brewster. She caught the flash in Fleet's eyes. Had he sensed an undercurrent in the question? There was a trace of impatience in Diane's answer:

"It will take most of to-morrow to get back to Meadow Farm, Boris. The next morning Judith is to play in the tournament; at noon on the exact stroke of the ship's bell we set sail in the houseboat. You can make it, can't you, Judy? You must."

"I will keep to your schedule, Diane, or perish in the attempt. Who am I to throw sand in the gears of your plan? I shall start for the Club before you are up. On my way over I will leave my bags on *The Blue Crane* that you may have no thought of me till I arrive. Peter McFarland will look after them for me."

"I have seen your Peter," observed Peyton. He was leaning on one elbow as with his free hand he buried Diane's shoe under a heap of pebbles. "He has the eyes of Barrymore's Hamlet, a touch of Keats about the brow, a suggestion of Cyrano about the nose and the magic of the Pied Piper in his flute."

"Why do you refer to him as Judith's Peter? Where has she seen him except when he is on duty?" demanded Stetson sharply.

Fleet's tone was light as he explained:

"He and Judith have been teaching the twins to handle a boat. Judy suspects that he is a genius, apparently he suspects that she is an angel in disguise. I shouldn't be surprised to hear that she was backing his musical education."

He colored to his hair. His eyes flashed to his cousin in quick apology. Evidently he had just remembered that never again could she back any one financially, Judith thought. Being unable to help would be the hardest part of having no money, she had so loved to give. At least Peter would have his flute. It was already paid for. With a quick little sigh of relief she turned her attention to what Stetson was saying:

"You will have great weather for your trip on *The Blue Crane*. Sorry that I am obliged to hie to the hot city instead of going along with you, Di."

"But you must go, Boris, if only to look after that hatchet-faced crew you yourself selected. Do they know the coast?"

"They know all they need know with Neil aboard. He is going, aren't you, Doc?"

"If the new medico holds on that long. I want the sea trip so much that I would go alone, if necessary."

"Then you will be safe with any crew, Di. Neil could navigate a dreadnaught along this coast in shine or fog. Be thankful that you have a crew, hatchet-faced or not. It is getting to be as difficult to secure the right men for a boat as it is servants for a house. I admit that this lot leaves much to be desired in the way of appearance, but what can one do when a man with a modicum of good looks is snitched by a movie-director re-gardless of the fact that there may be nothing behind his face but bone. It is a wonder that they haven't roped young McFarland."

"Postpone your trip, Boris. I have planned the cruise for you and Judith."

"I appreciate the delicate attention but I must go. I hop off the minute we reach Meadow Farm. I may row across the lake to-night."

"Hop off! Do you intend to fly to New York?"

"A mere figure of speech, Oliver. Fly! Not on your life. I shall leave the bus on the island. It will give that lazy Johnny Brewster something to do while I am gone. He can overhaul the engine. He's a wizard with a motor."

"Then he must get a lot of fun out of that generator you have in the hangar. It's a corker."

"What do you know about it?"

"Oh, I saw it one day when I landed."

"You can keep out of that hangar, Fleet. You seem to have a passion for minding other people's business. I have intended to express that opinion for some time. Now you've got it."

Boris Stetson's voice was harsh with fury. Diane Turkin breathed an incredulous, *"Boris!"* before she hurried into an explanation:

"That generator was my extravagance, Ollie. I had it put in to light the building. I am afraid of lamps on the island. There is too much valuable timber there to risk fire."

From under her long lashes Judith regarded Oliver Fleet. He was lighting a cigarette. Were his fingers unsteady? His voice was cool and unruffled as he ignored Boris Stetson's furious attack and inquired:

"Diane, how do you dare put so much money into that plant? Don't the inhabitants from all the country round about land there for picnics and hunting?"

"No. I paid the town of Seaboard a fancy price — so fancy that it was grotesque — for that island on the condition that it was to be considered by the townspeople just as much my private property as was the lawn of Meadow Farm. I wanted it for a bird sanctuary. That was before Boris built the hangar and brought his plane. I don't know what effect the airplane has had on the wild life there. I made sure that there was a comfortable room for him if he had to stay or for a mechanician, then I shed the responsibility. I don't like the island. When there I have a sense of being trapped."

Fleet tugged at his short mustache. A smile twitched at his lips; his eyes were on his cigarette as he sympathized:

193

"I'm not strong for islands myself. What the dickens would one do if one's boat drifted off?"

"One could always fly," suggested Stetson urbanely as though desirous of obliterating the effect of his angry protest a few moments before.

"You mean that you could, or Neil could. I never tried but once and that was when —"

Stetson sprang to his feet.

"Come on, Judy, let's shake the experience meeting."

The girl glanced at Peyton. He was leaning on one elbow as he laughed at an aside of Oliver's. She had planned the evening excursion to hurt him. It had proved a boomerang. He did not care and she would give her ears to side-step this canoe trip *à deux*.

"Won't you come with us, Di?" Judith invited eagerly.

"And spoil sport? Not I. Playing gooseberry always has left me cold. Remember what I said about an early return, Boris. Sing for us, Neil."

"Wait until these young people get off."

At the indulgent amusement in his tone Judith turned sharply away. As she stepped into the canoe and took bow paddle she looked back at the group near shore. Peyton

194

and Oliver were on either side of Diane. Her hair glistened like gold in the dim light. The fire indulged in a burst of pyrotechnics as it signaled to the pale stars with a shower of sparks. The donkey still sagged within radius of the smoke with his head on one side as though in contemplation.

The beast's near-human absorption in the group brought a smile to Judith's lips. At a low command from Stetson in the stern she dipped her paddle. Little chills of excitement raced to her finger-tips as with scarce a sound, scarce a break in the mirror-like surface of the lake the two blades dipped and turned in rhythmic unison.

As though a magic sower had skimmed across the water scattering mammoth golden seeds as he went, the purple-black expanse suddenly reflected a thousand low-hung stars. The yellow half-moon dangled on the tip of a gigantic spruce like a glinting ornament on the top of a Christmas tree. The damp fragrance of the forest perfumed the cool air. From the shore floated a man's voice singing.

The music grew fainter. Judith brought her teeth down hard upon her lip in an effort to shut out the vision of the group about the fire. Was Neil still covering Diane's shoe with pebbles, she wondered jealously. She paddled automatically. Fainter and more faint came the voice.

"After we round the next point stop paddling. No matter what you see, keep quiet."

Stetson's cautious whisper floated forward. Judith nodded assent without turning. The world was so still it seemed as though the tempestuous beating of her heart must be audible to the man behind her. Like a water wraith the canoe skirted the base of a jutting fern-covered rock. Tall grasses! At the first swish the stern paddle shot the canoe to open water. Then around another bend into the dense shadow of a pine-girted cove.

It seemed to Judith that for hours she held the bow of the canoe steady by her paddle. The world was drugged with silence. At a slight sound above she looked up in time to see a meteor flash across the sky and vanish. What a night! Indigo velvet spangled with gold! Was that a slight rustle in the underbrush on shore? She held her breath. As though in answer to her unspoken question a disc of light illumined the spot from which the sound had come. The girl shook with excitement. Standing in the glare, staring straight at her were a doe and fawn. Their fascinated eyes shone like gigantic rubies. The spell shattered. Underbrush crashed.

The light went out. Stetson's matter-of-fact voice announced:

"That is all we'll get to-night. Did you like it?"

"L-like it!"

Judith vainly endeavored to control the chatter of her teeth. Stetson laughed.

"A touch of buck fever, what? Shall we drift for a while?"

Judith was conscious of the note of panic in her answer. She had but one desire and that was to get back to camp as soon as possible. As sometimes on the screen the faint outline of a scene lingers after its successor has been projected, so the picture of Neil Peyton lounging on the shore beside Diane refused to fade out. What were the two doing now, the girl wondered.

"Back we go. Are your nerves sufficiently steady to paddle?"

In answer Judith dipped her blade and shot the frail craft out of the shadow into the moonlight. Her thoughts kept pace with the swift canoe. Intolerable shame at her own failure to stand by, jealousy of Diane — she might as well be honest with herself — anger at Neil — for what — the whole miserable business had been her fault. Now that her indifference to his advice had been demonstrated she was unbelievably eager to escape from Boris. Why? During the afternoon and evening he had been unobtrusively friendly. Just once she had caught a curious glint in the eyes bent on her. But that once had set her mind to clanging an alarm with the persistency of a grade-crossing bell.

Stetson kept up a running fire of impersonal chat as they paddled back. He beached the canoe. Judith jeered at her fears. She was quite off guard when in the shadow of a tall pine he drew her so close that she was too intent upon capturing her breath to struggle. He bent his head:

"I'll take that kiss now, Judy," he exulted.

"Sorry to be a spoil-sport, Boris," Peyton's cool voice separated them as adroitly as the slash of a keen sabre. "Diane sent me scouting for you. I have been waiting here ten minutes. She wants you at once. Something to open for a supper she is preparing for you adventurers."

With a growled protest Stetson moved away. Judith took a hurried step after him. A hand descended on her arm. In the dim light Peyton's face shone white, his eyes were brilliantly black as he demanded:

"You permit Boris to kiss you? Well, the more the merrier. If he — why not I?"

He caught her in his arms. The girl could feel the heavy pounding of his heart in the instant before he crushed her lips under his.

"Oh, Neil!"

The hail came from the cook-house. There was a possessive timbre in Diane's call. Judith twisted herself free. There had been no love, no tenderness in Neil's kiss she told herself, just revenge. It had been barbaric, horrible. He didn't love her. And — Diane wanted him. The girl's face was as white as the man's. Where his eyes were flames hers were ice. She touched her head appraisingly. Her voice was toneless as she observed lightly:

"Not a hair misplaced. Your technic has improved, Doctor Peyton. You do not muss one nearly as much as you did. Who is the lovely lady upon whom you are practising?"

"Judith!"

Peyton's voice was harsh with protest. The girl shook off his detaining hand.

"Tell Diane that — that I did not want to spoil the effect of my magic evening with anything so prosaic as eats," she endeavored to say lightly. "I am going to my cabin. We make an early start, you know."

She throttled a panicky impulse to run and walked to her log house humming as she went. Once inside she dropped the bar across the door and sank on a bench by the open window. She crossed her arms on the sill and hid her face on them to strangle a sob. Her mind named with anger at Boris' insolence, her lips still burned from the fury of Neil's kiss.

A forest-perfumed breeze laid a velvet touch on her hair. She raised her head and looked from the window. The moon was low in the west, the lake was an obsidian mirror, black, glassy. The fire on the shore blinked a dozen red eyes. She heard the murmur of voices. Then Boris Stetson's call:

"I am going across the lake to-night, Di. Good-bye!"

She heard steps on the porch of the cabin next hers, then voices. She recognized the inflections of Neil's and once she caught Di's in a quickly stifled exclamation. She flinched from the probabilities her too-ready imagination presented. She put her hands over her ears to shut out the sound. When she removed them the voices had ceased. She looked out of the window. A man was standing by the fire staring down at the embers. Neil!

As though drawn by her thought he turned and took a few steps toward her cabin. She barely breathed. He stopped at the sound of a boat being pushed into the water.

"Wait, Boris! I'm going with you!"

In the stillness of the night his quick call floated back to the girl. It seemed hours before she heard the soft dip of oars. She watched the white wake of the boat till it disappeared into clots of shadow. With her head resting against the frame of the window, fixed abstraction in her brown eyes, she sat there thinking, thinking, while frost as delicate as a baby's breath whitened the fern rim of the lake and a violet dawn stole above the eastern tree-tops.

CHAPTER XIV

The Blue Crane, Diane Turkin's seventy-five-foot houseboat fidgeted with an enticing what-a-day-to-be-free-and-away tug at its mooring. The sea sparkled and twinkled in intriguing sympathy. As the Club launch drew alongside Judith Halliday regarded the cruiser with speculative eyes. The boat seemed unusually low in the water. It gave the impression of a brooding hen huddled down on hopes if not on eggs. The girl smiled at the comparison. Chameleon-like her mind was taking on the color of its surroundings; already she was thinking in farm terms.

Boats had personalities, she decided. The house of *The Blue Crane* carried up from the hull proper gave an impression of homelike spaciousness. The large afterdeck with its wide divans and tempting chairs of gayly cushioned wicker presented the last word in seagoing luxury. There was no one on deck. One of the men should have been on hand when she boarded. Where was Peter McFarland? Evidently Diane's hatchet-faced crew was imperfectly trained in the amenities of service. How quiet — how sleek —

that was the better word — the boat seemed. Its square windows appeared to blink with well-fed drowsiness.

"Somehow you remind me of the sheriff's cat that swallowed the canary. I can sense you licking your chops," Judith mentally soliloquized as she stepped on deck. She watched the Club tender scoot away. The ship's clock struck eight bells. She was on time to the minute but she had had to take a short cut from the tennis court to the Club pier to make it. The davits which had held the motor launch dangled in the slight breeze. The men and boat must still be at Meadow Farm float. Diane was notoriously tardy.

So much the better, Judith congratulated herself. She was hot and tired after her triumphant bout at tennis. She would have time for a shower and change before the others arrived. Ought she to hunt up the captain and tell him that she had come? No, Diane had said that he would be on the watch for the arrival of the Club tender, so that they could start at once, that she was to take her time about dressing, that luncheon would be served on deck at one.

In the white and cretonned stateroom she found the belongings which she had left on her way to the Club. As she performed the difficult feat of slipping her white kasha frock over her head without ruffling a hair she heard the exhaust of a launch, then her cousin's voice. She looked at the clock set in the woodwork above the dresser. Only twelve-thirty? Her exercise, plus the shower, plus the fact that she had not slept the last two nights had drugged her with drowsiness. She had time for forty winks.

She flung herself on the berth, punched a pillow into a soft heap under her head, groped sleepily for the fleecy afghan and drew it over her. The comfort of it. To let herself go after propping her lids up — just to let herself go-o —

"Just — to — let — go-o," she repeated the words drowsily. She stretched luxuriously, opened her eyes, closed them, yawned experimentally and patted her lips with pink fingers. Her mouth remained half open, her slender hand poised in midair as she counted the strokes of the ship's bell. One! Two! Three! Four! Five! Six! Seven! Eight!

Four o'clock!

She stared at the timepiece over the dresser. She felt the slight vibration of the forty-fifty horse-power twentieth century motors as they worked with the rhythm of perfectly geared machinery. Under way!

Was it possible that she had slept more than three hours?

She sat up and blinked at the clock again. She stepped to the square window which took the place of a port light and looked out upon a moving panorama, upon an expanse of blue sky fluffed with pink swansdown clouds, a dancing sea broken by the black fins of a school of porpoise, a bunch of racing catboats, their white sails gleaming like paper cut-outs against the horizon. Land must be on the other side. There could be little wind *The Blue Crane* was making way so smoothly.

Judith nodded approvingly at her reflection as she adjusted her soft green hat before the mirror. She looked as refreshed as she felt and she felt equal to any situation which might arise, no matter how difficult. The last four days had been difficult. It had required all the courage and more, much more than she had thought she possessed to face the world with a smile when the solid ground of an ample income had been swept from beneath her feet, when she realized that never now could she go back to the crossroad where a year before she had taken the wrong turning. That way was barred. Neil would think that she wanted him because she had no money — because his chance had come to make good in New York. If only — the substitute had not come — if only she could have proved that she loved him enough to live with him anywhere. If — only — he didn't love Diane!

The last was the insuperable obstacle. Judith shut her teeth hard. Had she no more pride than courage? She had flinched from opening up the past with Neil. It must be done. They would be on the boat three days. Surely in that time she would find her opportunity. Her thoughts returned to the present in a rush. Even though her mind had been excursioning she still confronted herself in the mirror in the gay little stateroom.

"One day at a time, Judy!" she reminded her vis-à-vis. She had determined to keep all thought of finances in the background during the short cruise. She had a far more vital problem to solve. Oliver had promised that upon their return he would summon his lawyer to Seaboard for consultation. Little her cousin suspected that the money loss was the least of her trouble. She forced a smile and addressed the girl in the looking-glass:

"You thought that you could be as selfish as you liked and get away with it, Miss Halliday? Well, now that life has cracked back at you, be a sport and laugh no matter if it hurts you horribly." Her derisive smile touched only her lips as she slipped on a slim green coat with a snowy fur collar and left the stateroom. Diane's door was closed. It was tea-time. Doubtless she was on deck.

The living-room of the deck-house was unoccupied. Once more the cat and canary premonition tingled through Judith's mind. She gave an unconscious sigh of relief as she stepped out upon the afterdeck. The suggestion of nightmare which had tinged her consciousness vanished. At last she had discovered signs of life. At the extreme stern a pair of shoes were braced against the rail. From behind the tall back of the chair in front of them rose a thin whorl of pipe smoke. At last she had located Ollie and where he was, there would be others. Ollie liked company. The surge of relief which swept her was wholly incommensurate with the situation. It communicated itself to her voice as she called gayly:

"Messmate, ahoy! Where are the others? I had begun to think that I had boarded the *Flying Dutch*— What — why — who — *you!*"

The sentence dissolved in an unintelligible murmur in her throat as the shoes and pipe-smoke materialized into Neil Peyton confronting her. He might have posed as a model for the well-dressed-man page in his gray trousers and double-breasted blue coat. His eyes were blank with astonishment, his face was white, he gripped his pipe in one tense knuckled hand as he demanded with uncomplimentary emphasis:

"What are *you* doing here?"

Indignation submerged the teasing tingle of premonition which had again begun to function in Judith's mind. No wonder that Neil was embarrassed to see her after that last night at camp. Quite unconsciously she brushed her hand lightly across her lips before she shrugged and answered flippantly:

"Doing here? Oh, I ran out to cut the lawn."

"Don't try to be funny. Answer me."

Try to be funny! It was the last straw. Judith had thought her reply rather amusing.

"Aren't you being absurd yourself? Why pretend that you didn't know that I was coming on this cruise? I might be the pig-faced lady by the way you glare at me."

Her heart shook her with its pounding as she noticed the flame rising in his eyes, the color stealing back to his face. At The Junipers he had looked at her like that. Had he forgiven her at last? But there was Diane. What did it mean? He must not think that she was embarrassed. With simulated nonchalance she tapped her fingers lightly over her lips as she admitted:

"I am still half asleep. Don't tell Ollie if I confess that I have been napping all afternoon. I haven't slept for two nights and —"

"Why not?"

The rest, the tonic of the sea air, the stimulation of an electrically charged situation sent Judith's spirits soaring. She was possessed by the same unaccountable sense of gorgeous happiness that had seized her on the afternoon Neil had caught her in his arms as she dropped from the tree. Her voice was patronizingly audacious as she admonished:

"Physician, forget thy calling. Remember, thou art on a vacation. Where is Diane?"

"Diane did not come."

"*What!*"

The girl's insouciance vanished like a light smashed to earth. She sank into a deep-cushioned chair. Soft waves of pink eddied to her hair. Her eyes darkened to black as she demanded:

"Is that the truth or are you trying to frighten me?"

"Why should I try to frighten you?"

"Where is Ollie? I heard his voice — I *know* that I heard his voice after I came aboard."

"He went ashore just before we weighed anchor."

"Are you and I alone on this boat?"

The fingers in which Peyton held a match were not quite steady. He waved his pipe toward the deck bridge from which came the voice of the skipper.

"Except for the crew."

The girl's lips were white, her voice a mere whisper as she demanded:

"Did you plan this?"

Her lashes went down before the fierceness of Neil Peyton's eyes but his voice was rich with amused indulgence as he reminded:

"My dear Judy — as we are alone you will forgive the informality, won't you — must I repeat that I keep my promises to myself when it is humanly possible? Why should I plan this? You don't suspect me of an attempt at kidnapping, do you? As for an elopement — I was tempted once but since have come to the conclusion that I am not built on the caveman plan."

Wasn't he? Judith's heart raced as she remembered his kiss. The thought left its mark on the voice in which she demanded unsteadily:

"Why isn't Diane here?"

"After you left for the Club she received a

message from Mt. Desert that she was needed to close a real-estate deal. You know her well enough to know that she never allows pleasure to interfere with business."

"Did she forget me?"

"She asked Oliver to notify you at the Club of her change of plan. He was confoundedly busy with — some films and had Soki send the message."

"Then the Jap must have mixed signals. I did not return to the Club house after tennis but came directly to the houseboat. Why didn't they send the message on to the court?"

"I suspect that the Club budget does not provide for the service required to page its members. Diane, knowing that Oliver and I were keen for a few days' cruise, insisted upon our following out her first plan."

Judith looked up at him quickly. That last explanation did not ring true.

"When did Ollie decide not to come with you?"

"On the way out to the cruiser. He saw a boat coming in that he wanted to shoot and —"

The girl lifted a protesting hand.

"Don't tax your ingenuity further. I don't believe a word of your explanation. I know that there is something behind all this. Will you give the order to come about?"

Peyton looked at her with the oblique intentness which always caught at her breath.

"At once. Having inadvertently heard your confession of affection for Boris Stetson I can appreciate how unendurable the present situation must be for you."

Did he really believe that she cared for Boris, Judith demanded of herself turbulently. So much the better. She watched him out of sight. It seemed as though she waited for hours for the boat to come about. Had he not intended to give the order? Silly! Of course he wanted to turn back. He had more to lose from the situation than she. What would Diane think? Why — why had she not made light of the contretempts instead of accusing Neil of planning it? Her face burned. From that accusation he had every reason to conclude that she thought that he still loved her. She would disabuse his mind of that fantasy. From now on she would treat the situation as an uncomfortable but amusing predicament for them both.

The engine-room gong! The boat was coming about! On a sudden impulse she made her way forward. Through the window of the enclosed bridge she saw the captain at the wheel. His face was sullen but he touched his cap which tilted at an angle with unctuous politeness. His white trousers, his blue coat looked as though they might have recently returned from the tailor's creased where they should be creased, smooth where they should be wrinkleless. He suggested a fashion-plate or a millionaire yacht owner playing skipper. She didn't like him, she decided. He gave the impression of endeavoring to assure her — against the nudge of his conscience — that he considered it quite a matter of course that a man and girl should set sail on a houseboat unchaperoned.

From the bow she looked ahead. *The Blue Crane* was nosing straight for the reposing camel in the background of the village of Seaboard. A copper disc like a huge medal hung above its sharpest hump. Shadow Island was a dusky blur. The sea was satin smooth and rainbow hued. A tinted mackerel sky gave the heavens the effect of a spread of tasselated pavement. On the horizon a twilight shot with the flame and rose and purple of a fire-opal was stealing up.

Restlessly Judith returned to the afterdeck. For a while she watched the fleecy wake of the houseboat spread and diminish like a lacey court train frilled with sapphire ripples until merely a hint of white it was lost in the dark water. She curled up in a corner of the wide divan against the rail. She felt very young, very solitary, very insignificant. Chin on her arm she watched the moon coming up in the east. As it rose it took on a lovely light which filigreed the sea with golden motes. Soon there would be a path. Her thoughts flashed back to Gretchen's threat:

"Some day, Judy, when you all go off on a party Greg and I are going in the launch to find that treasure."

Funny little things the twins. But adorable in spite of their mischief. The moon's one eye seemed to grin understandingly down upon her. She stiffened and hurriedly set her feet on the deck side by side with stiff conventionality as Peyton spoke from behind her.

"The skipper assures me that at the rate we are going, we will make the Meadow Farm mooring at eight o'clock."

"Did you have difficulty in persuading him to bring the boat about?"

"Why do you ask?"

"I don't know — honestly I don't know. His expression perhaps when I went forward."

"Did he dare —"

"No! No! *No!* Don't look so angry. He said nothing."

"I have ordered supper served on deck at seven. I will join you then unless you prefer to be alone. I hope that you won't. Why broadcast the fact that we are not friends? I will be on the forward deck should you want me before then."

Judith restrained an impulsive, "Don't go!" Had he cared to stay he would not have waited for an invitation. Generally men did what they wanted to do, she reflected with uncharacteristic cynicism. She watched the color pale in sky and water. On the horizon was the outline of a boat. She picked up a magazine and read until it was too dark to see. As she laid it down she realized that she was ravenously hungry. She had had nothing to eat since breakfast, she remembered. She had an instant's thought of confronting Peyton with a theatrical demand for food — it might ease the constraint between them, might pave the way for her admission of regret. No. He had said supper at seven. After supper while he was smoking she would tell him. The deck would be shadowy and if his eyes were stern she would not see them.

What time was it now? She had been so immersed in her thoughts and in the story that she had not heard the ship's bell. She glanced down at her wrist. She had left her watch in the stateroom. She stole to the door of the deckhouse and looked at the clock. Almost half-past six. Thank heaven she wouldn't have long to wait. As she was tiptoeing back to the divan Peyton appeared. He regarded her in amazement. The suggestion of ferocity still lurked back of the laughter in his eyes as he demanded:

"Why are you gum-shoeing about the deck?"

The friendliness of his voice snapped the bands of resentment and fear which had held the girl's heart as in a vise. That temperamental organ stretched cramped muscles. In an hour she would be free of the burden she had carried this last year. Judith's eyes and lips reflected the release of her spirit as she acknowledged gaily:

"I was looking at the clock. If I don't have something to eat soon I shall bite." She clicked her lovely teeth.

Peyton's eyes met hers with steady friendliness though the cords in his throat stood out in strong relief.

"Then as a measure of self-protection I will hurry the steward. You have had neither luncheon nor tea, have you? I seem to have been forced into the position of host on this extraordinary cruise and I admit I have been a thoughtless one. Imagine Aunt Dot's disgust when she learns that a Sylvester, even once removed, has allowed a — guest to — go hungry."

The last words dragged. Peyton's eyes were intent upon a blotch in the pale moon-path. Judith's glance followed his. It was a boat. Doubtless the one she had noticed a while before. It was too far away to be classified but even at a distance one could tell by the froth of white at the bow that its speed was kicking up a tremendous spray. Neil uttered a low exclamation as he reached for the binoculars on the table. Could it be of relief, the girl wondered.

"What sort of a boat is she?" Judith inquired as she knelt on the divan. With elbows on the rail she strained her eyes in a vain effort to determine the type of the oncoming craft.

"She is a high-speed cruiser and she is stepping along at the rate of thirty miles an hour. Take a look at her. She is a pretty sight, isn't she?"

The girl put the glasses to her eyes.

"Won-der-ful!" For some unaccountable reason her heart tripped up her voice. "Is she following us?"

"More likely she is planning to flash by at a pace which will make *The Blue Crane*'s progress seem as rapid as a retarded cinema film. I am off to see if I can't get as much speed on that supper."

Left alone the girl watched the approaching boat. Was she mistaken or had the white foam about the bow stilled? Had the headlong pursuit been checked? Pursuit! What a silly thought to have come into her head. For what reason would anyone or anything pursue the stodgy houseboat?

Dusk was stealing up. Judith turned on the table light as the steward and Peter McFarland appeared with laden trays. She smiled radiantly at the boy. He acknowledged her greeting by a surly nod. Her eyes widened with amazement. What had happened? He was actually scowling at her. When she had given him the flute in the morning he had been overwhelmed, his face had been white, his voice hoarse with surprised appreciation. Now — his face was whiter than it had been then, and the one glimpse she had had of his eyes reminded her of Neil's comparison of them to those of the melancholy Dane. Their expression out-Hamleted Hamlet. She didn't care much for the steward. He seemed far more intent on watching the boy than on the proper service of the meal. Perhaps Boris was right, perhaps all the good-looking seagoing men were in the movies. As Neil Peyton stepped out on the afterdeck he dismissed the men:

"We will wait upon ourselves." He felt of his pockets. "McFarland, get the pipe and tobacco pouch in my room and bring them here, will you?"

The boy nodded assent and followed the steward forward. Judith regarded Peyton from behind the screen of her lashes. Was her hectic imagination responsible for the suspicion or was he white under the extra layer of burn he had acquired in the last few hours? The lines between his nose and mouth had deepened. Was he worried as to the consequences of her presence aboard *The Blue Crane*? Why should he be? Ollie was entirely responsible. He should have made sure that she received the message at the Club. If her cousin did not explain to Diane she would. She herself had made the initial mistake by treating the contretemps as a tragedy. Considering everything Neil had been wonderful. She would show him that she could be a good sport, too. She smiled up at him as she seated herself in the chair he drew out.

"Victory perches on your banner. You have retrieved the Sylvester reputation — once removed — There is food enough here for a near-army. Where are we now?"

"We are approaching Shadow Island.

From there it is not more than a thirty-minute run to *The Blue Crane*'s mooring. When you reach that you can sponge this unpleasant afternoon from your mind. What the dickens —"

His hand on the back of the chair opposite the girl tightened as the slight vibration of machinery which had seemed like the steady heart-beat of the houseboat stilled. Judith watched him as he stood tense, listening. There was the look of a hurt little girl behind her smile as she suggested:

"Evidently the engine, with that innate sense of the timely indigenous to engines, has balked. It looks as though this *unpleasant afternoon* refuses to be sponged."

CHAPTER XV

Judith's prophecy fell on deaf ears as Peyton's mind snapped out an explanation of the silent machinery. Stalled! Of course! Before his mental vision the events of the last weeks unreeled with incredible speed. Fleet had dropped down upon The House with the astounding intimation that Seaboard was being used as a port of entry for contraband goods. He had been sent by the authorities to investigate. Shocked but skeptical David Sylvester had urged him to make the White Cottage his headquarters. He had pledged his help and Neil's to prove the suspicion false or true. Only his nephew knew how the elder man had hoped that it would prove unfounded. He could believe no evil of his beloved people.

Under the guise of photography Oliver had visited every crack and cranny, every island on the surrounding coast. He had discovered no evidence of rum-running. The three men had decided to keep the sheriff in ignorance of Fleet's quest until something definite had developed. Cody was too bull-headed to be of use besides being addicted to gossip. There was that in the touch of the barber's fingers in the village which loosened men's tongues and reduced their bumps of caution to dents of garrulity. The sheriff was suspicious of every stranger who entered the county, but his imagination led him no further than possible violation of the game laws. He was obsessed by that phase of his responsibility. After Fleet's arrival Neil had tested him with the suggestion that Seaboard offered every advantage for eighteenth-amendment evaders, but Cody had growled:

"Mark my words the lawbreakers about here can make more and take less risk supplying the rusticators with lobsters at a dollar a pound."

Sylvester had proposed that Brewster be taken into their confidence. Lazy he was but in his way Johnny was a patriot, he contended. He could be trusted to keep a government secret even from his wife. When mere straws of evidence began to blow from the direction of Stetson, Sylvester had been incredulous, Fleet uneasy — he feared dragging Diane's name into the mess — and he himself skeptical. Boris had too much to lose to venture.

But gradually those irresponsible straws had piled into a solid stack of conviction.

Johnny had reported that the airplane and *The Blue Crane* occasionally advanced or retreated at a flashed signal from his cottage, he knew, he had watched — he was sullenly jealous of Pansy. Weight had been given to his suspicion by the fact that Stetson had importuned him to clear his field for a landing at the same time that Pansy had begun to hound him to make the place presentable for a garden. Sylvester had held him steady in his denial when he had wavered under his wife's reproaches. Until it was known just what Stetson's activities were safety lay in blocking an easy village landing. To the elder physician Johnny Brewster had confided:

"I'll hold out against her as long as I can, Doctor David. The government treated me white when I was wounded. I'll stand by the government."

On the day that Judith Halliday had fallen from the bleached oak Brewster had demonstrated that three flashes of light signaled:

"Turn back!"

Two weeks later following four flashes Stetson had written F O U R against the sky. That same day Fleet had observed the powerful reflector on his plane. It seemed quite unnecessary for practise flying. Was it for the purpose of catching signals from below?

Oliver had marshaled and dismissed one conjecture after another as to the significance of the flashed message. He refused to believe that Boris — no matter with what philosophy he doped his own conscience — would drag his sister into the vicious circle, and he would be dragging her in if he used her houseboat for transporting contraband. But the fact remained that *The Blue Crane* had come about at the three flashes from Kelp Reef, with which Johnny had experimented. He had seen it himself from the canoe. It might have been coincidence, Oliver had argued against his conviction, but when this very morning he had paddled noiselessly about the houseboat and had noted how unusually low she sat upon the water he had faced facts. This was the day Diane had set for the cruise. One — two — three — four. The fourth day following the signal.

White and tense-lipped Fleet had routed out Peyton to report the discovery. What should they do? Smash the slate at once or let it remain intact until they had gained more evidence? It seemed incredible that Oliver should ask advice when the most priceless asset among his tools-of-trade was his ability to make sharp, sure unassailable decisions. Concern for Diane had shaken his confidence in himself.

She and Judith must give up the cruise, they had decided. Oliver and he would accept the loan of the houseboat for the weekend. Without implicating her brother could they put the owner of *The Blue Crane* on guard?

When Fleet had reached Meadow Farm he had found Diane curiously indifferent to his intimations. Of course she could change her plans. She ought to go to Mt. Desert. Judith already had gone to the Club. Would he get word to her?

And Fleet had instructed Soki to telephone. Soki! Had he learned that his employer would be recalled? Had he intentionally forgotten that message? Had he schemed to get the girl aboard?

"Does this hold-up mean that we may have to *stay* here?"

Judith Halliday's question sent the torturing thought skulking to cover. How long had he been standing like a brazen image thinking back? If only she were safe on shore! Oliver was on the boat following. Should he tell her? Not yet. McFarland had handed Fleet a note as he set foot on the gangway. When the boy's back was turned Fleet had whispered that he must go back, that he would follow with the Coast Guard.

225

Time enough for her to know what they were up against when she could be reassured by the sight of her cousin. He had read her thoughts. Better for her to imagine anything rather than suspect that he had been rigid with fear for her when he had heard her laughing hail. Peyton's tone was reassuringly light as he answered her question.

"Stay here? Certainly not. We are not far from Shadow Island. Should *The Blue Crane* be held up for repairs it will take little more than three-quarters of an hour to make the Meadow Farm landing in the launch. The distant shore is beautiful in this light. Take a look."

He handed her the glasses. A brisk breeze had sprung up. The sea had roughened. The wind on her quarter sent the waves slapping impudently against the side of the houseboat, sent the girl swaying against him. With a murmured apology she straightened:

"There is so much motion I can't hold them steady."

"Let me help."

The veins at Peyton's temples knotted as he steadied her with an arm about her shoulders. His voice was stiff with repression as he inquired:

"Is that better?"

"Much. Boris said that you knew your way along this coast in the dark. You must. I cannot see the island."

Peyton released her and took the glasses.

"You will never qualify as an able seaman. The island is off the port bow, we are in the stern. Finish your supper while I investigate the reason of the hold-up. I will return in a few minutes."

"Wait! I want to tell you — Oh, of course, go," he heard the girl protest and assent in the same breath. What had she wanted to tell him? That she was suspicious of the crew? He would learn the cause of the delay as soon as possible. She must not be left alone. If the engine had been stalled as he suspected he would tell her the truth. In the companionway he came face to face with McFarland.

"I couldn't find the pipe, sir."

"Sorry that you had the hunt. It was on the divan aft. Peter, look at me! You know what's afoot, don't you?"

The melancholy eyes which met Peyton's squarely assented.

"You wouldn't let anything happen to Miss Halliday, would you?"

"Gee! No, sir!"

"I will trust you. It is her safety I am putting into your hands, Peter. A coastguard cruiser is following us. The moment you hear its hail take your stand beside the girl. No matter what happens. Don't leave her. Understand?"

The boy's dark eyes seemed like lanterns set in his white face.

"They'll have to get me first, sir." He lowered his voice to a whisper:

"Every man on the boat is armed, sir."

At a sound from the forecastle he moved away whistling softly as he went:

"Mar-che-ta, Mar-che-ta, I still hear you calling me!"

Every man on the boat armed! Peyton's lips whitened. He and Fleet had looked upon their seizure of *The Blue Crane*'s crew as a lucky chance which had come their way, as a blood-tingling adventure not without its humorous side. That had been before Judith had been catapulted into the mix-up. Oliver would be wild with anxiety if he knew. It would wipe the color from his face for a while. The girl's safety depended upon himself and McFarland. Unless he had lost his skill at judging human nature the boy could be relied upon where Judith was concerned. Had his whistle been intended to convey assurance? The situation was not unlike a Robert Louis Stevenson classic brought up to date. But this adventure instead of being conducted to the accompaniment of:

> "Fifteen men on the dead man's chest —
>   Yo-ho-ho, and a bottle of rum!"

was getting under way to the sentimental air of a popular song.

Hands in his pockets Peyton strolled into the engine room. For a moment admiration of the perfection of the equipment of the houseboat occupied his attention. There was abundance of room for auxiliary machinery, for electric lights including dynamo, storage batteries and the like. Brass and nickel gleamed in undimmed splendor. Two men were tinkering at the twin motors. They looked up and touched their caps. One had a crooked mouth and one blinked a wicked eye Peyton noticed as he inquired:

"What's the trouble?"

"Must be a short circuit somewhere, sir. We haven't found it yet."

"Let me have a look. I'm used to engines."

The man with the crooked mouth opened and closed it in a fish-like gasp. The evil-eyed one answered civilly:

"Beg pardon, sir, but it couldn't be done without the captain's orders. He's responsible for this boat and he —"

"Don't be an idiot. I can't hurt machinery by looking at it, can I? I represent the owner of this boat. Step aside."

The two men manœuvred into a line of defense. Their courtesy persisted even as they protested in unison:

"Captain's orders, sir."

Peyton regarded them speculatively.

"Go ahead! I don't wish to upset discipline. The captain wouldn't object to my watching your investigations, would he? I'm interested because it is mighty important that this boat gets back to her mooring soon." Hands in his pockets, feet slightly apart to steady himself in the roll of the boat he appeared oblivious of the look which passed between the two. Apparently they reached an agreement by wireless for the spokesman admitted:

"I guess there's no rule against your looking on, sir."

Had a spark of hope still smoldered in Peyton's mind that a short circuit had been the cause of the stopping of the engines of *The Blue Crane* the attitude of the two men would have extinguished it. He was up against brute force, his only weapon diplomacy. The automatic in his pocket would count about as much as a pop-gun in a machine-gun attack. The one chance of help lay in the oncoming boat. At the speed at which it was following the patrol would board before the crew of the houseboat had a chance to realize what had happened. He must get back to Judith. As he turned toward the door of the engine-room one of the men hailed him.

"We think we've found the trouble, sir. Will you take a look?"

"Not now. I —"

A hot oily hand cut off the sentence. Peyton struggled as four arms gripped him about waist and shoulders. In spite of furious resistance he was thrust into a small compartment. He flung himself against the door. A key turned.

Locked in! And Judith alone on deck! With shoulders heaving, with his breath tearing at his throat from the force he had put into the attack on the door Neil Peyton waited in the dark. As his breathing eased he groped for the light button. There must be one. He had it! Thank Heaven he could see. This must be the engineer's room and —

Was that a gong? Rigidly he listened. The signal to go ahead. Trapped! They had counted upon his coming below when the houseboat stopped. Now they had him. He felt the rhythmic throb of the engines. Another gong! *The Blue Crane* was coming about! Heading for the open sea again and Judith — where was Fleet?

He pulled the automatic from his pocket. He'd shoot out that lock! *No!* He might need every cartridge later. He would try every other way of escape first. The door must give. An emergency axe! Where? Not in sight! Under the berth? Queer place for it — but, everything was queer. Nightmarish! He dropped to his knees. His hand struck wood.

"They have even the staterooms loaded," he muttered as he dragged a heavy case to light. He stared at the printed side.

SELECTED BLUEBERRIES

EVERY BERRY AS BIG AS A CHERRY
(Trade Mark)

Peyton dropped his head against the side of the berth and laughed immoderately. Blueberries! Hot on the trail of a prince of bootleggers he had come up against — blueberries! Cases and cases of them. He and Oliver never would hear the last of it if the truth leaked out.

They could stand being laughed at. What a relief to know that Stetson was not the shifty traitor they had suspected. He was making a little money transporting native crops. Just like him to be ashamed to acknowledge his participation in so prosaic a venture. Judith ought to hear the joke at once.

Judith! — He looked at the door. Locked!

He had forgotten! An armed crew conveying a cargo of canned fruit! Blueberries? His brows met, his eyes narrowed. Cautiously he worked the lightly nailed down cover from the case. He pried out a wedged-in can. Its label was a triumph of imagination over fact. Berries big, blue, bulbous on a shield of paris-green over a caption done in crimson and gold:

SELECTED BLUEBERRIES

Every Berry as Big as a Cherry

(Trade Mark)

Peyton shook the can he held. His face was white from the shock of revelation as he admitted under his breath:

"Hooch! They almost had me fooled. Stetson and the canning factory! What a smokescreen!"

The crew must not suspect that he knew. They would drop him overboard in short order. Carefully he replaced the can. Soundlessly he adjusted the wooden cover above it. Cautiously he pushed the case under the berth. His face was still colorless as he rose to his feet. Boris had done a neat job. He had removed himself, his sister and Fleet to the wilderness while *The Blue Crane* was being loaded. Now he was in New York. He would have no difficulty in proving an alibi.

Peyton snapped out the light. Silently he swung open the window and looked out. Moonlight flooded the world. The wind whistled and whined and sobbed, it ruched ripples of dark water with white. Were those the lights of a high-speed boat bobbing off the bow of *The Blue Crane*? The Coast Patrol!

The houseboat leapt ahead as the skipper's signal for full speed was honored in the engine-room. Did the poor fool think that he could make his get-away? The boat forward whistled a sharp command. Peyton stripped off his coat. He sized up the dimensions of the window. Lucky it was square instead of the usual porthole. He visualized the outside of *The Blue Crane*. He could squeeze through the opening, climb to the deck or drop and board some other way. He must get to Judith.

One shot! Two! The Coast Guard had fired across *The Blue Crane*'s bow! Would the skipper heed that warning? Apparently he would. The twin motors stilled. Peyton heard the diminishing shuffle of feet. Evidently the engineers had scuttled to cover. He waited only long enough to see a launch shoot away from the patrol boat before he made a furious onslaught on the door. It was the quickest way out. The barrier groaned encouragement. As he drew back for another attack he heard Judith's voice:

"Don't try to stop me, Peter. I must find Doctor Peyton. He went below to investigate the trouble. Neil! Neil!"

The guarded, breathless call came from the engine-room. Peyton tapped lightly. He put his lips to the keyhole and demanded cautiously:

"Unlock this door! Quick!"

There was an apprehensive catch in the girl's answer:

"There is no key!"

"Stand aside! I'll break through."

Why had not McFarland reassured him, why was he standing there like a dummy, Peyton wondered as he stepped back to gain impetus. He ought to crash through the door with this attack. A man's mocking voice on the other side checked his onslaught.

"So-o, there's a woman in this game! Queen of the bootleggers stuff, eh? And a good looker too. I'll take you along with me, sister. You can tell the story of your life at Headquarters."

Headquarters! Peyton relaxed. The Coast Patrol had boarded! Where the dickens was Fleet while Judith was being subjected to the man's perfectly logical conclusions? He put his mouth to the keyhole. Before he could shout a command for his own release the girl's voice defied:

"You will take me nowhere! What do you mean by 'game'? The captain of this boat knows who I am. He —"

"The captain! He has a few questions to answer for himself. Here he comes! Stand him up there, boys. Looks like a dude yachtsman in that fancy wrapper, don't he? Now, my sporty friend, what's this boat carrying?"

Peyton could hear only a mumble. He would be willing to take his oath that the man who occupied stage centre was puffed with importance like a pouter pigeon, that he was rocking backward and forward on heels and toes as he pursued his cross-examination which took the form of a monologue:

"Cut that mumble! Can't we read skywriting as well as the gang down the shore a little way that's waiting for this cargo of blueberries? We've watched this houseboat. Thought you'd drawn a herrin' across the trail, didn't you, when you steamed back to the moorin' and settled down like a nice fat pussy-cat with its stomach full of grub?"

"What's that?" the speaker shouted in response to another mumble.

"Do you think the patrol is in business for its health? Do you think we don't know what you took on at that cannin' factory down the bay? Been there before, haven't you? I'll say you have. I'll take my hat off to your boss for that idea. Who'd ever think of lookin' under blueberry labels for hooch? But it don't go no more that way, no more!"

Peyton leaned rigidly against the door for fear of losing a word. Where was Fleet, he wondered uneasily as the rough voice in the engine-room commanded:

"Search the boat, boys. Chuck this skipper in ice-cream pants into the fo'castle and keep him there while we have a look around. You've got the two engineers locked up, haven't you? Didn't have a chance to pull their guns, did they? Hustle him out!"

There was a scuffle. Evidently the "boys" were having some difficulty with their hustling. As the rough voices drifted back more and more faintly the revenue officer rapped out:

"Now I'll deal with you, young fella. I saw you duck below with the girl. Thought you'd hide up something on us, didn't you? What have you got to say for yourself? Don't stand there gasping like a fish. Do you hear?"

"I'll say I hear. You've got me wrong. I didn't try to hide anything. Stetson hired me for a pleasure boat. You know him. He's a sly one. Do you think I would have signed up had I suspected what he was using this boat for? Not on your life! As for the girl, she's been mighty thick with him. Now he can look out for her. Catch me being pulled into jail by the likes of her."

Peyton longed for the chance to stuff the swaggering voice back down McFarland's throat. Traitor! He heard Judith's incredulous:

"Peter!"

The revenue officer indulged in a derisive snort. "Grandpa, you're a wonder! But just to make sure that your conscience isn't racked any more by these pirates we'll take you along with us. Got the millionaire skipper locked up, boys? Grab the girl!"

Judith's voice was low with fury as she defied:

"Don't dare touch me!"

"Touch you! Hear her! What can a little thing like you do against three men?"

Three men and the traitor McFarland in the engine-room! Where was Fleet? Peyton raised his clenched fist to batter on the door for his release. His arm stiffened. Suppose this were not the Coast Guard? Their job did not tend to develop Chesterfieldian qualities but would not the chief have known when he looked at Judith that she could have no affiliation with the hatchet-faced crew of *The Blue Crane*? It was the business of the patrol to know every pleasure craft on the coast and who sailed on them. He would not make himself known until he was sure. They would make short shrift of him if they were what he now suspected; then what would become of Judith? Had they already made way with Fleet? The thought blanched Peyton's face. He clutched the side of the window. He would squeeze through. He must. He paused for an instant as the girl's clear voice flung its challenge in Johnny Brewster's very words and intonation:

"*Little* thing! Understand if I am small I can — I can lick my weight in wildcats!"

CHAPTER XVI

Judith felt her face flame with color as the man in the uniform of a revenue officer threw back his head and roared with laughter. The two government stars of lesser magnitude who had returned to the engine-room after disposing of the skipper regarded her with silly grins. She ought to feel safe in the presence of Uncle Sam's administrators, she assured herself, but for some unaccountable reason she didn't. She turned her back squarely on Peter McFarland. Hot tears of disappointment stung her eyes. She had so believed in him.

The three men scowling at her seemed to be considering a method of procedure. Evidently finding a girl aboard *The Blue Crane* had upset their calculations. She couldn't have cowed them with that absurd boast. Only a psychoanalyst could explain why when she had met the glare of the revenue officer's eyes that ridiculous threat of Johnny Brewster's had hurtled from her lips. She crushed back an hysterical desire to laugh as she thought of it. Should she tell the men that Doctor Peyton was locked into the compartment behind her? No. Neil could hear. He would make himself known when he thought best. Curious that she should be so distrustful of this patrol crew. The features of the man in command had been assembled on the porcine plan. As she regarded his small eyes, his snoutish nose which jutted well over a receding chin a line from Alice in Wonderland flashed through her mind:

"If you are going to turn into a pig, my dear, I'll have nothing more to do with you. Mind now!"

Judith curbed a laugh. This was no time for her irrepressible sense of humor to grab the bit in its teeth. She leaned back against the door. Was it her imagination or did she hear stealthy sounds within the compartment? She would give Neil a hint as to the situation in the engine-room. He must be as suspicious as she or he would have demanded his freedom long before. She mentally formulated her sentences to convey as much information as possible to an interested listener before she defied:

"You three men and McFarland standing beyond the engines gaping at me braced against this door make an heroic group. You should be immortalized in marble."

The revenue officer-in-chief glowered.

"We don't want none of your highbrow patter. And you needn't shout as though you expected your voice would reach shore without wireless, neither. We are here to do our dooty and we don't take back talk from any of your gang."

"My *gang!*"

"Don't fool yourself. You can't pull that wide-eyed innocence stuff and get away with it — least-wise, not on me. This boy gave you away when he said you were thick with Stetson. He's been on board long enough to know who's what. My men report that this boat is loaded to the gun-wales with cases."

"Cases of *what?*"

"I said cases. You don't have to be told of what, do you?"

"But this is a pleasure boat!"

"Sure it is, liquid pleasure all done up in nice clean blueberry cans."

"Don't joke, officer. This is serious."

"I'll say it is. The Government's gettin' tired of playin' 'Puss! Puss, come out of your corner!' Givin' three years now besides the fine."

"But you've made a mistake —"

"Now see here, sister, you heard what I said to your skipper. We've been watching this boat for weeks. Three days ago she slipped away from her mooring and came back loaded."

Three days ago! While they were all at camp. Judith's startled realization was reflected in her face.

"I see you're beginning to remember. Well, you can come along with me and tell your story in court."

"But I prefer that she should tell it here," interrupted Peyton's voice from the door.

Judith plunged her teeth hard into her lower lip to shut back a cry of jubilation. Peter McFarland colored darkly and shuffled his feet as for an instant Peyton looked at him. How had Neil escaped from the compartment behind her, the girl wondered. He was without coat and waistcoat. There was a rent in the sleeve of his shirt, his gray trousers were smooched, his tie veered slightly to port, his black hair drooped in a Napoleonic point on his forehead. One hand was thrust into the pocket of his trousers. His eyes were inscrutable as he smiled at the three men.

"I heard your charge, Captain. If your statement is true, and I don't doubt it, someone has double-crossed the owner of this boat. Come here, Judith."

The last words were so like their forerunners in tone that the girl had dashed across the engine-room before the officer realized that they had been addressed to her. He made a futile grab. His failure darkened his face as he demanded:

"Just who are you, young fella?"

Peyton laid his arm across Judith's shoulders.

"You flatter me, Captain. It has been many years since I was called a young fellow. I am Neil Peyton, a physician at Seaboard. If that means nothing to you, the name of my guest may. Where is Oliver Fleet?"

He waited. The furtive roll of the man's eyes as he tried to find an answer to the question confirmed Judith in her suspicion that these men were other than they claimed. Had Neil expected Ollie on the boat which had followed them? His voice was suggestively friendly, as though he and the alleged revenue officers shared a secret as he went on:

"Evidently he didn't make connections. I am in entire sympathy with you in your job, Captain, but, as you know, this houseboat was headed for shore when the engines stopped."

"Stopped! What d'y mean? You were streaking it for the Azores when I fired my gun across your bow."

"And I was locked in that compartment

when the boat came about. You saw the manœuvre. A bunch of pirates is running *The Blue Crane*. You don't need to be told that, either. You are on to your business. We want to help in law enforcement but just at this moment Miss Halliday and I want to get back to Seaboard. We know nothing of how this boat came to be loaded with contraband. I take your word for it that it is. When you need us as witnesses, you can summon us."

His voice was cool but Judith could feel the hard throb of the pulses in the arm across her shoulders.

"You sound convincing, young fella, but I have my doubts about the girl. If Miss — is what you say she is what's she doing on a houseboat alone with you at this time of night? It don't look reasonable." Judith could feel Peyton's fingers bite into her shoulder but his voice was light as he answered:

"Chief, you're not provincial enough to object to a man and girl taking an afternoon sail together, are you? Would I have permitted her to step foot on this boat had I suspected that the crew were a lot of thugs? Land us at the village then take this cargo anywhere you d—n please."

Judith's heart flew to her throat at the fury

in Peyton's voice. He ought to be careful. It would be so easy to antagonize the man in command who glowered at them. His hand, caressing an unshaven chin, produced a sound not unlike an infant sawmill getting under way. It rasped Judith's taut nerves. Why didn't he do *something?* She hardly breathed as one of his companions caught him by the arm and glared at him meaningly:

"You're crazy wasting time like this, crazy to come way into this bay! You don't know it. Drop 'em overboard! Get rid of them! We ain't got no room for prisoners. Fer the love of Mike, get busy on yer own job."

The great one's face purpled. He shot a murderous glance at his underling before he demanded:

"Here you, boy! You've been round here for weeks. What's on that island astern?"

McFarland swaggered reproof.

"You can't leave a *girl* there, Captain. Even this kind. There isn't a house or a person on it."

"So much the better. I can't drop these two overboard; they *might* be worthy citizens and we'd get in wrong with the authorities. Dan, take 'em to the island and take 'em quick."

"Oh, no —"

Peyton's hand tightened warningly on Judith's shoulder as he interrupted:

"Be a good scout, Chief. Let your men take us to the village. One of them can stand guard —"

"Overboard or the island? Choose quick!" A man dashed into the room, mumbled something in the overlord's ear and rushed out.

"The island, you czar! Come, Judith."

Peyton's fingers pressed a warning before he released the girl. The deck of *The Blue Crane* was humming with activity when they reached it. The wicker fittings of the after-deck were piled in a ruinous heap. Men bent beneath the loads of heavy cases. Two were constructing a rude chute. Judith was reminded of ants swarming in and out of a hill.

Snuggled in the woolly softness of her top coat she huddled in the stern of the alleged revenue launch. With muffled engine it tossed forward through the rough water. Spray drenched her. Beyond the blur which was the island the village lights blinked like wary eyes. She gazed over her shoulder at the lighted houseboat. A nervous laugh caught in her throat. The cat had disgorged the canary.

The man at the wheel nosed the boat between two boulders on the shore of Shadow Island. Flood-time! The high water left but a precarious foothold. His mate caught at a rock in a futile attempt to steady the pitching launch.

"Here's where you get out," he shouted above the lash of the waves. "If you say a word I have my orders to dump you overboard." The moonlight set the nickel on an automatic in his hand agleam.

With a shrug Peyton motioned to Judith to step up on the rock. He steadied her until she found a footing. As he followed he pushed the launch offshore with one foot. Judith watched the boat back away, come about and streak ahead till the beat of the muffled engine was lost in the sound of the lashing waves.

The girl's heart knocked like a motor with a defective bearing as she glanced over her shoulder at the plateau. When last she had seen it in the sunlight it had stretched like a carpet of emerald velvet. Now its sinister gloom and quiet seemed daring her to approach. There was one chance in a thousand that Johnny Brewster might be at the hangar. Nine hundred and ninety-nine that there would be no boat, no way of getting off. She caught her lips between her teeth to steady them. She shut her eyes for a moment. When she opened them she could see the distant lights in *The Blue Crane* docilely following the alleged Coast Guard cruiser out to sea.

"Give me your hand! Watch your step!"

Peyton's command was a whisper. The minutes seemed hours to Judith as they made their cautious way from boulder to boulder. The wind had increased in volume. It flapped Peyton's white shirt sleeves — she should have made him stop for his coat, Judith reproached herself — it yanked the soft hat from her head and whirled it back the way they had come. It whipped spray over their feet. With a maddening display of temperament the moon whisked back and forth among the clouds. The girl's taut muscles relaxed as she felt the soft sward under her feet. She looked back at the dark water, ahead at the ghostly blur of white that was the hangar. The wind spread panic among the tops of the gigantic trees behind it. The swish and murmur and whine of the branches pressed upon her spirit like an iron hand. Never in her life had she been frightened enough to make her shake as she was shaking now. Neil must not know. She thrust her hands hard into the pockets of her coat in an effort at control. She forced a smile as she confessed:

"That was a perilous path we traveled. I feel as abandoned as Robinson Crusoe." She added with a reckless attempt at gaiety: "Will you be my man Friday?"

Judith's heart stood still. Why — why had she asked that flippant question? Wasn't the situation precarious enough as it was? Her heart resumed the day's work with a speed which choked her as Peyton seized her by the shoulders. His face was colorless. His eyes probed hers. His husky voice set her pulses hammering as he warned:

"Judy — remember that I said, 'If humanly possible.' If you want me to keep my promise — help. Don't smile at me again till this business is finished."

Her heart answered, "Oh, but I don't want you to keep your promise!"

Her voice quavered:

"What — b-business?"

"The business of checkmating those pirates and — and locating Fleet."

"Then you suspected the alleged Coast Guard, too?"

The buoyant note in the girl's voice indicated her relief at having safely skirted skiddy ground. There was a hint of amused comprehension in Peyton's eyes as they met hers.

"They were hi-jackers. Doubtless their

leader was telling the truth when he said that they had been watching *The Blue Crane* for weeks. They had not been watching in the interest of the government, however. They were uneasy at being so near the village. I must locate Oliver."

"You are anxious about him?"

"To be honest, yes. He was to follow in a Coast Guard cruiser. You'll have to know now that his photography has been a blind. He has been in Seaboard on government business. I must get in touch with him but I don't dare make a move till I am sure that that launch is not hanging around to see if we find a boat."

"I thought I saw it reach the houseboat."

"It could double back. McFarland —"

"Don't speak of him. I was so sure that he would stand by."

"The temptation of double wages and a bonus at the end of the job was too big for him to resist. Doubtless he was a spy on *The Blue Crane* for this second bunch of cutthroats. It infuriates me to stand here talking when I ought to be moving on."

"I can barely see the houseboat's lights."

"When they disappear we'll move. If only every person who is encouraging bootleggers by patronage could take his turn in that compartment on board *The Blue Crane*.

Locked in, his — a girl on deck — a gun in his pocket — for fear of her safety forced to appear smoothly oblivious of the truth of the situation!"

"They would laugh at us if we tried to make them understand."

"Laugh! It would be their last chuckle for some time could they be made to realize the extent of the network of lawlessness they are abetting, the perfection of the spy-system about them. The lights have disappeared. I must get in touch with Fleet. Di's name must not be dragged into the mess for which she is in no way responsible. Come!"

His first thought was always for Diane! Why not? She was loyal and lovable. Judith swallowed hard before she whispered:

"Suppose there is no boat here?"

"Stetson's plane is in the hangar. I'll fly."

CHAPTER XVII

Judith repressed the startled protest on her lips. She knew from the steel in Peyton's voice that it would be useless. Four years since he had had a control stick in his hand! Suppose — suppose — she shut her eyes in a desperate attempt to flag her imagination. If only they could find a boat at the float!

"There must be one there! There must be one there!" she kept repeating to herself as she skirted the island in Peyton's wake. "There must be one here!" she insisted as they came in sight of the float as though by her impassioned iteration she could will one there.

But no boat rocked at its mooring. After one quick look Peyton bounded up the incline. The girl followed slowly. Neil must not risk his life. If she begged him not to go for her sake she would be arraying herself against Diane — he would remind her by voice and eyes if not by words, that she had flung away her right to lay as much as a finger-tip upon his life. What had he meant by that warning that she was not to smile at him again?

The white door of the hangar swung out in ghostly silence. She heard cautious sounds within the building. Was Neil investigating the gas supply? Judith shivered with excitement as the mammoth head of the demoniacal darning-needle emerged from the building. The creature seemed to be holding its breath in suspense. Peyton appeared struggling into Stetson's leather jacket. The straps of the helmet on his head dangled with every motion. He spoke in a low voice as he came close to the girl:

"If I have luck I shall be in communication with Uncle David five minutes after I land on Brewster's field. Fleet must be located. No use mincing matters to spare you anxiety. The authorities must be informed that he did not follow *The Blue Crane*. I will come back for you."

"Come back! I'm going with you."

"*No!* I haven't piloted for four years. The take-off will be a cinch but I am not sure of Johnny's field for a landing."

"Is it more of a risk for me than for you?"

"More of a risk for us — together. I should have your safety on my mind. Help by trusting me. Would I leave you on the island were I not sure that you would be safe? Every solid citizen of Seaboard sleeps on summer nights with only a screen door between his household and chance marauders, which fact goes to show his feeling of security. Besides I ought to be back here within thirty minutes."

"I am not afraid neither am I anxious about Oliver. I am sure that he is following some new clue. Find him. Save *The Blue Crane* for Diane. If it is so safe for you to fly why can't I —"

"Safer for me — alone. After I have tried out the ship I will come back for you. As you suggest — we must save Diane's boat. You and I owe that to her. Your coat is wet. Wait for me in the room at the back of the hangar. Oliver discovered a radio outfit there. You can entertain yourself with that. There is a transmitting set and a receiving set. One more talent to be credited to your paragon."

Peyton caught the girl by the shoulders.

"Judy, when I come back there's a reckoning due between you and me!"

He had his voice in hand again as he announced:

"I will show you how to help me off. It will save time."

"You won't have to show me. I helped Boris. Try me."

"I will. I wish the ship were black," Peyton deplored as he looked at the great white wings glistening in the moonlight.

"You have no lights."

"I don't want them. Take this flash. Don't use it till the drone of the engine is out of hearing. I'll circle before I land."

Before Judith could answer Peyton had swung her into the pilot's seat. She touched the switch. Motioned as though to throw it over. He nodded. He ran to the front of the plane. She could barely hear his low call:

"Off?"

"Off!"

He gave the stick two complete turns. He stood back.

"Contact!"

Judith threw the switch. Peyton whirled the propeller. She throttled the engine to warming speed. As she stood up he caught her in his arms and lifted her out.

"You can't climb in and out of one of these things in a skirt," he explained close to her ear. Did he press his cheek against her hair? As he climbed into the seat his face was the face of a man who for the moment has conquered the unconquerable. He pulled down his goggles. She could barely hear his voice above the roar as he leaned toward her and held out one clenched hand.

"Take this, Judy. I'm coming back — remember."

He dropped something into her outstretched palm. He pulled on his glove, drew open the throttle and thrust forward the control stick. The plane taxied a few rods, then touching the ground with the lightness of a toe-dancer it tripped down the field and took to the air.

With her heart in her throat, her face drained of color, Judith watched the aeroplane sail and circle and disappear. She strained her ears to catch the diminishing whine of the engine. Her heart still pounded from the moment when she had watched the great wings rise into the air. Four years was a long time between drives. Neil had stepped into the pilot's seat as calmly as though he were about to start in his roadster. She had hoped that at the last moment he would show some sign of forgiveness for her but there had been no tenderness in his:

"I am coming back — remember."

His tone had been that of a conqueror dictating terms. Quite as frosty as that in which he had said only a few weeks ago:

"I don't care for quitters. They leave me cold."

A reckoning, he had said. The sooner the better. Why — why, when he had been thinking only of Oliver had she been possessed to drag Diane and her boat into the foreground?

She opened her clenched hand and looked down. In the palm lay a fine platinum chain. In the uncertain light the diamonds in a narrow circlet attached to it twinkled up at her. So Neil, not Fanny Browne had taken it from her neck the day she had fallen from the bleached oak. She remembered clutching it as she had felt herself going. She had known nothing more till she had looked up at the nurse standing over her. Her brain had cleared quickly enough then. Why had Neil taken the chain? Why had he kept it? Once he had flung the gleaming ring into the fire.

Judith leaned her head back against the white building and closed her eyes as she visualized the room at The Junipers on the afternoon she and Neil had parted. She heard again his furious exclamation as he had flung the ring she had drawn from her finger into the red heart of the hot ashes on the hearth. Without another word he had left the room. She had dropped to her knees and begun a frantic search for the circlet. It was dim and smoky when she found it. She had had it restored to its original beauty and had worn it on a chain about her neck. She had felt it to be a sort of talisman that would bring Neil back to her. The day that she had lost it had been the day upon which she had first suspected that he loved Diane.

She opened her eyes and looked down at the glittering ring. What was it that Doctor David had said:

" 'Little fires grow great with little wind.' A spark of anger, a tiny flame, presto, a conflagration and something priceless reduced to ashes."

She shrugged and brushed her hand across her wet lashes. It was most evident that Neil's love for her had not burned up, it had frozen. She fastened the chain about her neck. Quite of its own accord it slipped under her frock. As she felt the ring against her soft flesh she whispered:

"Diane never will have you!"

The rattle of the shutters of the hangar shook Judith out of her revery. Where was Neil now, she wondered. She listened. She could hear nothing but the sighs and moans of the trees, the dash of waves against the shore. There was a wicked wind. She could smell salt in it. In a lull she heard the chirp of crickets and the monotonous plaint of a tree-toad. The tide would turn soon. The sea had left little margin for foothold on the boulders when the launch had marooned Neil and herself. How dark the sky had grown. Even the moon had for a time deserted her.

Where was *The Blue Crane*? Judith's

thoughts traveled back over the afternoon. They dwelt on Peyton's explanation of her cousin's presence in Seaboard. She had been too engrossed in her own discoveries to suspect that he was working for the government. Had he been in the canoe the day that Brewster had signaled from Kelp Reef? Had Peter McFarland been in the dory? In spite of his well simulated innocence a few hours ago she was convinced that he had known for what he was signing up when he engaged for service on the houseboat.

Neil had said that the bootleggers had a marvelous organization, a fool-proof spy-system. How could it be permitted to exist? She knew men — scores of them — who had fought gallantly in the Great War, others who had given until they were impoverished, who would thrash a man who called them traitors, who now thought it extremely humorous and clever to aid, abet and encourage these twentieth century law-breakers.

Where was their sense of values? Couldn't they see that this same machine could be turned easily — oh, so easily — against them, against their households, could be a menace to their wives, their mothers, their daughters? David Sylvester's words again flashed through her mind:

"Little fires grow great with little wind."

Why, these men, these friends of hers who were so merrily and cockily flouting the law were setting little fires from one end of the country to the other. Would they awaken to a knowledge of the conflagration they were staging before it was too late? Couldn't they realize that these modern buccaneers were just as much pirates as were the men who, in the days when rum-smuggling was a profession, swarmed over the sides of vessels, cutlasses in hand, pistols in belt, stripped to the waist, attired in red petticoat breeches, bandanas on their stringy hair, gold rings in their ears, and sheath knives dangling at their sides? Suppose — just suppose Neil had not been on *The Blue Crane* this afternoon? She shivered and glanced surreptitiously over her shoulder.

She broke into her colorful imaginings with a laugh. Her hectic memory showed the ineradicable influence of Howard Pyle and Wyeth. Ollie had brought her up on their illustrations. Her thoughts were too lurid for comfort. She would tune-in on the radio. Music would cool her heated imagination. It would help pass the thirty interminable minutes before Neil's return. Centuries to wait — alone.

Judith used the flash sparingly as she

groped her way through the dark hangar. Neil had warned her to be cautious with the light. She stumbled over a gas-can or two before she located a door. She turned a handle and opened it. Her light revealed a small room, a cot-bed with immaculate spread, two chairs, a wash-stand, ruffled muslins at the windows — how like Diane to add that homey touch — and on a bench along the wall a radio outfit.

She closed the door, groped her way to the windows and drew the shades. She flashed her light about the walls. Electricity! She remembered now, Diane had said that she had had the hangar equipped with it for fear of fire on the island.

Judith snapped on the hanging light and heard the responsive hum of the generator. She peeled off her wet coat and spread it over the back of a chair. The white fur collar reminded her of a bedraggled Persian kitten. She crossed to the bench and thoughtfully regarded the radio outfit.

The sight of the transmitting set at the right with its knobs and coils resurrected the sickish sensation which she recognized as the emotional state in which she had lived and worked during the war. She had learned to operate an instrument not unlike the one before her. She had been young but not too young to realize tragedy, not too young to have her heart stop at every ring of the telephone. Ollie was all she had and he was in the midst of the fighting. She laid the tip of one finger on the key between the transmitting and receiving sets. She touched the transfer switch. Was it thrown back to receiving or had she forgotten?

She seated herself before the bench and turned a dial. Instantly the small room was filled by a voice emerging from a pair of earphones:

> "How d'you-do! How d'you-do!
> How d'you-doodle-doodle-
>   doodle-doodle-do!
> How d'you —"

The song ceased abruptly. Judith slipped on the ear-phones and reached for the dial. Before she could touch it a voice announced in her ears:

"Stand by for police report! Children missing!"

The girl's eyes softened in sympathy. Could any words strike greater terror to a mother's heart than those? Her thought flew to the Turkin twins. They would be tucked snugly in their little beds by this time. How adorable they looked asleep. They —

"Watch for two children. Twins. Names Gretchen and Gregory Turkin —"

"Oh, no, no, *no!*"

With the terrified denial Judith sprang to her feet. Almost she touched her lips to the machine as she bent close as though to drag that gruff voice from its depths.

"Last seen at five o'clock this afternoon. Six years old — plus. Light hair. Blue eyes. Girl in pink, boy in blue rompers. May have strayed into the woods. May have been picked up by passing automobile for reward. Communicate information at once to nearest county-seat."

Missing! The twins! The adorable twins!

"They can't be! They can't be!"

Judith denied vehemently. She glared at the machine before her as though defying it to refute her strained protest. She pulled off the earphones and mechanically shut off the current.

Why — *why* was she standing like a dummy when Di's children were lost, she demanded of herself. "Picked up by a passing automobile — for reward!" The sinister suggestion was unendurable! What should she do? What could she do marooned on this island? Her mind which had seemed to explode into a thousand fiery splinters of fear rallied from the shock.

"Stand by, Judy! You can't help if you let imagination run away with you," she admonished herself. She could do nothing until Neil came for her. She would wait for him outside the hangar, be ready to leave the moment he landed. He would whiten with anxiety when she told him. He loved the twins as much as she. But he would know what to do. He would be cool and assured. Just his coming would be like a steady hand to grip.

As she left the hangar she heard the lash of water above the wind, the flutter of leaves, the creak of trees. The moon emerged from behind a silver-rimmed cloud. It gilded a path on the sea.

"Oh, my —"

Judith pressed the back of her hand against her mouth to stifle the terrified cry. The golden path! Could it be possible? Gretchen had threatened:

"Some day, Judy, when you all go off on a party Greg and I are going in the launch to find that treasure."

She could see the child as she had proclaimed her independence, could see her eyes big and darkly blue, the gold of her hair, the aggressive defiance of the little figure. And to-day they all had left the twins! Where was Toinette? Ineffectual as usual against the determination of her charges? Suppose they had escaped her. They had been forbidden to go near the shore alone. Intrepid lawbreakers, the twins. She and Peter had taught them to handle the launch. Diane had been insistent that they learn. She pushed them far ahead of their years. They had been so quick. Their chubby fingers could unknot a painter. Gretchen had become adept at the easy-turning wheel, Greg had been fascinated by the engine. He had plied McFarland with questions as to its mechanism.

Judith laughed shakily. She was absurd. Even had the children evaded Toinette and stolen to the float they could not start the boat. The announcer had not even suggested looking for them on the water. If only Neil would come to laugh at her fears. Memory roughly ousted reason:

"Some day, Judy, when you all go off —"

The girl shut the ears of her mind against the shrill little voice. Absurd as her fears were had she a boat she would follow the shore along the mainland near Meadow Farm. She knew the coves. Suppose the children had succeeded in freeing the launch? It would drift ashore on the incoming tide. The tide must have turned.

The wind was blowing straight out to sea. The thought blanched her face.

Where was Neil? Thirty minutes must have passed since he flew away. It seemed hours. Why of all days in her life had she forgotten her wristwatch to-day? She left the shadow of the hangar and ran out into the patch of moonlight. She stopped. Surely by this time she should hear the rising whine of the engine of the plane. The wind stopped to take breath. The lull seemed full of whispers, snickers, warnings.

What was that sound? A billion or two Lilliputian ice-barbs quivered in her veins. Silly! Her imagination-complex was stalking her again. She put her hand to her heart. The bushes at her right had rustled. Not the wind! A *human* rustle! Pirates! Back! For Neil? For her?

Better to know what she had to face. She tried to swallow her heart which clamored in her throat. She took a step forward. Stopped. She caught her lips sharply between her teeth.

A head stealthily emerged from the bushes. A bit of nickel glinted in the moonlight!

CHAPTER XVIII

Each bound of the plane across the field increased Peyton's confidence in himself. He listened to the throb of the engine. It was humming in full-toned unbroken rhythm.

"Good ship," he commended and took to the air.

As he climbed his thoughts flashed back to the lovely white face of the girl he had left on the island. He had forced himself away. Tempted. Horribly, to break his promise. He'd keep it. She must come to him. Only chance of happiness. In love with Stetson? She couldn't be. Not after today. He shouldn't have her.

Fleet! Where was he? Was Judy worrying? Couldn't be helped. Had had to make her realize that only for a matter of life or death would he leave her alone on that island. Alleged Coast Guard crew easily could have tricked Oliver aboard. And then — He'd better shake that thought. Oliver would be furious when he knew that Diane's boat —

Diane! That night at camp! Her call! Judy in his arms. Diane's voice. Fool not to have seen — unbearable! On her porch — later —

he had told her. One girl in the world for him. Never had been anyone else. Never would be. Had she known whom he meant? Her white face! Her eyes! The memory scorched him! He had felt like a thief! Had left that night. Couldn't trust himself near Judith. Fleet loved Diane. She must love him. She would in time.

The plane banked. Better keep his mind on his present job, Peyton thought as he brought it back to its course. In level flight he turned toward the village. The moon had disappeared. He could see lights in the houses on the mountain, lights in the woods of Meadow Farm. What could those mean? Some of Diane's blooded stock must have strayed.

It was good to be in the air again. From years of navigating the bay below in fog or shine he could locate the Brewster field with his eyes shut. Chancy, attempting to 'phone from Pansy's house but it was nearest the landing field. He must take the risk. He must get word to his uncle that Fleet had not boarded *The Blue Crane*. He might have an explanation. If Johnny were at home it would be smooth sailing — if his wife only — he would use the telephone just the same.

It seemed barely a moment since he had left the island when beneath him he made out the white fence about the Brewster cottage, could see the blur that was the float on the shore of the field. He kept on westward, circled, closed the throttle and put the plane's nose down. Wheels and tail-skid touched earth together in a landing which would have done credit to his war descents.

He left the engine humming softly. He might have to make a quick get-away. He would chance no delay in the start. He glanced toward the island. Judy must be safe. He should count the minutes till he got back to her. He swung his legs over the side of the plane and jumped out. A hand gripped his arm.

"Boris! Boris! I heard you coming! Why did you risk it?"

Peyton reached a quick-fire conclusion. Through his disguising goggles he stared down into Pansy Brewster's white face. Her fierce whisper had cleared his mind of a clutter of suspicion. Pieces of a puzzle slipped into their sordid places. She would not let him into the house if she suspected who he was. His voice was muffled as he whispered:

"Holy smoke, don't stop me! I've got to 'phone. Where's Johnny?"

The woman's tone was equally guarded.

"Someone at the Farm sent for him. What has happened? Why are you here?"

"Can't stop to explain. Serious. Watch the ship. Don't leave it a moment." That last injunction had been an inspiration, Peyton congratulated himself as he ran toward the house. It would keep Pansy busy until he got his message through. Thanks to his professional visits he could locate the telephone without waste of time.

He pushed back his goggles as he took the receiver from the hook. He called guardedly for his number.

"Line's busy!"

He paced the floor as he waited. Each moment counted! He rang again.

"Line's busy!"

How long, how long before Pansy would discover the truth? He listened. The engine of the plane was droning rhythmically. He rang again. After an interval his uncle's voice answered. Peyton whispered into the receiver:

"Neil speaking. Where's Fleet?. . . . . .Of course I'm all right. . . . . .Shouldn't have worried, Uncle Dave. No danger. . . . . .Oliver safe! . . . . . .Orders changed?. . . . . .Get word to him *Blue Crane* seized. . . . . .Pretended to be. Hi-jackers. . . . . . Left Judith on the island. . . . . .On the houseboat. . . . . . Didn't get Di's message. . . . . .Perfectly safe. . . . . .Going right back to her. . . . . . Don't

271

worry. . . . . .Flew. . . . . .Don't get excited. It had to be done. . . . . .What —"

Peyton clapped his hand over the receiver. Was someone breathing hard in the hall? He listened. The house was uncannily still. Lucky that he had got his message through before his imagination had tricked him. Fleet was safe. His uncle's voice had been keyed to excitement pitch. Had it been due to concern for his nephew or for Judith?

His next move was to make his get-away from the field without arousing Pansy's suspicions. He adjusted his goggles. He pulled the helmet down to meet them. As he stepped out of the house the wind shrieked at him. It bid fair to be a wicked night on the water.

Pansy Brewster was standing in the shadow of the plane when he reached it. The moon turned traitor and burst through the clouds. Even through the smoked glass over his eyes the woman's face seemed startlingly white. As he put his foot on the step she clutched his arm and drawled:

"What's the rush, Doctor Peyton? Thought you'd get away with it, didn't you? You fell down when you called this machine a ship. Boris calls it, 'The bus.' "

Hand gripping the side of the pilot's seat, foot on the step Peyton regarded her. He had assured himself of Fleet's safety, reassured his uncle as to his own, he had reported the seizure of *The Blue Crane*. He was free to return to Judith. It would take something bigger than Pansy to stop him.

"I couldn't stop to correct your mistake, Pansy. I —" His face went white. What had happened to the engine? He listened. He stared at it. He had left it humming smoothly. Had she dared — His face was white with fury as he demanded:

"Did you touch that plane?"

The woman shrugged. She opened her gold vanity and in the moonlight regarded herself in the mirror.

"I only threw a little sand into the intake."

Sand! And he had boasted to himself that it would take something bigger than Pansy to keep him from Judith. A few grains of sand! He couldn't believe it. How would she know —

"You what?" he demanded incredulously.

"I *threw* — a little *sand* — s-a-n-d, into the intake — I have the right term, haven't I?" she inquired with malicious flippancy. "I guess I have lived with Johnny long enough to know the vital parts of an engine. That's all he talks about."

Peyton seized her by the shoulders. He'd like to shake her as he would a rat. Because she was a woman he couldn't.

"You — Do you realize what you have done? Miss Halliday is alone on Shadow Island."

Pansy twisted herself free and applied the powder puff before she snapped the case shut.

"So I heard you say over the telephone. Let her stay there. It is a good place for her. You won't bring her back in this bus, Doctor Peyton."

What had set her against Judith, Peyton wondered. Only a few days ago they had cleared the field together. He had no time to inquire into the idiosyncrasies of Pansy's mental processes. He must get back to the island. He started for the float.

"I'll take Johnny's boat."

"The engine's locked. I have the key. Try to get it!"

Try to get it! Neil shut his teeth hard. She knew that he wouldn't use force with her. He knew too well the condition of her tricky heart. He would have to use diplomacy. Diplomacy! Diplomacy on *The Blue Crane* — diplomacy here. Would he ever be placed where he could beat someone to pulp? There was an undertone of fury in his voice as he placated:

"Pansy, I want the key to that boat and I

intend to have it. Give it up peaceably. Put yourself in Miss Halliday's place. Suppose that you had been left alone on Shadow Island."

The woman took a step nearer. Clouds scudding across the moon cast fitful shadows on her face.

"Serves her right. So you too are after her and her money, are you? Vamp! She came here with her Frenchy clothes and her high and mighty air to marry Boris Stetson — folks say. Who's — coming?" Her angry voice dwindled to a whisper as she struggled for breath. Peyton sprinted for the float. He reached it as Cody came alongside in *The Husky* and hailed him:

"Dave said I might find you here, Neil," he panted as he jumped out and began to make the painter fast. "Mark my words, I haven't rushed so —" Peyton jerked the rope from his hand and stepped into the boat.

"I want this."

"You can't go now, Neil. You can't. Don't you know what's happened?" The sheriff held the tossing cabin-cruiser by the gunwale as he protested.

"*Fleet?*"

"No. It's the Terrible Turks. Missing."

"The twins. Missing? How long?"

"Don't know. Them servants up at the Farm are scared purple. That Toy-nette is 'Mong Dooing!' all over the place."

Peyton flung off helmet and leather jacket. His torn shirt sleeve fluttered in the wind as he switched on the self-starter.

"Where were they seen last?"

"The French woman declares she left them playing in the garden just before supper. When she went back to call them they were gone."

"Go on!"

"She thought they were hidin', just to be mischievous. Give a dog a bad name — She hunted and called and called, mark my words; when dusk came she was about crazy. Then she set the whole caboodle of servants to hunting. They were scared to let anyone outside know for fear they'd lose their fat jobs. Besides which they were pretty sure that 'twas only one of the Terrible Turks' pranks."

"Fools!"

"We can't blame them too much, Neil. They've stood for a lot. They reckoned that the kids were watching from somewhere, tickled pink to see them swarming like ants out of a hill which has been stepped on."

"When did you hear about it?"

"About thirty minutes ago they had a rush

of common sense to the head and 'phoned Johnny Brewster. He cut up there in his flivver and when he found the Meadow Farm launch wasn't at its float he telephoned me to come over in the speedboat. But I wouldn't start out in that. Them fast boats are too much like a high-strung woman. They go to pieces when most you need 'em."

"The launch! Gone!"

"There's a search-party combing the woods. I had a hunch when Stetson yarned to those kids about bears we'd have trouble. They've gone huntin' them. They ain't afraid of nothing. Brewster's turning the village inside out. Dave Sylvester got an alarm radioed for fear some automobile had picked them up. Their mother isn't home from Mt. Desert yet. Hope she won't hear."

"Who is looking for them on the bay?"

"Nobody. Johnny Brewster and I decided that the twins couldn't start the boat, let alone run it. It must have worked free in the rough water the wind kicked up. Mark my words, suppose they'd pried the painter loose someone would have seen the launch a-drifting —"

"Get into *The Husky*!"

"But, Neil —"

"Get in!"

"Well, I'm in. You needn't grit yer teeth at me —"

"Pansy, telephone —"

Cody gripped Peyton's arm.

"She can't hear you, Neil! Look!"

The woman had crumpled in a little heap. Back of her in the field the white wings of the aeroplane shone whitely. Peyton shut off the engine and jumped to the float.

"Make the boat fast, Sheriff. We may have to take her to the house if — she isn't tricking us."

He knelt beside Pansy Brewster and lifted her hand. He looked up at Cody looming over them as he admitted cryptically:

"She stopped me. We'll carry her in."

The few moments seemed hours to Peyton before on a couch in the living-room of the cottage the woman opened her eyes. Was there a glint of malevolence in their light blueness as she looked up into the tense face above her? Peyton's voice was strained as he prescribed:

"Pansy, don't move from this couch to-night. I'll send for Fanny. She can come over in the roadster, make you comfortable and — I'll tell her the rest myself."

He spoke to Hiram Cody before he took down the receiver.

"She's all right now, Sheriff. Start the

boat's engine. I'll be with you as soon as I get Fanny. I want her at the Meadow Farm float with my bag in case the twins —" he left the sentence unfinished. His voice was rough as he gave the number of his office.

When a few moments later he jumped aboard *The Husky* the tide had turned. Wind and water and the ledges would make short work of a drifting boat, he thought as he headed the cabin-cruiser straight for the island. Judith first. By this time she must be frightened at his delay. She would be broken-hearted when she heard that the twins were missing. But she would keep her head. They adored her. Better than anyone else she knew the children's haunts. She would know where to find them. How the boat crawled!

Peyton's shirt was drenched. The Napoleonic lock of hair on his forehead dripped salt water into his eyes and mouth. Between the shriek of the wind and the clop-clop of waves against *The Husky* he could hear the jingle of the sheriff's insignia. Bull-headed as he was, it was a comfort to have him aboard. After what seemed to him an eternity of time he reversed the engine and ran alongside the bobbing float on the island shore.

"Make her fast, Sheriff! Get out the

slickers while you wait."

"You don't expect the Terrible Turks are camping here, do you?" Cody's question was edged with sarcasm.

"No. I left Miss Halliday here when I flew across the bay."

"Well, I'll —"

Peyton abandoned Hiram to his reflections and dashed up the incline. He slowed down as he crossed the field. He would frighten Judith if he burst in on her at the rate he was going. She had been alone long enough to justify nerves. He'd reassure her. He forced himself to a walk as he sang softly:

"Mar-che-ta, Mar-che-ta,
In dreams I can see you —"

The words diminished to a hum as he entered the hangar. How quiet! Too quiet. Why hadn't Judy rushed out when she heard his voice? He turned the knob of the door of the room. Locked! Against possible pirates? Or — against him?

A smile amazingly tender kindled in his eyes. He knocked peremptorily and called:

"Judith! Judy!"

There was no stir within. No slightest sound. Peyton shook the door.

"Judith! *Please!* We must get away — the twins!"

A sound on the other side of the barrier started beads of moisture on his forehead. A moan? Suppose she couldn't answer? Suppose the pirates had returned? In a moment he was at the back of the hangar. He tried a window. It opened. He swung his legs into the room. Perched on the sill his heart stopped. Judith's green coat hung over the back of a chair. The clothes from the cot bed lay in a torn heap on the floor. In their midst stretched a man, face down. One outflung arm from elbow to shoulder was bound with a bloody bandage.

In the clenched hand was a key.

CHAPTER XIX

Hardly had Judith realized that the head and the glint of nickel had appeared among the bushes before they vanished. Pirates! Had the man seen her? Could she steal back to the radio-room? Once there she could barricade doors and windows. She would be safe until Neil arrived. He must come soon. He had said that he would be in communication with his uncle within five minutes. Was that a rustle in the bushes? She kept her eyes steadily on the spot where the head had appeared. She backed away. If only her heart would settle down instead of thundering. Boom! Boom! Boom! like a Bigger, Better, Busier, Bertha!

Was she near enough to the hangar to make a dash for it? She didn't dare turn to look. She must remember the gas-cans. They could easily lay her low and then — What was that? She put her hand over her heart to hold it still.

A flute? The notes of "Mar-che-ta!" A bit hoarse from exposure to sea air, but a flute!

McFarland! Judith's pulses changed tempo. Peter who had denied her on the houseboat! Why had he come? Not as an enemy. No foe would attack to the accompaniment of a love-song. The glint of nickel? The flute of course. Silly! The girl's voice was vibrant with relief as she called softly:

"Come out, Peter!"

Furtively the boy edged from the bushes. He seemed grotesquely tall and thin as he approached. Somewhere he had lost his swagger. His face shone white in the dim light. He seized Judith's arm and pulled her into the hangar. She opened her lips to protest. His grip tightened.

"Don't speak!"

He bent forward and listened. What did he fear, the girl wondered. She could hear nothing but the wind and the waves and the beating of her own heart. The boy relaxed and loosened his hold.

"We're safe. I thought they might have followed me. Sorry that I had to lie about you, Miss. I took a chance of helping you that way. If they'd suspected me of being your friend I'd never have escaped."

Judith's spirit cast over a sandbag of disappointment and soared. It had hurt to think that the boy had deceived her. She patted his arm.

"Now I understand — why — what — ?"

She looked down at her fingers. The shirt sleeve she had touched had been wet but this was not water.

"Come into the radio-room at once, Peter. Don't talk," she commanded as he made a sound of protest.

He swayed as he turned. She steadied him through the hangar. She left him sagging against the door while she snapped on the light. She eased him into a chair.

Just for an instant the bottom seemed to drop from her stomach, her ears tuned-in on a Niagara or two. No wonder that the boy was weak. One sleeve of his shirt had been neatly slashed to the cuff. The opening disclosed the arm furrowed from shoulder to elbow. McFarland's great dark eyes met hers. The panic in them steadied her. She smiled as she encouraged:

"Nothing but a nasty little flesh wound."

"Little!"

"It looks more serious than it is, Peter. I'll have you comfy in a jiffy." As the tinge of color in his face turned to chalk she added, "Hold your arm this way, Peter."

She flung back the spotless counterpane, pulled a sheet from the cot and tore it into strips. She brought a basin of water from the stand. If she didn't distract his thoughts from the ugly wound at which he was staring he would faint, then what would she do, Judith thought feverishly. She must keep cool. She smiled up at him as though dressing a man's arm on a lonely island were a part of her daily schedule.

"Tell me what happened, Peter?"

The boy's eyes and body relaxed.

"After you and Doctor Peyton left I hid among the piled furniture on the afterdeck. The crew was fighting. About dividing the loot — they'd forgotten me — The men who brought the launch back didn't stop to take it up — too eager to join the pow-wow. Saw my chance to get you off the island — Tied flute tight in my coat — dropped it into launch — waited — went over the side — Gee, but the water was cold." He flinched.

"I will be careful, Peter. What happened next?"

"I floated for a while, thought they might have heard me. Then I climbed into the launch — cut her adrift — didn't dare start the engine — wind was high — took a chance they wouldn't see — heard the signal to go ahead — someone must have remembered the launch — shouting — more shouting — reckon some wanted to get the boat — others objected to wasting time. Someone fired — they must have found my shoes by the rail — hit me — I laid flat and the cruiser went on. I started the engine — steered for the island — saw the plane go up — figured you and Doctor Peyton had made your get-away — stole up here to send a message — heard sounds in the hangar — hid. Aren't you almost through, Miss?"

"Just a bandage now, Peter. You've been a lamb. Where is the launch you came in?"

"At the float."

"How can you send a message from here?"

"I'm a radio man, Miss Halliday. No harm in telling you now. Mr. Fleet had me sent to Seaboard. Told me to apply for a job aboard *The Blue Crane*. He suspected that someone round here was coding to the ships outside the twelve-mile limit — never guessed that the houseboat was mixed up in the mess — wouldn't believe me when I said the owner's brother had tried to bribe me."

"Boris Stetson!"

"I fell for him, all right. I learned his code."

"But there is no aerial visible outside the hangar, Peter."

"It's there. Hidden by tall trees — this is no fan outfit, it's professional."

"The flashes of light?"

"Stetson's idea. Suspected someone was on to the code — had messages 'phoned to the Brewster woman — she heliographed — Through? Then I must send to the patrol." He looked down at his right arm in a sling. "If I can."

He shivered. The chill of the water, the wound, the excitement were getting in their work. He struggled up from the chair and twisted back to the seat.

"Gee, my head spins! Why should it? That little scratch. I must get to the set."

Little scratch! Judith wondered if she had been wise to make light of the wound. She put her arm about his waist and steadied him as he swayed across the room. She eased him into the chair before the bench. She adjusted the earphones for him. He twisted in his seat to reach the transfer switch.

"Shall I throw it to sending position, Peter?"

McFarland stared at the girl in dazed incredulity.

"You know —"

"Enough to help you. Like this?"

She pulled the switch forward and slipped on a head-piece.

"Keep me steady while I get the patrol."

She put her arm close about the boy's shoulders as with his left hand he pressed the key. A blue-white flash followed his touch. As he sent the roar in the small room was deafening. Even in his weakness how accurate he was, the girl marveled. His hand fell to his knee.

"Back," he commanded thickly.

Judith threw the switch to receiving. They listened breathlessly. McFarland nodded.

"Got the patrol. Signaled 'Go ahead with message.' Ready to send! Quick!"

Judith pulled the switch forward. It seemed as though the thunder of sound must burst out the walls before the boy finished his message. His fingers dragged from the key. His voice seemed strangely hollow in contrast to the din which had preceded it as he weakly directed:

"Back."

Judith kept her eyes on his white face with its sagging chin as she listened for the patrol's answer. Was he conscious enough to understand it when it came? She held her breath as the dots and dashes buzzed in her ears. McFarland nodded and made a futile effort to remove the 'phones.

"They've got it. That's all!"

"Peter — don't stop! Tell them that you are — here — wounded — quick!"

Judith pulled the transfer switch forward.

"We have the launch — No need —"

"Send — quick — *please!*"

The girl sensed the effort he made to hold his mind to the message — could see him cringe at the first roaring spark. She watched him closely. As his hand dropped she switched to receiving. Would the patrol reply? Had they lost the boat? She kept her eyes on McFarland's face as the answer came. They had not been too late, thank heaven! She removed the head-piece and gently drew the 'phones from the boy's ears. His head fell forward on the switch.

"O K," he muttered.

Judith flew for the water-pitcher. She filled a glass.

"Drink, Peter! Not so fast. Now come over to the cot and I'll make you nice and comfy."

She steadied him on the side of the bed with one arm as with the other hand she swept blankets and counterpane to the floor. She lowered his shoulders to the pillow. She lifted his feet to the cot. As she stood looking down at him her mind seemed to split, to run on parallel tracks. One branch followed the boy, one switched to the twins. In the excitement of helping McFarland she had forgotten them. There was a boat at the float! She would make Peter comfortable then she would search for the children. She couldn't wait any longer for Neil. Where was he? Thirty minutes! He had been gone hours! Had he —

She put her hands over her eyes in a vain effort to shut out the vision of a tangle of wires, crumpled wings, a heap of junk. Of course Neil was safe! He had been so sure, so cool as he had started off. She must keep her grip! There were a dozen logical reasons for his delayed return. He would see the light of her launch. He would follow. She opened her eyes. McFarland was smiling at her faintly.

"A — lot — better. All right in a — min—" He closed his eyes.

Judith regarded him critically. He was better. Already the chalky pallor had left his face. He would sleep for an hour or two. She placed a glass of water on the chair beside the cot. She opened a window. As she drew a blanket over him he looked up.

"Don't go."

The girl hesitated. Should she tell him? She laid a tender hand on his hair.

"Peter, keep your mind on what I am saying. *Please!* I must go. The twins are missing."

McFarland struggled to his elbow and attempted to swing his feet to the floor. Judith gently pressed him back to the pillow.

"Keep quiet if you want to help, Peter.

The woods are being searched for the children, automobiles are being held up. The alarm has been radioed up and down the coast. I think that they are on the water. You can help me by staying here quietly —"

"Quietly! D'you think I'm a fish?"

"No, Peter, I think that you are a sensible boy. Haven't I shown that by telling you the truth about Gretchen and Greg? Promise to stay here so that my mind will be easy about leaving you. Doctor Peyton will land in the plane. He must come soon. Tell him that I have taken the launch you came in —"

"Not alone in this wind. You —" He made another futile effort to get to his feet and dropped back.

Judith bent over him and listened to his breathing. He had not fainted. His eyes had closed from weakness. The patrol had O K'd his call for help. Someone would come. She must get away.

She tiptoed to the door. She stopped. Peter might follow her, might faint again when he got out. She locked the door on the inside. She laid the key on a chair beside the cot. If the Coast Patrol arrived before he was clear-headed enough to use it the men could get in through the window. She would leave the light. She bent over the boy. He was sleeping. She stole to the window and climbed out.

As she rounded the corner of the hangar the wind almost lifted her from the ground. An off-shore breeze! Out to sea! The thought whitened her lips. Where was Neil? He had said that he would be in communication with his uncle five minutes after he landed on the Brewster field. How she reiterated that! Had he landed? She stood quite still. There was no sound of an airplane engine. Surely she would hear it if it had left Johnny Brewster's field.

With all her strength, with all her determination she routed the recurrent vision of a wrecked plane. Neil was not a novice. He might have been obliged to rush to the help of Ollie. Ollie! Of course! Silly! Why had she not thought of that before? Neil knew that she was safe, knew that she would understand that he was following Oliver, gave her credit for common sense. McFarland, Fleet and Neil out of the running. It was up to her to find the twins. Hadn't Providence provided a boat? She would accept that as a good omen.

The wind whipped her skirts, roughened her short hair, snatched at her breath as she raced toward the float. A launch tugged at its painter. She tumbled aboard. She inspected the engine. It was identical with the one on the Meadow Farm boat in which she and Peter McFarland had instructed the twins. She could manage it. In the weeks she had been in Seaboard she had spent many hours navigating among the reefs of the inner bay.

With startling suddenness the moon emerged from behind a cloud. It illumined the opposite shore. Judith almost pitched overboard in surprise. Was the streak of white in the cove across the bay a boat? It was too easy! Had her imagination tricked her? It wouldn't take long to make sure. There was no sign of a reef, no betraying ripple of white in the rough water which stretched between the island float and that cove. Nothing but waves — big waves. She could make it. She must make it while the light held. It would be something gained to make sure that the twins were not there. If they were she would be the only safeguard between them and the open sea.

She forgot McFarland, she forgot Peyton. She loosed the painter, threw on the self-starter, put the engine into reverse and gripped the wheel. She backed away from the float. As the boat came about she put on full speed ahead and strained her eyes to make out the streak of white in the distant cove. It was still there. The village clock struck. Only three-quarters of an hour since

Neil had left the island? It seemed years. An incredible number of years.

The moonlight held. The powerful launch made sport of combating wind and tide. The girl was drenched to the skin. Straight for the white streak she steered. As she neared the shore she brushed the salt water from her lashes. She had been right. A boat rocked in shallow water. She could see the colors at the stern whip back and forth in the wind.

Judith increased the speed of the engine. She looked up at the sky. She must make the most of the light. The fickle moon showed symptoms of a retreat behind swift-moving clouds. It would not do to beach her boat. She might be unable to push it off. The tide was on the ebb. As she approached the gently rocking boat she closed her eyes for an instant. Suppose — suppose the twins were not there!

"Don't be a quitter," she rebuked herself sharply as she slid alongside the other launch. She caught the gunwale. The two boats tossed and bobbed and banged as she looked down.

The twins! Safe! Hand clasped in hand they lay in the bottom of the boat. They slept as sweetly as though they were in their own beds at home. Curled up between them was a mass of rough black fur. From it blinked one bead-like eye. Scotty whined feebly.

"Thank God! Oh, thank God!" Judith whispered fervently. What should she do next? Wait for Neil? How could he come? He would return to the island. There would be no boat. Peter would tell him where she had gone — what good would that do? She would take the children back. She could locate the channel buoy! The rest would be slow but comparatively safe.

Should she transfer the twins to the pirate launch? She did not dare leave them where they were alone. Rousing sleepy children to make the change safely would take time. She couldn't trust the tricky moon for light. There would be plenty of gas in their boat. Even had they succeeded in starting the engine it could not have used up the supply. It was an inflexible rule of Di's that tanks were to be filled immediately upon return no matter how short had been the trip. She would take no chance of being stranded gasless.

Judith made the painter of the launch in which she had crossed the bay fast to the stern of the Turkin boat. The two danced impishly as she climbed from one to the other. Safely beside the children she threw on the switch. The engine responded promptly. She regarded the launch tugging at the stern. It would be a tremendous drag through rough water. Dared she cast it adrift? She answered her own question by unfastening the rope and dropping it overboard.

She left the engine running softly while she rummaged in a locker. She pulled out a slicker and laid it gently over the children. So much depended upon keeping them asleep. Slowly, cautiously, mindful of possible snags near shore she steered for deep water. Once in the channel her way would be clear.

She had wind and tide in her favor. The moon disappeared. Her heart skipped a beat. She turned on the search-light. From the shore astern came the creak of trees, the swish of branches. Wave crests about her broke into white foam. The boat bobbed and skidded and pranced with near-human skittishness. The light revealed the buoy.

The channel! She was safe from the ledges about Kelp Reef! If only the children slept it would be plain sailing. They must be desperately tired to remain undisturbed by the motion of the boat. She suspected that poor little Scotty was desperately seasick. Judith smiled as she looked at them over her shoulder. She would have the three snug at home —

What had happened? She listened. She drew a half-sob, half-laugh of relief. For one horrible moment she had thought the engine had skipped. A case of nerves. Was it? The sound again! She put her hand to her throat to quiet throbbing pulses. The machinery ran rhythmically on — skipped — picked up — skipped — on — skip — on skip — still!

A cyclone of panic spiraled counter-clockwise through Judith's mind. Valiantly she fought for self-possession. She was not frightened, she reiterated. If she were it was not for herself but for the twins. She shivered. She caught her lip between her teeth.

"Don't be a quitter, Judy! Remember that quitters leave Neil cold," she reminded herself sharply. "Tackle that engine, my dear, and give thanks on your knees that Peter taught you how."

Fortified by a sense of efficiency she switched on the engine light. Left at the mercy of wind and wave the boat performed the whirling-dervish act and topped-off with a few weird improvisations. Spray drenched the girl as time after time she ran the self-starter. The engine failed to respond. She tested the ignition and patiently searched for loose wires.

"O K there," she sighed in relief.

She removed the spark-plugs and carefully cleaned the points. Again she tested the engine. No response. She sat back on her heels and contemplated the silent machinery. She sniffed. Gas? A leak? She looked down. Oily pools floated about the base of the engine. Buffeted by wind and spray, intent upon her investigations, secure in the conviction that the tanks were full, she had been too absorbed to notice it before. Greg! Greg had been experimenting! He had turned the outlet on the carbureter. Before he could turn it back he must have practically emptied the tanks. Most of the gas had run through to the bilge. Quite distinctly above the wind and water Judith heard the sheriff's voice saying:

"Sooner or later everyone gets let in by their pranks."

They had let themselves in this time, the girl thought as she struggled to her feet. She clutched at the wheel to steady herself. The world was dark. She tried to get her bearings. How much had the boat drifted? The beam from the searchlight danced upon the water like a flame-sprite. Thank heaven for that! Someone in the village would see the curious light. Someone would come to their rescue.

The children stirred. The slicker over the dog billowed as the little body writhed. Poor, miserable Scotty! If only they would all stay asleep. She had not dared sound the whistle for fear that she would rouse them. Awake they would be a greater menace to their own safety than wind and waves.

On hands and knees Judith breathlessly inspected the indicator of the forward tank. Empty! With difficulty she made her way to the aft tank. Empty! She bit her lips to control their quiver. Evidently Greg had succeeded in stopping the flow in time to leave enough gas for the short run the launch had just made from shore.

What next? How many times to-day had she asked herself that question, Judith wondered as she lurched back to the wheel. She glanced at the compass. She could try to keep the boat headed toward the village; she would feel that she was doing something even when she knew that it would be useless with the engine still. Neil — someone would come to her aid. The wavering light on the water would indicate something wrong. Curious that long before this she had not heard the whine of the plane. Neil must have returned to the island unless —

"Oh, *darn* my imagination," the girl choked under her breath. She must not think of Neil. She must not. In her heart she prayed wildly:

"Please don't let anything happen to him, God! Please keep him safe until I've had a chance to say I'm sorry! I will. I promise. Take care of him and help me to get the twins home safe. I don't care what happens to myself. I've made such a mess of things. Honestly I don't!"

The impassioned appeal steadied her, warmed her cold heart. As she gripped the wheel she forced her thoughts from her peril back to Peter McFarland. Had the Coast Patrol reached him? His arm was horribly gouged. Was Neil with him? How the spray glittered in the rays of the search-light. Glorious colors. Like a rainbow. The load lifted from her spirit. Always color did that for her. It was a tonic. She would keep her mind on the beauty of the sparkling drops, not on tragic possibilities. The light! Where was it? Gone?

A dash of spray in her face, the smell of brine dripping from her hair answered the question. Short-circuited by water! Not surprising. There had been gallons of it. For one stunned moment Judith stood rigid. Perhaps she had gone a little blind from the strain of staring ahead. She closed her eyes. She opened them. No light. Only indistinct white ridges on the dark water. She winked furiously. She must face the truth. The lights of the boat were out!

From behind her came a startled cry. Another. Then the voices of the twins in unison:

"Mother! M-Mother dear! Where are you, Mother?"

CHAPTER XX

Judith dropped to her knees and caught a twin in each wet arm. The little dog huddled close against her drenched skirts. The children buried their heads in her shoulders as the boat dipped and pitched and rolled. She held them tight as she encouraged:

"Gretchen, Greg, you are safe with me. Who, *who* do you think is on his way to find us? Doctor Neil!"

The twins raised their yellow heads. She felt their little bodies flinch as a shower of spray fell on them but they looked at her with wide, happy eyes as they chorused:

"Really, Judy?"

"And I shouldn't be surprised if Hi Cody came along, too. Perhaps they'll come in the chunky old *Husky*."

Numbers inspired courage, the girl reasoned. How confidently she had spoken of Neil's coming. How did she know — With all her strength of will she smothered her apprehensions. She would keep control of her mind!

"I guess old Mark-my-words will scold this time, Greggy, worse'n he did about the eggs. How soon will they come, Judy? Can't you hold this boat still? It makes me feel funny in my head."

"F-funny in in-my head. I — I want M-Mother," whispered the boy. He made a valiant attempt to keep his chin steady.

Judith tightened her hold.

"Mother will be waiting on the float when we get in, just you see if she isn't. And Toinette will be there and before you can say Jack Robinson you will have had something, oh something hot and luscious to eat and you'll be snug in your little beds. And Scotty, Scotty will wag that stub of a tail off. Now we'll listen for the boat. Greg, you keep the whistle going."

"I want to blow the whistle, Judy."

"Let Gretchen take her turn, Greg. Judy will take the wheel and try to keep the boat headed for the village. You keep as quiet as two little mice in a pantry, won't you?"

"Why don't you make the engine go?"

"There is no gas in the tanks, Gretchen. Greg turned it on, did he not?"

She could feel the constrained silence which dropped between her and the children like a smoke-screen. She hugged them gently to stimulate their memories. The girl answered:

"Yes — a little. You all went off and left us

so we ran away and started to find out what was at the end of the moon-path, Judy. We put up the flag and untied the painter and paddled the launch along with sticks and then Greggy —"

"I — I just turned on the gas for a minute to see if I could and the old t-thing s-stuck and it t-took a long time to t-turn it o-off," the boy's voice caught in a sob. Judith laid her cheek against his wet hair. He needed comforting, not discipline.

"We won't think of that now, Greg. Instead, let's pretend — let's pretend that you are the knight who was the crowning glory of his house and name. Keep close to Gretchen. We'll pretend that she is the lovely lady clad in white samite all glistening with silver threads and that even in the dark your shining eyes can see ahead."

"B-but I d-don't feel like a c-crowning g-glory, Judy, I only f-feel my s-stomach."

"Lie flat in the bottom of the boat, Greg. Gretchen, keep the whistle going. Watch for the light of *The Husky*. Shout when you see it, shout as loud as you can. Promise that you won't move, Sir Knight. That you won't leave the lovely lady."

"I p-promise," agreed the boy gravely. Stretched in the bottom of the boat he clutched a fold of his sister's once pink rompers. Gretchen was stiff with responsibility as she laid her finger on the button of the whistle.

Judith crept forward. The lurch of the boat almost pitched her over the wheel. She gripped it and vainly attempted to bring the launch head on to the village. In a lull in the gale she heard the oily lash of the sea. The ledges! The boat had drifted from the channel.

She caught at her fleeing courage and jerked it back. Nothing could happen to those lovely children, she assured herself sharply. God wouldn't allow it. God? Quite suddenly from being a remote, awesome tradition the Deity became a warm, pulsing personality. Back to the girl's mind stole her childhood idea of the Father, of a benign, flowing-bearded giant sitting on a gold throne. The wind seemed to hold its breath as she pleaded:

"Please bring us safe to shore! Please bring us safe to shore!"

"Who you talking to, Judy?" Gretchen called. "Listen!"

Judith held her breath. Was it — it was the distant put-put of a power boat. Neil? It couldn't be. The sound came from the direction of the island. There was no boat there. But it was a boat! There must be a skipper. Would he hear them? Would he see them? As though to prevent the possibility the wind howled like a horde of prairie wolves. In the lull which followed Judith called:

"Keep tight hold of the lady, Sir Knight. Don't move! Someone is coming. Keep the whistle going, Gretchen! Harder! Louder! Longer, dear, lon-ger!"

The girl's heart was in her throat as she watched a search-light illumine every crack and cranny of the shore. Hunting for the twins, of course. Why — *why* didn't someone *think* to look toward the ledges? Would the light ever pick up the launch? She blinked in a sudden glare. She heard a triumphant shout. Then a voice through a megaphone. Neil's voice! Her knees crumpled.

"We'll come alongside! I'll board —"

"Not this boat!" Judith shouted frantically. As a white cabin-cruiser crawled up on them she called again:

"No gas — here —"

Her voice splintered on the last word. Silent, white, tense she watched *The Husky* edge between the launch and the ledges. Neil realized their danger. He grappled the side of the launch with a boat-hook. She could see the sheriff straining at the wheel.

"Throw your painter! Quick!"

Judith reached for the coil of rope on the bow. The launch pitched, ducked, twisted itself free. Peyton made a futile grab for it. His face was livid, his eyes were like black coals as he shouted an order to the man at the wheel. As the distance widened the twins held out their arms.

"Please don't leave us, Doctor Neil! Oh, please don't leave us! We — we want Mother," they sobbed.

Judith steeled her heart against their terror. She could not go to them. She must stand by with the painter. She tried to keep her voice light, but leaden weights seemed to drag it down as she called:

"Doctor Neil can't help us if you cry, children. See! *The Husky* is catching up with us again!"

Judith's mind and heart and pulses stood still as the cabin-cruiser crept up. The faces of both men gleamed ghastly in the light of the engine lamp. The oily lash on the ledges sounded nearer. They hadn't many chances, the girl told herself. She shut her teeth into her lip. As *The Husky* sidled up she cried sharply:

"Catch it!"

She flung the painter. Peyton caught it. She could see the veins knot in his hands as he made it fast. He pulled the launch close.

"Grab it, Hi!" he shouted.

The sheriff gripped the gunwale in a vain endeavor to steady it. Peyton tumbled in.

"All right!"

The Husky increased speed cautiously. As the painter tightened and the launch settled into its stride the cabin-cruiser shot ahead. Peyton laid his hand lightly on Judith's shoulder. She looked up into his white face, into his glowing eyes which for the first time in a year smiled freely into hers.

"Just to assure myself that you are real — darling!"

His rich voice broke in a husky whisper. He released her and caught the wheel.

"Don't think of the boat. Look after the twins."

"I — I've s-said J-Jack Robinson over and over and I'm n-not t-tucked in yet, Judy," sobbed Gregory.

"Only a few moments more and you will be, dear," comforted Judith tenderly.

Cautiously she piloted the twins to the stern. With a slicker across her shoulders she sat on the broad seat with a child held close in each arm. Scotty huddled into her lap. She was unconscious of cold or wet clothing, her body tingled. The thrumming pulse in her throat caught at her breath as over and over in her mind echoed Neil's voice with that husky break in it. He had forgiven her. He still loved her. Would he tell her — to-night?

"What you drawing in your breath so for, Judy?" inquired Gretchen sleepily. The warmth of the oilskins, the sense of safety were getting in their work. Already Gregory's head had fallen heavily against the girl's shoulder. His eyes were closed. His breathing was softly regular.

"Watch for the float light, Gretchen," Judith whispered and returned to her turbulent thoughts. Never could she remember how long it was before the search-light of *The Husky* illumined the Meadow Farm float, before it cast its glare on Diane Turkin clinging to Oliver Fleet's arm. Both faces were livid with fear.

"Call, children! Call!" Judith prompted eagerly.

She helped them scramble to the seat. She held them firmly as they waved their chubby hands. Judith heard Diane's strangled cry. Saw her hide her face against Oliver's shoulder, saw his smooth head bend over hers. Behind them stood Pansy Brewster. Judith could see the glint of the gold vanity in her hand. Fanny Browne in her striped uniform gripped a bag. She stood close to her sister. Her face was like a plaster mask with tiny blue flames burning in the eye sockets.

"I hadn't supposed you could show so much feeling. You must be really fond of the twins," Judith thought as she watched her.

The water inshore was quiet. The moon's one eye beamed down upon the group on the float. The stars blinked shrewdly. The damp air was sweet with the fragrance of balsam. From the woods above the shore came a plaintive call:

"Whip-po'-will! Whip-po'-will!"

As the launch slid alongside the float a man stepped from the road into the circle of light. Quickly he backed into the shadow. Judith saw him and wondered. She shook from reaction as she loosed her hold on the twins. Gretchen looked up at her. She patted her wet sleeve.

"Judy's just shaking with cold, Doctor Neil."

The girl's hand over the child's lips was too late. Peyton looked back over his shoulder. He laughed. The flash of white teeth in his grave face brought youth and ardor surging back to it. His eyes between his slightly narrowed lids were brilliantly, possessively demanding as they met the girl's. He answered the child:

310

"We'll have you all snugly, safely at home in a minute."

His look sent the blood flaming through Judith's veins. Gretchen smoothed her cheek.

"You are warm enough now, Judy. Your face is all red."

Judith was grateful that Neil was too absorbed in making a landing to hear. The launch made fast he turned to the twins. One after the other he swung them to the float. The girl's eyes brimmed in sympathy with the sob which tore up from Diane's throat as she dropped to her knees and caught the children close. Peyton held out his hand.

"Next!"

Judith was stiff from cold. Her wet, bedraggled frock clung to her like a clammy skin. As she stepped forward it tripped her. Peyton flung an arm about her just as Diane Turkin looked up at Fleet and admitted passionately:

"Ollie, you're the comfort of my life! You said that the children would come back safely." Still on her knees she hid her face against the pocket of his coat.

"Diane!"

Fleet's ardent exclamation was quite audible to the man and girl on the boat. Judith felt the arm about her tighten. There was a curious light in the eyes which met hers as Peyton observed quizzically:

"There goes your last line of defense — Miss Halliday. Watch your step," he cautioned tenderly as she stumbled. As he followed her to the float Boris Stetson emerged from the shadow. He looked about him in exaggerated surprise and demanded gaily:

"What's the commotion? I got back to the house. No one there but the servants flapping round like headless hens. What happened? The Terrible Turks again, I'll bet my hat. Di, you'd better get those kids into a school or —"

His sister seemed to grow inches as she faced him. In her white frock with a fair-haired child on either side clinging to her skirts she reminded Judith of Abbott Thayer's Caritas. Her face was colorless. There was no anger in her eyes only infinite pity as she interrupted his flippant suggestion.

"Boris, *The Blue Crane* has been seized by the authorities. You know why."

Her brother spluttered into virulent denial. She held up her hand.

"Don't perjure yourself. I *know*. I won't go into details now." She lightly touched Gretchen's soft hair. "Your trip to New York and back was made in record-breaking time. You didn't go there, did you? I advise a vacation in South America. You had better start to-night. I don't want to know where you are. Your monthly allowance will be deposited with your bank as usual. Go."

Boris shrugged and laughed.

"All's fair in love and Volstead, Di. I rather like your advice. I'll go at once." He caught Judith Halliday's shoulder. "I'll wait long enough for you to get your things together, Judy. Will you come?" his voice was brazenly flippant.

With savage force Peyton struck off his hand. Pansy Brewster caught Stetson's arm. Her blue eyes glittered, her voice was shrill as she warned:

"Don't trust her, Boris. She's —"

She stared down at the hand which had gripped hers. Her lips remained parted as she looked up into her sister's white face. Fanny Browne's voice had the tinkle of ice against glass as she cautioned:

"You would come with me, Pansy. Keep quiet. Don't batter away your life against Boris Stetson's selfishness. For Johnny's sake —"

Pansy Brewster flung off the restraining hand.

"Fanny the beautiful but dumb! Pleading

for Johnny! Johnny! So that's why you stayed in this dead place! To look out for him! Ask him whether you should trust Judith Halliday, Boris. He knows that she spied on him. I saw her hiding in the bleached oak. Folks said she had come to marry you. I pushed her off. She thought that Fanny did it. I wore the nurse's uniform so that Johnny wouldn't know that I was watching him as he stole down to Kelp Reef with that mirror. He and that man Fleet thought they could fool me. I'm not as simple as Hi Cody. Not quite!"

Her laugh was a taunt. She flippantly opened her gold vanity, and regarded herself in the mirror as she applied powder to her nose.

Judith brushed her hand across her eyes. Pansy had pushed her from that tree! Not Fanny! Was she in a nightmare? She looked from one to the other of the group illumined by the search-light on the rocking boat. Boris Stetson was staring down at Pansy Brewster. Fleet had thrown an arm about Diane. Her blue eyes were abnormally large as she watched her brother. Wide-eyed the children pressed against her skirts. The sheriff might have been a stone man as with one foot in and one foot out of *The Husky* he gripped the gunwale. His china teeth glistened in his open mouth. Neil Peyton's eyes were on Pansy Brewster. Stetson's face was livid as he gripped her shoulder:

"Fiend! To push that girl!"

"Fiend! *Me!* I like your line!" Pansy's voice rose in frenzied invective. "Who told me to make Johnny jealous of Neil Peyton? *You!* Who bribed me into nagging him to clear that field so you'd have an excuse if you were seen round the cottage? *You!* Who —" she caught her throat as the shrill word broke.

Peyton sprang forward. Before he could catch her she had crumpled to the ground. He dropped to one knee beside her. Fanny Browne lifted her head. Boris Stetson slunk into the shadow. The rocking search-light begot weird effects. The wind moaned in the tree-tops, the tide lapped monotonously against the float. From the village came the tinkle of the piano in the motion-picture house. Peyton loosed the powder-pad gripped in the long, capable fingers. Softly he closed the gold case over it.

"Such a trivial thing to outlast a life," he said gravely and laid it against the woman's hand.

CHAPTER XXI

Four o'clock shadows in the fragrant garden. Shifting purple and blue tints on the sea. Murmur of tide. Somewhere a robin twitting garrulously. White hair as silvery as the silk of milkweed. David Sylvester in a wicker chair, a cane against his knee. Diane Turkin in a frock of blue as charming as her eyes. Oliver Fleet with arms crossed on the high back of a rustic bench. Dorothy Sylvester knitting placidly as she kept one eye on the fern-bordered pool. On either side of it crouched a twin. All luminous gold and pink and blue, their faces screwed into grotesque puckers, they dangled bread-baited pins attached to lines of linen thread to tempt the darting streaks of living gold in the water. The Scottish terrier with forepaws hanging over the edge of the pool watched in head-tilted absorption.

Fleet crushed the smoldering tip of a cigarette under his foot.

"Here we are, Doctor Sylvester, to give you a first-hand account of yesterday's thrills. That is, to fill in what you have not already heard from Neil."

"He hasn't had time to tell me much. He had to hunt up a nurse to take Fanny's place for a few days. This morning he heard from the steamship company, in answer to a wire he sent a few days ago, that he could get accommodations on a boat sailing for Liverpool in forty-eight hours. He has had to do some hustling. Why was he sent off alone on the houseboat yesterday, Oliver?"

"I don't wonder you ask. As he stepped to the deck McFarland slipped me a message from my boss. 'Keep off houseboat. Peyton go on.' I had but a moment in which to make Neil wise to my change of plan, to intimate that I would follow with the Coast Guard when their picket-boats swooped down on *The Blue Crane*."

"And the hi-jackers slipped in between?"

"They did. They also slipped into the trap the patrol had set for them. They were in riotous control of *The Blue Crane* for thirty minutes before the trap sprung. Now they and — the blueberry cans are snug under government seal. When I got into communication with the authorities I found that I was to keep out of the dénouement. My work in Seaboard was finished. I was needed somewhere else. You can imagine my state of mind. Even though I knew that the Coast Guard would follow the houseboat I felt like a deserter."

"Why didn't you come to me?"

"Why frighten you? All afternoon I was fit to tie when I thought of Neil starting off alone on that boat. Then I heard that the twins were missing. I smashed all speed regulations trying to reach Di before some interested party had scared her to death. Oh, it's a great life if you — don't — weaken."

Fleet's words wavered as he fixed his eyes on the tree behind Sylvester's chair.

"Missing! The word twists my heart to pulp."

Diane Turkin put her hand to her eyes as though trying to shut out the memory of her terror.

"What has Hiram Cody to say —"

"Just a moment, Diane. We'll clear this mystery up now." Fleet finished the sentence as he grabbed for an angle of black protruding beyond the trunk of the apple tree. He dragged the Japanese in front of Sylvester. His hazel eyes seemed to bore into the man:

"Soki, Doctor Peyton and I have tripped over you every time we've moved. What's your game? Who's your boss?"

The Oriental's smile was bland.

"You, Mr. Fleet, yes."

318

Oliver jerked a small book and pencil from the man's hand.

"What's this? Spy, are you?"

Sold's denatured smile exposed his slightly yellow teeth.

"Spy? Yes, I guess. I learn Eenglish. I say Mr. Fleet speak with great pepper, yes. Doctor Peyton laugh and say, 'Mr. Fleet use advance models. You should take notes, Soki.' I like to learn. Darn fast. Yes. I do as he say. I listen all time you talk. Each chance. I write." He motioned toward the book in Fleet's hand.

Oliver opened it. His face was crimson as he scanned the pages. He snapped it shut. As he returned it he acknowledged:

"I hadn't realized how — how peppy my language was, Soki. Toddle along."

"Yes. Thank you. I toddle. I get Doctor Peyton's bags."

Fleet watched him as he passed through the opening in the hedge which separated the grounds of The House from those of the White Cottage. As he disappeared he drew a long breath:

"That man had me worried. I began to think that I was getting stale. He dogged my footsteps. I suspected that he was crabbing my plans but I couldn't find a thing to pin on him. To return to Cody. What has he to say about the seizure of *The Blue Crane*, Doctor Sylvester?"

"He is too chagrined to talk much. He told me that he had discovered that Johnny Brewster had flashed signals from Kelp Reef. He suspected that he was working with the lobster gang which has been operating without a license. He had been watching for developments along that line. He spent considerable time with McFarland this morning after which he left The House too depressed to twirl his insignia."

"Peter was the only card I kept up my sleeve. I didn't tell you. I didn't tell Neil that he was my man. He was in the dory the day Johnny tried out the 'Turn back' signal. When he saw the flash he came about to watch the houseboat. How is he?"

"Normal and more Miss Halliday's humble adorer than ever. She did an expert piece of first-aid in that room at the hangar both on the arm and at the radio set. Why didn't she come with you?"

"She dashed off early this morning in the roadster, Doctor Sylvester. She had not returned when we came away. I left word that we were coming here for tea," Diane Turkin answered. She rose and crossed the green turf. She knelt between the twins as they hung over the pool. Fleet watched her help the children bait their hooks before he turned to David Sylvester and admitted:

"Judith had an overdose of excitement yesterday. I found the youngster who took Soki's telephone message for her at the Club. He claims that he wrote it on a slip of paper and left it at the desk. She did not go back to the Club-house. Had I known that she was on that boat —" he steadied his voice. "She is such a good sport. Since she lost her money —" he stopped abruptly.

"I know. Neil told me that her uncle had absconded."

"How the dickens did he know?"

"I suspect that he keeps himself fully informed on all matters concerning Miss Halliday. I hope that she will come for tea."

"She will. She will want to see McFarland. He was a pretty sick boy when Neil and I deposited him in your guest room. When we reached the island last night or rather early this morning two men from the Coast Guard were hanging over him. Neil had lifted him to the cot and rebandaged his arm before he rushed off to find Judith. Peter had been clear-headed enough to tell him of the wild party on which she'd started. We stayed at Johnny

Brewster's till long after midnight."

"What do you make of the affair between Boris and Pansy?"

"Money — nothing but money. She was his tool but from indications a darned expensive tool. She was preparing for something, the big city I suspect. Fanny Browne was shocked white when she found a lot of expensive jewelry and a few choice furs locked up in Pansy's dresser last night. Evidently she took her pay that way."

"I am glad that there was nothing else. I —"

Sylvester snapped off the sentence as he looked toward The House. Judith Halliday was coming down the garden path. The deep pink of her cheeks was accentuated by the whiteness of her close hat and frock. The ends of a scarf of delicate green floated back like gauzy wings as she approached. Her vivid lips suggested strain. The hint of appeal in the brown eyes which met Sylvester's set his heart pounding. The air which had been so mild before she came seemed to vibrate. He held out his hand.

"Welcome, my dear."

The twins looked up from their fishing. With shouts they dropped their lines and flung themselves upon the girl.

"Where you been all day, Judy?"

Before she could answer David Sylvester interposed.

"Gretchen! Greg!"

The children faced him intrigued by the hint of mystery in his voice. Feet sturdily planted apart, mouths slightly open they fixed their blue eyes upon him expectantly as he whispered:

"What do you think is in the barn? A — brand — new — bossy. Ask Hi Cody to show it to you."

With a whoop of anticipation Gretchen caught her brother's hand.

"Come on, Greggy! We'll grab old Mark-my-word's pitchfork and make the bossy show his speed!"

"S-show his s-speed!" echoed the boy.

Dorothy Sylvester rolled up her knitting as she watched the flying figures. Scotty yelped diabolical encouragement at their heels. She sighed.

"I'd better make sure that Hiram is in the barn, Davie, before I bring out the tea."

Sylvester laughed as she hurried after the children.

"Hi will look out for the calf. He may be a poor law-enforcer but he can be trusted to protect anything on four legs." He smiled at Judith Halliday seated in the peacock chair beside him. "Didn't I hint to you that life in

Seaboard might not prove as uneventful as you apprehended?"

"You did. I have experienced thrill enough in the last twenty-four hours to satisfy for some time my craving for adventure."

"Judy, had I known that you were on *The Blue Crane* —" Fleet crammed his hands into his pockets and turned his back. Diane Turkin's voice was as turbulent as his as she implored:

"Don't think that I do not appreciate what you did for my children because I have not spoken of it, Judith."

"Please, Di —"

"Let me say it now, Judy, then we'll forget it forever. Had I suspected that Boris was deceiving —"

"Deceiving!"

Judith sprang to her feet as she echoed the word. Two crimson spots burned in her cheeks, her eyes were black with emotion. Her voice was shaken as she protested:

"I can't let you blame Boris for deceit when I have been living a lie. I was married to Neil Peyton over a year ago." For an instant she closed her eyes as though to gather her courage for further confession.

Sylvester leaned forward in his chair, his blue eyes flames. Fleet was white as he lighted a cigarette with fingers which were none too steady. Diane Turkin was colorless as she protested:

"*Married!* Are you the girl! Neil told me —"

"Let me finish, please, while I have courage. I have no apology to make for the secrecy of our marriage — I had no one who cared for me but Ollie, and I knew that he would understand. Had I had a mother or father I would have cut my heart out before I deceived them. But what was I to Uncle Glenn or Uncle Glenn to me? Ever since I was a child he has combated everything I wanted to do, before he gave his consent. I would not battle for the most wonderful thing that ever had come into my life. Neil demurred but I overruled him. The secret would only remain a secret until after the ceremony, I promised him, then Uncle Glenn could make all the fuss he wished. I would be free. I didn't think of Neil's side of it, Doctor Sylvester, that he might want you to know." She bit her lips to steady them.

"Don't think of me, child. Go on."

"There isn't much more to tell. After the ceremony we drove directly to The Junipers to tell Oliver and Uncle Glenn. As Neil stepped into the hall your letter asking him to come here to take your practise was handed to him. You know the rest. I told you how I failed to stand by. I waited and waited for Neil to write to me. He had vowed that never would he be the one to remind me of our marriage, but I thought that when his anger had cooled I should hear from him. He seemed to — to care so much." She put her hand to her throat as though to still the pulse beating there. "I went abroad expecting at any moment to see a headline in the paper blazoning the fact of the secret marriage. I have never understood why it didn't come out. Oh, how I wished it would." The last sentence was a whisper.

Fleet threw away his cigarette.

"It didn't come out because Uncle Glenn did not want it to, Judith."

"*Uncle Glenn!* What do you mean, Ollie?"

"I was in the wing chair in the living-room when you and Neil parted. Before I knew what was going on I had heard what had happened. I couldn't escape without crabbing everything. I thought if you had your quarrel out you would kiss and be friends. Half a dozen times I have been tempted to let you know that I had heard. As many times I have decided that you must work out your own salvation without my interference."

"But Uncle Glenn?"

"After you had pulled your ring from the

fire and left the room I sneaked out as though I had been stealing sheep. As I stepped into the hall Uncle Glenn confronted me. You can picture him. Wisps of hair brushed carefully over his bald head, pale shallow eyes, hooked nose and chin, his middle finger stroking his thin mouth as he palavered:

" 'We can be trusted to keep the secret of those dear foolish young people, can't we, Ollie?'

"I bolted without answering. He had every reason to keep the truth suppressed. He had influence enough to do it. With you married his paying job was gone. Had I suspected that he was dishonest I should have told the truth. It might have saved your property. Judith, when you came here you must have known, must have seen that Neil still loved you. Why, why didn't you tell the truth?" Fleet's eyes were stern.

"But you said yourself —" Judith's voice caught in her throat. She looked at Diane Turkin who sat with hands clenched in her lap, her eyelids lowered, then at her cousin. Fleet crimsoned. He met Sylvester's eyes. He cleared his throat.

"We'll leave Doctor Sylvester to deal with Judy, Di. I hear the clang of battle from the direction of that brand new bossy. I suspect that Hiram Cody and the twins have crossed swords. Let's go arbitrate."

Diane Turkin rose. She hesitated for a moment then with face averted turned into the path which led to the barn. Fleet slipped his arm within hers as they walked away side by side.

Judith looked after them then at the man who had caught her hand close in his. She dropped to her knees beside Sylvester's chair.

"Please — please do not be so kind to me. Diane — Diane was right. She wouldn't speak —"

The sentence was broken by little gasping sobs. The girl's head went down upon the man's knees. Gently he removed her soft white hat. Tenderly he laid his hand on her lustrous hair.

"Cry out your heartache, child. Di did not mean to be cruel. She was stunned by surprise. I confess that your acknowledgment shocked me into speechlessness."

"The marriage — was all my — fault. I honestly felt that Uncle Glenn would oppose — I urged and urged Neil before — he would — consent. And then — I thought he loved Diane — I did not know how to set him free."

Sylvester's laugh was tender.

"Looking at you I can't believe that you

had to urge very hard. When my boy stared down at you as you lay unconscious under the apple tree I knew that you and he had been more than friends. Little I thought that my sudden wish that you might belong to us Sylvesters already had been granted."

"Do I really belong?"

The muffled voice was little more than a whisper.

"Try to get away from us — again, my dear, and you will find that you 'belong.' "

Sobs still shook the slender shoulders against his knees. David Sylvester put his fingers to the whistle hanging against his waistcoat. Once before he had used it to summon help for the girl. Should he call Neil? No. Let her work out her own solution. He could feel the effort she made for control as she apologized:

"I'll get my grip in a minute, Doctor Davie. Never in all my life have I shed so many tears. But when I found that you did not hate me —"

"Hate you! My dear! Dorothy and I love you." Time was flying. Sylvester yielded to temptation. He gave the situation a push.

"Did you hear a car? Probably my imagination. Neil and I have had our farewell talk but he will try to come for tea before he starts."

Judith sprang to her feet.

"Farewell! Starts! Where is he going?"

Sylvester pulled out his watch.

"To London via New York. He will have to leave Seaboard in just one hour to make the ship."

"Going! Without a word to me?"

"Is he the one to say the word? Again you are at a certain crossroad, my dear."

"I understand. This 'faulty human' is being given another chance. Where is he?" Judith demanded breathlessly.

Excitement burned up David Sylvester's voice. He nodded in the direction of the hedge. The girl looked toward the White Cottage. There was a hint of laughter behind the tears in her eyes as she whispered:

"Would you advise me to — to beard the tyrant in his hall?"

The tender charm of her, the wistfulness in the beautiful voice tightened Sylvester's throat but his tone matched hers in lightness as he deliberated:

"Of course there's a chance that he may put you on bread and water for a week — but I'd risk it. Go!"

CHAPTER XXII

Judith's steps lagged as she entered the drive which curved in front of the porch of the White Cottage. A roadster waited before the steps. Her cousin's Japanese valet was lifting a bag into it. Neil really was going! At every step of her way from the Sylvester garden she had denied the possibility of his leaving without seeing her. Didn't he care? The remembrance of his eyes, of his voice as he had touched her on the shoulder last night sent the blood throbbing in her veins. The house seemed uncannily still. Almost as though it were holding its breath — waiting — waiting for what? For her?

She put her hands to her face as she approached the car. Her cheeks were burning. The Oriental bowed low.

"Is Doctor Peyton at home, Soki?" Would the man notice the panic in her voice, she wondered.

"Yes, Mees Halliday. He inside. Telephoning in room right hand of door. He go darned soon. Better hully."

Judith ran up the steps. On the porch she stopped to collect her breath. What awaited her on the other side of the door? She looked over her shoulder. A glorious world this side. Beauty! Color everywhere! Clouds blotched the amethyst sea with purple shadows. Among the deep green of pines and cedars an occasional touch of flaming crimson and the gold of maple attested the passing of summer. A copper sun nearing the top of the mountain was preparing to punch the time-clock and end the day's work. Across the burnished disc a winging heron drew a long slim silhouette. The white bulk which was *The Husky* snuggled against the float at the shore of the Sylvester garden. A riot of gold and tan and crimson there. The slender length of the speed-boat curveted at its mooring.

The sight of the cabin-cruiser was like a tap of reminder on the girl's shoulder. The room at the right, Soki had said. As though a little demon were at her heels, claw out-stretched to snatch her courage, she pulled open the screen, dashed through the hall and stopped abruptly just inside the living-room door. With one arm resting along the mantel stood Neil Peyton. He slipped the watch he held into his pocket.

In the instant Judith waited to get her breath, the book-lined walls, the pink rose in the low bodice of the simpering lady over the mantel, the swinging pendulum of the carved Swiss clock, the smell of burning cones, the rose light of the fire were indelibly impressed on her memory. She shut her eyes, opened them and plunged:

"I'm here," she announced in a small voice.

Peyton laughed. Something in the sound set little fires along the girl's veins.

"So I see. You seem very far away. Come in!"

Judith took a few halting steps forward. Neil put his hands behind him. The smile left his lips. His eyes were fiercely intent as he demanded:

"Well?"

The girl attentively regarded the priceless hooked rug beneath her restless white shoe.

"I — I have told them, Neil."

"What?"

"That —"

"That you liked Boris Stetson better than any man you ever met?"

With an incredulous protest Judith looked up into his eyes. Her panic vanished. That silly thrust of hers had been rankling all this time! The boy of him! Color came stealing back to her lips and face as she corrected:

"I said liked — not *loved*. But that was not

what I told your uncle and Diane and Ollie. Won't you help — *please?*" She caught the lapel of his coat.

"Bend your head "

She felt his fingers — unsteady fingers at the back of her neck. A slender platinum chain serpentined to the rug and coiled in a shining heap.

"Hold out your left hand."

Peyton slipped the gleaming circlet on to her third finger. He turned it round and round as he asked with amazing boyishness in the question, with amazing huskiness in his voice:

"Want to go to London?"

"With you?"

"With me."

"I'd love it."

She pressed her hand against his shoulder as he caught her in his arms.

"But — but — Neil — so soon! How can I get ready?"

"An hour ago I telephoned Diane's maid to pack the things you would need on a ship."

"Were you so sure?"

"That you would go? Yes. That you would come here? No. There are times when keeping a promise to oneself ceases to be a virtue. I had allowed you ten minutes more in which to get here. After that I was going for you. But — you came!"

ONE! TWO! THREE! FOUR! FIVE!

Boomed the tall clock on the stair-landing. Instantly from somewhere at a little distance a lighter gong intoned:

One! Two! Three! Four! Five!

One! Two! Three! Four! Five!

Chimed a bell from the next room.

The doors of the Swiss chalet on the wall clanged open. A bird hopped to the threshold as though guiltily cognizant of the fact that he was a second late.

Cuck'-oo! Cuck'-oo! Cuck'-oo! Cuck'-oo! Cuck'-oo!

He lustily proclaimed to the two absorbed humans who seemed as one before he clattered back into obscurity.

"Five o'clock!"

With the shocked exclamation Judith freed herself from Peyton's arms. There was a tormenting gleam in the tender eyes which met his for a moment as she patted her hair smooth and reproached unsteadily:

"I take back what I said that night at camp. Your technic has not improved, Doctor Peyton."

"Give me time. With constant practise I may be able to do better. If we are to have tea in the garden before we pick up your luggage —"

"Tea! Face Ollie — now! Oh, can't we steal away?"

"It's chancy, but we'll risk it. We will 'phone Uncle David from Meadow Farm. He will understand."

"He always understands. Curious that he should have warned me against Uncle Glenn —"

Memory shocked the lovely color from the girl's face.

"I had forgotten to tell you! I haven't any *money!* Uncle Glenn has lost it!"

Neil caught her close.

"I know, dear. I'm sorry."

Hand under her chin he tilted her head back against his shoulder that he might see her eyes. There was laughter, ardor, possession in his voice as he assured:

"I have plenty. Suppose we split fifty-fifty — Mrs. Peyton."